Acclaim for Mike Resnick and
A Gathering of Widowmakers

"Resnick is in fine form, returning his Widowmaker character to print after too long an absence. The guy is a brutal pragmatist, unswayed by sentiment or greed, with a direct and lethal response to most problems. The challenges he faces are remarkable and his solutions are equally inventive. He doesn't go out of his way to kill—the violence is never gratuitous—but he doesn't shy away either. In bits and pieces, his philosophy and backstory are both revealed...and a killing machine becomes human beneath many layers of emotional armor and detachment.

At the same time, the clones show how differently people can turn out, even with the same genetic profile. Each one has a distinct personality, even though some of the same qualities recur in all three. Kinoshita proves an excellent sidekick, his questions (like those a reader might have) shot down like clay pigeons by The Widowmaker.

Fans of loner heroes in SF probably already know about the Widowmaker, but if they don't...well, here's a great place to start."—*SFReview*

"Resnick's usual gifts for hard-boiled space opera, including even plausible future weaponry and not too much cynicism, keep things humming toward an ending indicating possible sequels."—*Booklist*

Praise for
Mike Resnick

"Resnick is thought provoking, imaginative...and above all galactically grand."—*Los Angeles Times*

"Resnick's tales are ironic, inventive, and very readable."
—*Publishers Weekly*

"Nobody spins a yarn better than Mike Resnick."—*Orson Scott Card*

"Resnick occupies a peak all his own in the mountains of science fiction"—*Analog*

"Resnick is a polished story teller."—*Library Journal*

"Top-notch science fiction."—*Kirkus*

"Woe to the reader who needs to rise early the next morning. When you start a book by Mike Resnick you're there to the very end, and damn glad you were."—*Classic Bookshop Book Review*

"Mike Resnick has never failed to deliver a good, satisfying read and can always be counted on to serve up some good food for thought."—*Strange Horizons*

"Resnick has written a highly entertaining series which provides a thorough look at the meaning of self-identity."
—*BookPage*

A GATHERING OF
WIDOWMAKERS

MIKE RESNICK

Meisha Merlin Publishing, Inc.
Atlanta, GA

A Gathering of Widowmakers Copyright © 2005 by Mike Resnick

A Gathering of Widowmakers

Published by Meisha Merlin Publishing, Inc.
PO Box 7
Decatur, GA   30031

Editing by Stephen Pagel
Interior layout by Lynn Swetz
Cover art Jim Burns
Cover design by Kevin Murphy

ISBN: Hard Cover 1-59222-085-1
ISBN: Soft Cover 1-59222-086-X

http://www.MeishaMerlin.com
First MM Publishing edition: December 2005 HC
First MM Publishing edition: July 2006 SC

Printed in the United States of America
0 9 8 7 6 5 4 3 2 1

A GATHERING OF
WIDOWMAKERS

MIKE
RESNICK

Prologue

THE OLD MAN looked up from his garden, shaded his eyes from the sun, and stared off into the distance. The clouds were gathering in the west, obscuring two of the three moons; the rain would be here in another two hours, three at the most. He'd have to hurry if he wanted to finish planting his flowers today.

He walked to the potting shed, picked up the seeds, stuffed them in a pocket, grabbed a hand trowel, and returned to the section of black dirt where he planned to work. But before he could start digging, a woman's voice called to him.

He turned toward the house. "What is it?" he called out.

"Lunch is ready."

"I'm busy," said the old man. "I'll be along in a couple of hours."

"You'll come right now," said the voice firmly. "I didn't cook this so that it could sit out on a counter and get cold. Whatever you're doing, it can wait."

The old man looked regretfully at the unturned dirt, then laid his trowel down on the ground with a sigh. He felt a tiny shooting pain in his back when he bent over, and he straightened up very carefully.

He wiped the sweat off his face with a shirtsleeve, paused for just a moment to watch a flock of avians soaring overhead, and then trudged off to the small house to join his wife.

He seemed a perfectly ordinary old man. Tall, lean, wrinkles around the eyes and the jawline, hair gray and well on its way to white, a few liver spots on the back of his hands.

To look at him, one would never guess that he was the most dangerous man alive—or even how many times he had lived before.

1.

THE TWO BOYS looked out through the store window.

"Are you sure it's him?" asked the first.

"I've got his holo on my computer," said the second. "It's him, all right. And see that little guy? They say they always travel together."

"Why would he need any help?"

"*Him?*" was the reply. "He doesn't need any help, not now, not ever. Maybe he just wants someone to talk to."

"But why would he come here to Dominion?" asked the first boy, still unconvinced. "Who do we have that he'd want to come after?"

"Why don't you go out and ask him?" shot back the second boy.

"Not me," said the first boy firmly. "They say he kills people just for staring at him."

The object of their attention suddenly turned and began approaching the store where the two boys were speaking.

"Omygod, omygod, omygod!" said the second boy, terrified. "He heard you! He's coming in here!"

"He couldn't have heard me, not through that window."

"He's the Widowmaker!" said the second boy, almost crying. "He can do anything!"

"He's too young," said the first boy. "Look at him. He couldn't have killed half as many men as they say. You're wrong; it's not him."

"The hell I am!"

"We'll find out soon enough," said the first boy. "Here he comes."

The door irised, and the young man and his companion entered the store.

"Welcome to Flynn's Emporium," said the robot clerk. "May I be of service?"

The young man walked over, disassembled his laser pistol, and placed the battery on a counter in front of the robot.

"I need half a dozen of these," he said.

The robot's eyes extended on long metallic stalks and examined the battery.

"Model H-314," it intoned. "We have seventeen in stock, sir."

"Six will do."

"I have already ordered them from the stockroom. They will be here in approximately forty seconds, sir."

"Thanks." The young man looked around the store. He spotted the two boys; they were crouched behind a large holographic landscape projector, created especially for use during long voyages in spaceships that didn't possess Deepsleep chambers. "Who are you hiding from?" he asked pleasantly.

The second boy stood up, hands straight above his head. "We didn't do anything, sir! Honest we didn't!"

"Nobody said you did."

The first boy stood up and approached him, eyes wide. "Are you really the Widowmaker?"

"That's what some people call me."

"Some people?"

"My friends call me Jeff."

"I know," said the second boy, his hands still reaching for the ceiling. "Jefferson Nighthawk."

"That's right."

"Who are you here to kill?"

"No one," said Jeff.

"The Widowmaker never lands on a planet unless he wants to kill someone," insisted the second boy. "If you tell us who it is, maybe we can tell you where to find him."

Jeff looked amused. "Sometimes I go a whole day without killing anyone."

Both boys looked unconvinced.

Jeff noticed that his batteries had arrived, and he turned back to the counter. "How much?"

"Four hundred eighty credits," replied the robot. "I can also accept payment in New Kenya shillings, Far London pounds, and Maria Theresa dollars."

Jeff nodded to his companion. "Give him his money and let's go."

The first boy approached him. "Can I have your autograph, sir?"

"Are you sure you want it?" asked Jeff. "I'm not an athlete or an actor."

"Yes, please, sir. This way when I tell people I saw you, I can prove it."

Jeff shrugged. "All right. What do you want me to sign?"

The boy seemed suddenly distressed. "I don't have anything."

"It's all right." Jeff picked up his discarded battery, took a stylus from his companion, and signed his name on it. "Here," he said, tossing it to the boy. "Now you can tell your friends you've got the battery from the Widowmaker's burner."

"Wow!" said the boy. "Wow!"

Jeff and his companion walked to the door. When they reached it, he turned to the second boy. "You can put your hands down now."

"Thank you, sir," said the second boy, looking as if he might faint at any moment.

"Don't you ever get tired of it?" asked Ito Kinoshita as he and Jeff stepped out onto the slidewalk and let it take them south.

"I'm eighteen months old," replied Jeff. "I'm not tired of *anything* yet."

"Right," replied his companion. "I've been serving Widowmakers for so long I assume you've all had the same experiences."

"We share the same DNA, not the same lives," said Jeff. He paused. "I wonder if the old gentleman is keeping track of how his latest creation is doing?"

"You make yourself sound like some Frankensteinian monster," said Kinoshita. "You're a clone, that's all. And in answer to your question, yes, he knows what you're doing."

"I thought you didn't keep in touch with him."

"I don't. I'm only to contact him in an emergency, and—knock wood—we haven't had one."

"Then how does he know what I'm doing?"

"He's the Widowmaker," said Kinoshita, as if that explained everything.

"He used to be," said Jeff irritably. "*I'm* the Widowmaker."

"I just meant that—"

"I know what you meant."

They rode in silence for two more blocks, and then came to the end of the southbound slidewalk.

"I guess this is where we catch the transit back to the spaceport," said Jeff.

"Looks like it," agreed Kinoshita. "You know," he added thoughtfully, "Dominion's got a couple of hundred thousand men living on it. As long as we're here, we might as well check and see if there's some serious paper on any of them."

"Not interested. Leave it to the locals. We've got business on Giancola II."

"But—"

"I was created and trained to go after the men no one else can take," said Jeff. "If any of them were here, we'd have known it before we landed."

"You don't *always* have to go after the most dangerous men on the Wanted list," said Kinoshita.

"If I don't, who will?"

Kinoshita sighed. "Counting you, I've served four Widowmakers—and I don't remember ever winning an argument with any of you."

Jeff smiled. "Don't give up. There's always a first time."

They became aware of four more boys peeking at them from behind buildings.

"More autograph seekers," suggested Jeff.

"Or advice seekers," said Kinoshita. "Every kid out here wants to grow up to be the Widowmaker. You'd make their whole year if you'd stop and talk to them for a minute."

"What would I tell them?" asked Jeff with a wry grimace. "Say your prayers, eat your greens, listen to your parents, study hard in school, go to church, shoot first, and don't miss."

Kinoshita chuckled. "Well, two out of seven isn't bad."

"Depends which two," replied Jeff. He waved at the boys. Three of them immediately ducked out of sight; the fourth waved back.

Then the transit vehicle floated down the street, hovered a foot above the ground while the two men got on it, and headed off to the spaceport. When the passengers realized who had boarded the vehicle, they practically fell over each other to climb off at the next stop.

"Does that bother you?" asked Kinoshita.

"In the beginning it did," admitted Jeff. "I'm getting used to it."

"After we finish this," suggested Kinoshita, "what do you say to taking a vacation, maybe go out on the Spiral Arm where no one knows us?"

"If you need one, take one."

"I was thinking of you."

Jeff shook his head. "I've got too much work to do."

"The bad guys will all be here when you get back."

"And there'll be another hundred or thousand corpses, too."

"Don't you get tired?"

"I don't work that hard," said Jeff.

"You've worked every single day since I teamed up with you."

"I work about ten or twenty seconds every couple of weeks. The rest is just busywork and travel time."

"That's an interesting way of looking at it."

"I love my work," said Jeff. "I'm the best there is at it, and more to the point, if I stop working people die."

"When you work, people die," said Kinoshita.

"The *right* people die," said Jeff. "How many men can truly say that they've made the galaxy a safer place?"

"Doctors, soldiers, lawyers, politicians, clerics, police— the same people who said it while we were still Earthbound."

Jeff looked his contempt. "If they were telling the truth, they wouldn't need me, would they?"

Kinoshita smiled. "I keep forgetting."

"Forgetting what?"

"You seem like such a nice, friendly young man," said Kinoshita. "I keep forgetting that you're a younger version of *him*."

"Not really," said Jeff. "I only knew him for three or four months."

"But you've got that same steel beneath the surface. Your experiences are different, maybe even your thoughts and beliefs, but the core is the same." Kinoshita looked at the young man. "Don't be so quick to take offense. There are worse people to be like."

"So you keep telling me."

"Have I ever lied to you?"

"You don't understand," said Jeff.

"Enlighten me."

"He's not my father, or my teacher, or my mentor."

"He's all three," said Kinoshita.

Jeff shook his head. "He's much more than that: he's my *creator*. I'm like Adam's rib. I'm part of him in a way no one else will ever comprehend. And sometimes it's a very uncomfortable feeling, to be an exact replica of someone else, an artificially created replica, and to know that somehow you'll never quite be your own person."

"I think you're looking at it all wrong," said Kinoshita. "He gave you life, he trained you to take over for him, and he turned you loose. You haven't seen him or heard from him since then. He's kept his distance, and kept his hands off. He has no control over you, and he doesn't want any."

"I know," said Jeff, as the vehicle left the city and turned toward the spaceport. "I can't explain it—but how would you feel if you came face-to-face with your god, your creator, if you knew he wasn't on some higher plane of existence but was made of flesh and blood and was probably watching your progress through the life he gave you?"

"Honored."

"I'm honored. But it's also disturbing to know that everyone else came into life one way, and I came from a blob of protoplasm in a lab."

"You ever see a holo of a sperm and an egg?" asked Kinoshita. "On those occasions that they're lucky enough to crash into each other, the next step is to become a blob of protoplasm. All you did was eliminate one step from a generally disgusting process."

"You're probably right, but I can't help feeling uncomfortable when I think about it."

"If it was me, I'd be much more uncomfortable knowing that so many men and women out here on the Inner Frontier want me dead."

Jeff shrugged. "That's just business."

"You're the third clone of Jefferson Nighthawk," said Kinoshita. "I've never asked you before, but doesn't it ever bother you that the first one was killed by his enemies after just a few weeks on the job, and the second got shot up pretty badly in under a year? That's what I'd be worrying about."

"Then you'd die," said Jeff.

"I don't follow you."

"If you feel any uncertainty, any fear at all, you hesitate for a fraction of a second. You can't help it—and that's all the edge most of your opponents need. As the old gentleman explained when he was training me, every man and woman walking around with a weapon is undefeated in mortal combat. You can't afford to ever underestimate them or give them an advantage, and that's what you give them the second you think about what might happen if you lose."

Kinoshita stared at him for a moment. "That's why you're the Widowmaker and I'm just the hired help."

"I don't pay you anything."

"All right, then—I carry your water."

"I don't understand that expression."

"It doesn't matter," replied Kinoshita as the spaceport came into view and the vehicle approached the main entrance.

"Stop putting yourself down," said Jeff. "The old man told me you were a good lawman and a successful bounty hunter."

"That's what I thought, too," said Kinoshita. "Ten seconds after I saw the first Widowmaker clone in action I realized that I was out of my depth and damned lucky to still be alive. What if one of the bad guys had those skills? That was when I pledged my life to serving the Widowmaker." He smiled ironically. "Little did I know just how many of them there would be."

"How did you choose which one to serve?"

"There's never been more than one Widowmaker around at a time."

"What about—?"

"The old gentleman, as you refer to him?" said Kinoshita. "He turned the Widowmaker franchise over to you. He's off growing flowers and watching birds."

"I was about to say, what about the clone who survived? Only the first one died."

"He's out of the Widowmaker business too. Pity, too—the two of you would have made one hell of a team."

"I work alone," said Jeff. "Except for you."

"We have arrived," announced the robot driver as the vehicle came to a stop at the spaceport's main entrance.

"Which way to the private ships?" mused Kinoshita, searching for the correct color codes.

"Freeze," said Jeff softly.

"What is it?" asked Kinoshita, suddenly motionless.

"MacKenzie Platt," said Jeff, staring at a tall man who was walking toward an exit.

"Son of a bitch! There's paper on him—seventy-five thousand credits last time I looked!"

Jeff nodded. "As soon as we get to the ship, I'll send a message to the local authorities that he's here."

"He didn't spot you," said Kinoshita. "Why don't we just follow him until the crowd thins out and burn off the back of his head from a nice safe distance?"

"He hasn't killed anyone. They want him for robbing a couple of banks on Winslow IV—the wrong people's banks, obviously."

"I'm almost certain they want him dead or alive."

"That's *their* business."

"If you don't want him, why did you tell me to freeze?"

"I didn't want him to spot us, or I might have had to kill him here in the spaceport. There's too much likelihood that some civilians would get in the way."

"Civilians?" repeated Kinoshita. "You make it sound like we're in a war."

"Damned right we are," said Jeff, heading off to the private-ship hangar. "And the next battlefield is Giancola II."

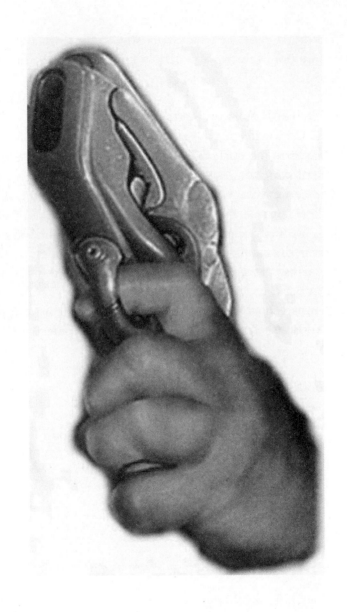

2.

GIANCOLA II WAS an unimpressive little planet, as were so many of the worlds of the Inner Frontier. The soil wasn't much good for farming, the ground didn't hold a lot of treasure, the mountains were too low for climbing and too lacking in snow for skiing, the oceans and rivers were filled with fish that humans couldn't metabolize, there were no indigenous sentient species, the climate was unexceptional.

"Why did anyone ever settle here in the first place?" muttered Jeff as he checked the computer's readout prior to disembarking.

"It was a neutral world where we held a lot of meetings with various alien species at the end of the Tamorian War," answered Kinoshita. "Some of the folks involved just stayed here. It does some banking, a little shipbuilding, and it has a pretty good hospital for cases that either can't make it back to the Oligarchy, or don't want to."

"It's a dump."

"You've spent your whole life out here on the Frontier. This looks like most of the other worlds you've seen."

"That's right."

"Then what are you comparing it to?"

"I was created on Deluros VIII," said Jeff, referring to the Oligarchy's capital world.

"I didn't think you'd know what you were seeing," said Kinoshita.

"I was born a fully-formed adult with an adult's education and memories. The memories weren't mine, and I soon began replacing them, but I was always cogent, always aware of my surroundings and what I was doing." Jeff paused. "You lived there for years. Do you ever miss it?"

"The conveniences, sometimes. The crowds, the cost, the corruption, the total impersonality of it, never."

"Then Giancola II should be just your speed."

They emerged from the ship and walked into the small spaceport. A robot that was literally part of the Customs kiosk greeted them.

"Welcome to Giancola II, garden spot of the Inner Frontier," it said with minimal inflection while Jeff fought the urge to argue with it. "Are you here for business or pleasure?"

"Business."

"May I inquire the nature of your business?"

"That all depends," said Jeff.

"On what, sir?"

"On whether the laws of Giancola II say that I am required to tell you."

"Yes, sir, you are."

Jeff placed a disk on the counter. It began to glow as the robot scanned it with a long metallic forefinger.

"I am a licensed bounty hunter. As you can see, the particulars of my license are appended to my passport."

"Still checking…" murmured the robot. "Your passport and license are in order. I have transmitted this information to our local law-enforcement officials, so that there will be no interference in the execution of your duties."

"Nice choice of words," remarked Jeff dryly.

"I do not understand, sir."

"That's all right. Check my friend's passport and we'll be on our way."

The robot examined Kinoshita's disk. "Sir, I must alert you that your bounty license will expire in forty-three days."

"I know," said Kinoshita. "I'll take care of it."

"You are cleared to pass through the spaceport. Enjoy your stay on Giancola II."

Jeff and Kinoshita, tired of eating in the ship's galley, stopped at a small restaurant in the spaceport, then took an aircar into the only city on the planet, which was also called Giancola, after the member of the Pioneer Corps who had originally opened and mapped the world.

"You'd better make a note to renew your license," remarked Jeff as they skimmed a few inches above the surface.

"I'm thinking of letting it lapse," replied Kinoshita. "If you ever need my help, we're in deep shit."

"Whatever makes you happy," said Jeff with a shrug. He looked ahead and saw they had almost reached the city. "Take us to the best hotel in town," he instructed the aircar.

"I am incapable of making value judgments," replied the aircar.

"Okay, take us to the most expensive hotel."

"Yes, sir," said the aircar, altering its course and heading off to the southwest. In another moment it came to a halt in front of the Da Vinci Hotel and hovered motionless until its occupants stepped out.

A robot doorman walked up to take their luggage, then froze when it saw they didn't have any. Jeff walked by it without giving it a second look and approached the front desk.

"May I help you?" asked a middle-aged woman.

"A real live human being," said Jeff. "You're the first I've seen since I landed."

She smiled. "There are a lot of us, really there are. But the spaceport is fully automated. Have you a reservation?"

Jeff shook his head. "No. I'd like a suite if you have one available, and my friend will take a room." He pressed his thumb down on a Spy-Eye scanner. "Charge both and all extras to my account at the Far London branch of the Bank of Deluros."

"Yes, sir. Suite 319 will respond to your thumbprint or voiceprint. If your friend will please give me his print and say a word or two."

"Beautiful day," said Kinoshita, placing his thumb on the scanner.

"Room 320, sir," she said. "You'll be right across the hall from each other. How long will you be staying?"

"I'm not sure," answered Jeff. "I wonder if you could do me a favor?"

"If it's within my power," responded the woman.

"I'm looking for someone, and I have reason to believe he may be on Giancola II."

She glanced down at a hidden screen on her side of the registration desk, then looked up disapprovingly. "You are a bounty hunter, Mr. Nighthawk."

"My credentials are in order. I'm here after a very dangerous man."

"May I ask what he's done?"

"Murder, extortion, probably treason. He's killed at least nineteen people, including a couple of kids."

"He sounds like a terrible man," she said. "I wonder what makes someone do things like that?"

"I don't know," replied Jeff. "I tend not to meet them until after they've committed their crimes."

"It sounds like an awful way to make a living."

"It has its compensations. And its satisfactions. Anyway, let me give you his name and—"

"Just a minute, Mr. Nighthawk," she interrupted. "If he's all that you say, then he doubtless deserves whatever you're going to do to him. But we don't want any violence in the hotel. I'll tell you if he's registered here, and if he isn't, I'll try to help locate him—but in exchange, I want you to promise not to do anything on the premises. That's my quid pro quo."

"Fair enough," agreed Jeff. "The man I'm looking for is Jubal Pickett. If the name is unknown to you, I can show you a holograph."

"Jubal Pickett?" she repeated, surprised. "You must be mistaken."

"Why should you say that?"

"He's an wonderful man! He donated a wing of the hospital, he paid for improvements in the spaceport, and he doesn't even live here permanently."

"There's paper on him on a dozen worlds, ma'am," replied Jeff. "The last three lawmen and bounty hunters who tried to bring him in are dead."

"Mr. Pickett?" She shook her head. "I'm sure there must be some mistake."

"I'm afraid there isn't." He turned to Kinoshita. "Have the ship's computer transmit some of the warrants to the desk here."

Kinoshita gave a brief order to his pocket computer, and an instant later the woman stared at her hidden screen, her eyes wide in disbelief.

"I don't believe he could have done those things—not Mr. Pickett!" she said adamantly.

"With all due respect, that's not my concern," said Jeff.

"That I don't believe it, or that he didn't do it?" she said quickly.

"Both."

"And what if he's innocent?"

"They don't put out dead-or-alive warrants on innocent men," said Jeff. "He's been judged, and he's killed the first three men who tried to bring him to justice." He paused. "I assume he's staying here?"

"I will not be a party to this," she said adamantly. "And I hold you to your promise: you will not kill or harm anyone on the premises."

"As far as I'm concerned, you've answered me," he said. "Since you kept your part of the bargain, I'll keep my part. No violence in the hotel or on its property." He walked to the airlift, followed by Kinoshita. Just before it took them to the third floor, he turned back to the woman. "If you were to warn him, I would consider that an abrogation of our agreement."

A moment later he entered his suite, motioned Kinoshita to join him, and sat down on a couch made from the leathery hide of some alien animal.

"Tomorrow morning we'll go hunting for his house," said Jeff.

"But he's staying here."

"Not a chance," replied Jeff. "He knows there's paper on him. Any bounty hunter who comes to town is going to stay in this hotel, and his holograph is all over the Inner Frontier. He might chance it for a night, but we know he's been on Giancola for at least six days. No, he'll have a place out of town, and since he's been an angel to the hospital and spaceport, none of the locals are going to tell us where it is."

"Then why didn't the woman downstairs tell us he was here and buy him a little time?"

"She kept her mouth shut because for all she knew you had a Truthtell pen trained on her and would know if she was lying. If she was a little smarter she'd have lied about something trivial when we were checking in, and then she'd have known for sure." He paused. "And she won't warn him, because she's sure if she does I'll come back and kill her."

"Would you?"

"Probably not. You don't kill an uninformed person for misguided loyalty."

"Then what's the 'probably' about?"

"If she refuses to tell me where he is, or even if she warns him to get off the planet, she gets a pass. If she's complicit in trying to set me up for Pickett, she doesn't." He looked out the window. "It'll be dark in about half an hour. I think we'd better go out to the ship and bring back some clothes."

"The hotel can clean the ones we're wearing in twenty minutes."

"And if some friend of Pickett's has spotted me or works in the laundry, I could wind up going after him in the morning wearing nothing but my shoes."

Kinoshita sighed. "We'll go to the ship." He paused and looked at the young man. "He taught you well. He was always the most careful, meticulous man I ever met. At first it surprised me, a man with his reputation—but I guess that's how he lived long enough to get that reputation."

They took an aircar to the ship, picked up what they needed, and came back to the hotel. The woman at the registration desk stared at them when they returned, but didn't say a word.

Kinoshita went to his own room, and Jeff entered the suite, activated the room's computer, had it bring up maps, building permits, tax records, anything it could find that might help him figure out where Pickett was staying. When he was finally satisfied that he'd learned all he could, he went to sleep.

He was up with the yellow-orange sun the next morning. After he'd showered and shaved he stopped by Kinoshita's room, waited a few minutes for him to finish his ablutions, and then went with him to the hotel's restaurant for breakfast.

"Have you got any idea where he is?" asked Kinoshita as he finished his coffee.

Jeff nodded. "Yeah, I think so. There's an unimpressive little house about six miles east of town, not near anything. Gets its water from a well. I think that's where we'll find him."

"Any particular reason why?"

"Yeah," said Jeff. "A house like that on a world like this can't be worth much more than twenty or twenty-five thousand credits."

"So?"

"I checked the real-estate tax rolls. It's being taxed on an estimated value of four hundred thousand credits."

"Maybe it's sitting on a couple of square miles," suggested Kinoshita.

"It's on three barren acres," said Jeff. "That means most of it is hidden from view. The guy has built himself a luxury home for when he's here, and he obviously doesn't want certain people to know. Now, the locals are aware of how much he's worth, because he donated a wing of the hospital, so it's obviously not an attempt to mislead them. Put it all together and you've got someone with a pile of money who doesn't want any off-worlders to figure out he's living there."

"Not bad," said Kinoshita, visibly impressed.

"You ready?"

"Yes, I suppose so. I just keep wondering if the desk clerk warned him. She's not here this morning."

"Just how many hours a day do you want her to work?"

"You're not worried about it?"

"Would worrying help?" asked Jeff.

Kinoshita sighed deeply, feeling out of his depth, as usual. "Let's go."

They walked out the front door and summoned an aircar. Jeff gave it the coordinates—the place was too far out of town to have an address—and then they sat back and rode in silence across the brown, empty countryside until the vehicle approached the house.

"Stop here," said Jeff when they were eighty yards away.

The aircar stopped and hovered above the ground while Jeff and Kinoshita got out.

"Wait for us," Jeff ordered the aircar, then turned back to the house. He stood perfectly still for a long moment, then began walking. "Okay, I don't see any booby traps. It sure doesn't look like much of a house, does it? If I didn't know how much of it was hidden under the ground, I'd say a team of robots built it in less than a day."

When he was fifty feet from the house a lean, well-muscled man, his hair starting to turn gray at the sides, stepped out of the house and stood on the sparse grass, facing them.

"Stop right there," he said, "and tell me why you're here."

"I'm looking for Jubal Pickett," answered Jeff.

"You don't want him."

"I'll be the judge of that," said Jeff.

"Then let me put it another way," said the man. "You can't have him."

Where have I heard that voice? thought Kinoshita. *I know it from somewhere.*

"There's paper on him, dead or alive," said Jeff. "He can save a lot of wear and tear on all of us if he'll surrender—but one way or another I'm taking him back with me."

"Don't believe everything you read or hear," said the man. "Jubal Pickett has never killed anyone in his life."

"Of course he did," said Jeff. "Along with everything else he's wanted for, he killed two lawmen and a bounty hunter who were after him."

"No he didn't."

Jeff stared at the man. "*You* did," he said at last. "Who are you?"

"My name is Jason Newman," replied the man. "As for who I am, I'm the guy who's not going to let any harm come to an innocent man."

"An innocent man who pays you to protect him."

"With people like you after him, he needs all the protection he can get" was the response.

He's so familiar, thought Kinoshita. *The way he carries himself, even his choice of words. Where the hell have I seen him before?*

"Enough talk," said Jeff ominously. "You're standing between me and the man I've come to collect."

"I've already told you: you don't want him."

"What gives you an insight into what I want?" said Jeff sardonically.

Newman looked amused. "Tell him, Ito."

"*Omygod!*" exclaimed Kinoshita.

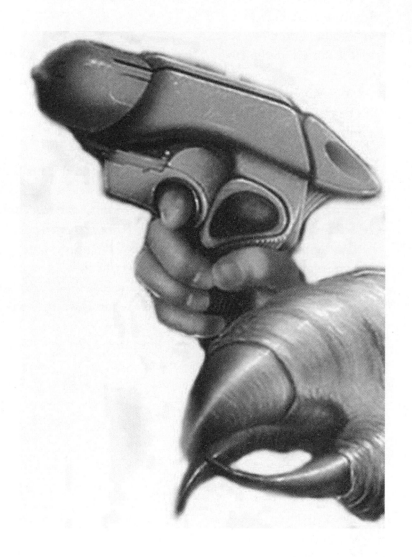

3.

JEFF TURNED TO Kinoshita, puzzled.

"It's *you*, isn't it?" said Kinoshita, never taking his eyes from the man facing them.

Jason Newman nodded. "It's me."

"But...but you look so different!"

"The last time we saw each other I told you that I was going to change my face," said Newman. "And of course *this*"—he held up his left hand—"is prosthetic, thanks to our friends back on Pericles. And since so much else was new, I thought I might as well take a new name too."

"Jason, son of Jefferson," said Kinoshita. "And Newman for the new identity. I approve."

"Are you who I think you are?" said Jeff.

"Probably," replied Newman. "It all depends on who you think I am."

"The clone who survived—the one who overthrew Cassius Hill on Pericles V."

"That's right. And since the first clone died before I was born, I have to assume you're a new one."

"I was created, to quote our progenitor, to take over the family business."

Newman looked at Kinoshita. "How's he been doing?"

"He's the Widowmaker," said Kinoshita, as if that was answer enough.

"The galaxy can use one," said Newman.

"Why did you stop?" asked Jeff.

"Being the Widowmaker, you mean?" replied Newman, as a sudden wind blew clouds of dust through the air. "I

completed my assignment. I was created to earn enough money
to keep the original alive and frozen in his cryogenic cocoon
until they came up with a cure for his disease. Once I'd done
that, I figured I'd earned the right to live my own life." He
stared curiously at the younger clone. "Haven't you ever felt
that way?"

Jeff shook his head. "This *is* my own life. Your mission
was performed with the knowledge that if you were successful, the original Widowmaker would be revived and live again,
so your term as the Widowmaker had a finite limit. Me, I'm
here so that he could retire from the Widowmaker business.
My mission is permanent; there's no time limit on it."

"So are you just a bodyguard called Jason Newman now?"
asked Kinoshita, brushing the dust from his tunic as the breeze
died down as suddenly as it had begun.

"Not exactly."

"Then what are you doing here?"

"After I recovered from the injuries I suffered on Pericles,
I got myself a new face and a new identity, and Cassandra and
I moved to the Outer Frontier, way out by the Rim. It seemed
a good place to start a new life."

"How did you team up with Jubal Pickett?" asked Jeff.

"A man named Willis Nordstrom tried to hold me up at
gunpoint out on a world named Mistover."

"Not smart," commented Kinoshita.

"I killed him. And two weeks later I saw that there was
paper on Jubal Pickett for killing Nordstrom and half a dozen
others. I flew to Mallachi VII, where the warrant was issued,
to explain that whatever else he'd done, he hadn't killed
Nordstrom." Newman paused. "They didn't give a damn. They
wouldn't even take Nordstrom's name off the warrant."

"Why not?" asked Kinoshita.

"I wondered about that too," said Newman, "so I began
looking into the matter. I learned that Pickett was a very
wealthy man, that his primary residence was on Mallachi
VII, and that a handful of local politicians had tinkered

with the tax code so that the government—all seven members of it—could confiscate the entire holdings, even the off-world holdings, of any citizen convicted of a felony. And a month after the law was passed, they found Pickett guilty of killing nineteen men, women, and children, and issued paper on him. I found him before anyone else did, and he convinced me that all of the charges were as phony as the one about killing Nordstrom." He paused again. "And here I am."

"So he's paying you to protect him?" asked Jeff.

"He's not paying me anything," answered Newman. "I don't need the money. I'm doing it because I'm in the justice business, and I'm not going to stand by and watch some bounty hunter kill a man I know to be innocent."

"I've studied that warrant," said Jeff. "Seven of the murders he's accused of committing occurred on Mallachi, including his wife's."

"So what?"

"The fact that he didn't kill a man half a galaxy from home doesn't mean he didn't kill his wife."

"He says he didn't do it. I believe him."

"Let him say it to me, and I'll decide if I believe him," said Jeff.

"And if you don't?"

"Then I'll do what I came here to do."

"I won't let you kill him," said Newman.

"Don't stand in my way," said Jeff. "I'm younger than you are, I'm quicker, and I've still got both the hands I was created with."

"I'm *you*—a version of you, anyway. If I vouch for him, that should be enough for you."

"I'm not in the judge or jury business," said Jeff. "The warrant's been issued, the reward's been posted, and my job is to bring him in."

"Look," said Newman. "I can prove he's innocent of one murder, and no one else has proven he's guilty of anything except being rich and living on the wrong world."

"Then let me take him back. You can come along and testify on his behalf in court."

"On Mallachi?" said Newman with a harsh laugh. "They'll convict him before he has a chance to sit down. If he sets foot on that planet he's a dead man." Jeff looked dubious. "Why are you having such a difficult time believing me?" continued Newman. "We share the same DNA, the same fingerprints, the same retinagram. You're the last person I'd lie to."

"That doesn't mean your judgment isn't distorted," answered Jeff. "You've been in Pickett's company for some time now. He's probably become a friend. You've killed three men on his behalf, men in our own profession. It would be very uncomfortable for you to think you killed them for a man who'd murdered his wife and a bunch of others. It's a lot easier to convince yourself he's innocent."

Suddenly the door to the house opened behind Newman, and a gaunt, balding man stepped out into the harsh sunlight.

"Jubal Pickett, I presume?" said Jeff.

"What are you doing out here?" demanded Newman angrily. "I told you to stay put!"

"I've been listening, Jason," said Pickett. "It's clear he isn't going to leave without me, and I won't have you dying on my behalf."

"I have no intention of dying," said Newman, never taking his eyes from Jeff. "And if you'll get inside, there's a possibility that you won't die either."

"I'm tired of running and I'm tired of this world," said Pickett. "Nothing grows on Giancola. It hasn't rained since I've been here, and I haven't seen a bird in two months. I'll take my chances on Mallachi."

"Your chances are slim to none," said Newman. "You know that."

"What are *your* chances against a younger, fitter version of yourself?" said Pickett. "Come to Mallachi and testify. Bring the press with you. Maybe it won't go so badly." He turned to Jeff. "I'm ready, young man."

Newman positioned himself between Pickett and Jeff. "*I'm* not ready," he said.

"Damn it!" said Jeff irritably. "We don't have to fight! He's *willing* to go back to Mallachi."

"Only because he thinks he's saving my life," said Newman. "Not quite the behavior you'd expect from the killer of nineteen men and women, is it?"

"Let me go with him, Jason," said Pickett, starting to walk forward. "I'm through letting you put yourself in danger on my behalf."

"You heard him," said Jeff.

"Yes, I did," replied Newman. "That's why I can't step aside."

"One way or another I'm taking him back. There's paper on him and it's my job."

"*He* turned you loose before you'd learned all your lessons," said Newman. "Killing innocent men isn't what you were created for."

"It's not my job to judge them," repeated Jeff stubbornly. "Someone else has already done that. I just bring them in."

"Not this time."

"Don't make me do this."

"You don't have to do anything," said Newman. "Just turn around and go home." He paused. "Ask yourself what the *real* Widowmaker would do."

"I *am* the real Widowmaker," said Jeff angrily. "Don't make me prove it."

"You're going to have to."

"I'll try not to kill you," said Jeff. "You're *me*—a version of me, anyway."

"Not anymore—or do I *look* like a foolish and pigheaded young man?"

As if by mutual consent they went for their weapons. Jeff's burner ripped through Newman's torso, melted his prosthetic hand, and incinerated most of his left ear. Newman, the tiniest fraction of a second slower, fired a blast of solid sound into the air as his screecher flew out of his hand.

Kinoshita raced forward and dropped to one knee to examine Newman. He was alive, his breathing and pulse erratic, the trunk of his body covered with third-degree burns, an unknown amount of damage to his internal organs, blood seeping out through the cauterized flesh on what remained of his ear.

"You son of a bitch!" roared Pickett, picking up Newman's sonic pistol and aiming it at Jeff. The young man was too fast and too accurate, and an instant later Jubal Pickett fell to the ground, dead.

"Shit!" muttered Jeff disgustedly. "None of this was necessary! He knew he couldn't beat me. And the old man..." He shook his head and shrugged, then walked over and hefted Pickett's corpse to his shoulder. "We might as well get back to the spaceport with him and drop him off at the bounty station on Binder X." He paused and stared at the badly wounded clone. "Newman will keep. I'll put in a call for an ambulance on the way to the ship." Kinoshita remained kneeling beside Newman. "Are you coming or not?"

"Not," said Kinoshita.

"If I leave, I'm not coming back for you."

"I don't expect you to."

Jeff stared at him. "I'm sorry it has to end like this. I'll miss you."

Kinoshita looked up at the young man. "I'll miss you too," he said sincerely.

"I thought you were sworn to serve the Widowmaker."

I am, thought Kinoshita. *And after I get Newman to the hospital or the cemetery, that's what I plan to do.*

4.

THE STILL-ATTRACTIVE middle-aged woman stood above Nighthawk as he knelt in the dirt.

"Why don't you just give up?" she asked.

"It's not my nature to give up," he replied.

"Every expert you've spoken to has told you that roses won't grow on Goldenhue."

"If I paid attention to what people said I could and couldn't do, I'd have died a century and a half ago."

"You've been working all morning," she said. "Won't you at least come in for a beer?"

He considered it, then rose slowly to his feet. "Yeah, I think I will. I'm getting a little old for all this kneeling." Nighthawk stretched to loosen the knotted muscles in his back, then stared ruefully at the drooping leaves and branches. "One of these days they're going to blossom."

"Why don't you take the afternoon off?" she suggested.

"Do I look *that* tired?" asked Nighthawk.

"You don't look tired at all. You look frustrated."

"I am," he replied. "Stupid roses."

"How stupid can they be?" she asked with a smile. "After all, they're winning."

"You know, you're the only person I've ever met who can talk to me like that." Suddenly he returned her smile. "That's probably why I let you stick around."

"Stick around?" she repeated sardonically. "That's as interesting a euphemism for marriage as I've heard."

He followed her past the bird feeders that were scattered around the yard, then into the house. They went to the kitchen, where she opened two canisters and handed one to him.

"Thanks," he said. "It was probably time to knock off anyway. I saw a ship coming down about an hour ago."

"So?"

"It might be the books I ordered from that dealer on Antares III. If it is, I don't want to be covered with dirt and sweat when I open the package."

"You could wait until you've showered." He simply stared at her. "No," she amended. "I guess you couldn't."

"One of them was published when we were still Earthbound," said Nighthawk.

"You could just have your computer tie into the library…"

"I read *books*, not electronic impulses or holographs."

"It would be less expensive."

"If we need more money, I'll go out and get it."

She had no argument for that, so she changed the subject, and they spent the next few minutes discussing the birds they'd seen at the various feeders that morning and making plans for their next birdwatching excursion to the planet's rain forest, a thousand miles to the south. Then Nighthawk saw a vehicle approaching the house.

"Looks like my books are here," he said. Suddenly he frowned. "Shit!"

"What is it?" asked Sarah, peering out the window.

"Someone I hadn't expected to see again."

"Bad news?"

"These days any news that can find me is probably bad news." He got to his feet and walked to the front door, opened it, and stepped out onto the broad veranda.

The aircar stopped in front of him, and Ito Kinoshita stepped out.

"What the hell are you doing here?" said Nighthawk.

"I'm delighted to see you too," replied Kinoshita wryly.

"I'd love to think this is a social call, but you don't make social calls and I don't accept them."

Kinoshita pulled his luggage out of the aircar and set it on the ground. "Have you still got that extra room?"

Nighthawk looked surprised. "He fired you?"

Kinoshita shook his head. "I left."

"Why?"

"Because it's my function in life to serve the Widowmaker."

"You're a little confused. The Widowmaker's out there somewhere." Nighthawk waved a hand toward the sky.

"That's what we have to talk about."

The woman stepped out onto the porch. "Hello, Ito." She walked over to him and gave him a hug. "How nice to see you again."

"I've missed you, Sarah," said Kinoshita.

Her gaze fell on his luggage. "How long will you be staying with us?"

"That's a matter of some debate," said Nighthawk.

Sarah studied his expression for a moment. "I'll leave you two to sort it out," she said. Before she went back inside the house, she turned to Kinoshita. "He's retired, and he's staying retired."

"You heard the lady," said Nighthawk as the door closed behind her.

"Do I have to stand out here in the sun, or are you going to invite me to sit on the veranda?"

"Do whichever you please."

"I see you're as gracious as ever." Kinoshita climbed the three stairs, walked over to a wicker chair, and sat down. "We've got a problem."

"*You've* got a problem," said Nighthawk. "My only problem is feeding you until you leave."

"Are you going to let me tell you about it?"

Nighthawk looked amused. "Has anyone ever stopped you from talking?"

"Let me get right to the point," said Kinoshita. "He's out of control."

"That doesn't sound like the kid I trained," said Nighthawk. "What did he do?"

"He may have killed an innocent man."

"Collateral damage?"

Kinoshita shook his head. "No, it wasn't collateral damage. He's you at age twenty-four. He hits what he aims at."

"Was there paper on the man he killed?"

"Two million credits."

Nighthawk frowned. "Well, then?"

"I told you: the man may have been innocent."

"They don't offer that kind of money until they're sure," said Nighthawk.

"Look, it's a long story," replied Kinoshita. "Maybe I'd better start at the beginning."

"Don't bother. There was paper on a man. Jeff killed him. End of story."

"Goddammit, Jefferson, you sound just like him!" said Kinoshita. "Let me explain! I didn't come all this way without a reason."

Nighthawk stared at him for a long moment, then walked over to a wooden rocker and sat down. "All right—talk."

"You taught him well, Jefferson," began Kinoshita. "I've been traveling with him since you sent him out, and he's everything you must have been at twenty-four or twenty-five. He's got the quickest reactions I've ever seen, he's as good with his hands or weapons as you were, his eyesight is unbelievable, and he's totally fearless. He's taken the Kimani Twins, and Jimmy Three-Eyes, and—"

"Okay, he's good. Get on with it."

"He's good because he has all the natural gifts he needs, and because you trained him to do what the job requires." He paused. "But you sent him out too soon."

"Explain."

"He sees everything in black-and-white. There are no grays in his world. If there's paper on a man, the man is to be killed, no questions asked."

"You stop to ask questions in this business, you don't celebrate too many birthdays."

"In general I agree with you, but there are always exceptions."

"I assume you're about to tell me of one."

Kinoshita nodded. "He went after Jubal Pickett, and he found him."

"Pickett, Pickett..." said Nighthawk. "Didn't he kill his wife and kids and a couple of dozen others?"

"He didn't have any kids. He was found guilty of killing his wife and eighteen other men, women, and children. After the paper was issued on him, he was accused of killing a lawman and two bounty hunters who tracked him down."

"Sounds like just the kind of man Jeff should go after," remarked Nighthawk.

"I agree," said Kinoshita. "That's exactly what he sounded like."

"But?"

"But an unimpeachable source told us that he'd been set up by some greedy politicians on his home planet that the whole thing was a scam to appropriate his property."

"Easy to say," noted Nighthawk.

"This source could prove at least part of it, which certainly cast doubt on the rest."

"I take it Jeff didn't listen to him."

"Jeff put him in the hospital and killed Pickett."

"Obviously your unimpeachable source wasn't very convincing."

"I don't think Jeff gives a damn whether Pickett was guilty or not," said Kinoshita. "There was paper on him, and that was all Jeff cared about."

"These things happen," said Nighthawk.

"That's all you've got to say about it?" demanded Kinoshita angrily. "It happened once. It could happen again, or ten more times!"

"It's possible," agreed Nighthawk. "Not likely, but possible."

"That isn't what you created him for. You've got to talk to him, explain why what he did was wrong. There's no way that he's going to listen to me."

"Forget it," said Nighthawk, as Sarah brought out a beer for Kinoshita. "Stick around," he told her. "Ito's talking about our whatever-the-hell-he-is."

"You mean Jeff?" she asked.

"Yes."

"Is he all right?"

"He seems to be."

"He's *physically* all right," said Kinoshita. "Jefferson taught him how to kill, and he's the best I ever saw at it. Now he's got to teach him *when* to kill and when not to."

"What did he do?" asked Sarah.

"He made a mistake," said Kinoshita.

"He *may* have made a mistake," corrected Nighthawk.

"Who did he kill?" asked Sarah.

"It's not important," said Nighthawk. "That's not why Kinoshita's here."

"What are you getting at?" asked Sarah.

"You didn't come halfway across the galaxy just because the kid killed a man with paper on him," said Nighthawk. "That's exactly what I trained him to do, so it's got to be something more."

"You're as sharp as you ever were," said Kinoshita admiringly.

"Whatever the reason, you're wasting your time here. If it was all that important, go find the clone who survived that mess on Pericles and get him to talk to—" Nighthawk stopped in midsentence, as a look of comprehension suddenly crossed his face.

"What is it?" said Sarah, puzzled.

"That's the only thing that could bring you here," said Nighthawk. "Is he dead?"

"Is *who* dead?" demanded Sarah.

"The clone I've never seen." He turned back to Kinoshita. "Is he?"

"Not quite," answered Kinoshita. "He's calling himself Jason Newman these days. He'll be in the hospital on Giancola II for a long time. They're growing him a new spleen and liver, and he'll need some cosmetic surgery, and a new ear, but he'll live."

"And he was me at what—maybe forty?"

"Somewhere around there, maybe a couple of years older."

"If *he* couldn't stop the kid, what makes you think *I* can? I'm an old man, in case you hadn't noticed."

"He'll listen to you."

"And if he doesn't?"

"You're his creator. You'll seem like a god to him—and people don't kill their gods."

"I'll bet that line got a lot of laughs on Golgotha," replied Nighthawk grimly.

"I'm serious, Jefferson," said Kinoshita. "I serve the Widowmaker. There were three versions of him in the galaxy. One's been shot all to hell and is in the hospital, and one's disqualified himself from the job." He stared at Nighthawk. "Like it or not, you're the Widowmaker again."

"The hell I am. I'm sorry about what happened, but it's not my problem."

"Excuse me, Jefferson," said Sarah, "but you're wrong."

He turned to her with a puzzled expression on his face. "What are you talking about?"

"A clone of Jefferson Nighthawk who gave his hand, his face, his very identity, to keep you alive while they were trying to find a cure for your disease is fighting for his life in a hospital, put there by another clone of Jefferson Nighthawk, who killed a man he was told was innocent. Jason Newman was created to raise enough money to keep you alive while medical science was developing a cure for your disease; you were cryogenically frozen at the time, and had nothing to do with that decision. But the younger clone, the one who put him in the hospital and killed an innocent man, is entirely your creation. You owe it to—"

"To the galaxy?" he interrupted sardonically. "I've paid the galaxy in full a hundred times, and Jeff has been paying interest on it since I sent him out."

"I was going to say that you owe it to the clone who's in the hospital," said Sarah. "The one who risked his life to save an innocent man from your creation. If that's not your problem, whose is it?"

"The kid is just doing what I taught him to do," repeated Nighthawk stubbornly.

"And Jason Newman—what was *he* doing?" said Sarah. "I know, it might never happen again. But it might also happen tomorrow, and next week."

"The kid's already put one Jefferson Nighthawk in the hospital. What makes you think he won't do it to me?"

"Who else is there?" said Kinoshita.

"Let me ask you a simple question, Jefferson," said Sarah. "If someone who had no reason to lie told you that a man you were about to kill was innocent, would you kill him before trying to find out the truth? If the answer is yes, then you're right and you should stay here. If the answer is no, then you'd better pay a visit to Jason Newman and learn what you can from him, and then find Jeff and correct the errors you made when you were training him."

Nighthawk uttered a sigh of defeat. "All I ever wanted was to live out my life in peace and obscurity. You wouldn't think that was so fucking hard to do, would you?"

"It isn't, for normal men," said Kinoshita. "But you're the Widowmaker."

Sarah stared at him with compassion and regret. "I think it's probably time to stop pretending that you were ever anything else."

5.

THE SHIP TOUCHED down on Giancola II, and Nighthawk and Kinoshita emerged.

"Ugly world," commented Nighthawk, surveying the bleak, barren brown landscape.

"Thank you," said Kinoshita.

"What for?"

"Those are the first words you've spoken to me since we took off."

"I wasn't saying them to *you*."

They entered the spaceport. Kinoshita kept his distance. Nighthawk had been in a black mood for the entire trip. Kinoshita knew, or at least thought he knew, that the old man wasn't going to shoot the messenger, but he was making the messenger very uncomfortable.

Nighthawk approached the robot/kiosk, tossed his passport disk on a counter, and let it read his fingerprints and retina.

"Welcome to Giancola II, garden spot of the Inner Frontier," said the robot. "Name, please?"

"You read my passport. You know my name."

The robot froze for a few seconds, then spoke again. "There is a problem, Mr. Nighthawk. You have identical fingerprints and retinagrams to a Jefferson Nighthawk who was here earlier this month, yet you are not he. Your ages and passports are different."

"Is my passport in order?" asked Nighthawk.

"Yes."

"Then the problem is yours, not mine. Let me pass through."

"Are you here for business or pleasure?"

"Pleasure."

"May I inquire—"

"You may not," said Nighthawk. "I have no legal obligation to tell you what I plan to do, as long as I'm not here on business."

"You may pass," said the robot. "Welcome to Giancola II." It rattled off the temperature, time of day, gravity, atmosphere content, and acceptable currencies, but Nighthawk was out of earshot before it was halfway done.

Kinoshita went through a different booth and fell into step behind Nighthawk as they made their way to the exit. An empty aircar glided up and Nighthawk got in, followed by Kinoshita.

"Hospital," Nighthawk instructed the aircar.

"It's the Admiral Miguel Riccardo Cordobes Memorial Hospital," said Kinoshita.

"Is there more than one on a planet like this?"

"No."

"Then be quiet."

They rode across the dreary landscape in silence. The aircar reached the city limits in five minutes, and pulled up to the small hospital in another five. Nighthawk walked up to the reception desk and learned the location of the clone's room. Then he and Kinoshita took an airlift to the fourth level, and walked down the hall until he came to the proper number.

Jason Newman was asleep. There were tubes connected to his arms and legs, he was connected to an artificial spleen and liver, a dozen machines controlled his breathing, heart rate, blood pressure, and other vital functions. They hadn't fitted him out with a new prosthetic hand yet—in fact, Nighthawk noted, he'd need not just a hand but a wrist and most of a forearm—and the place where his ear had been was covered with opaque ointments to promote healing of the burned flesh before any attempt to restore his hearing could be initiated.

"Jesus!" muttered Nighthawk. "How did you keep him alive long enough to get him here?"

"Jefferson Nighthawks have remarkable vitality," said Kinoshita.

"I've never been shot up this badly."

"You managed to live with a disfiguring disease for more than a century."

"I was frozen for all but a couple of years." Nighthawk studied the clone's face. "He doesn't look like me at all. The cosmetic surgeon who worked on him did a good job."

"He could afford it," answered Kinoshita. "He sent me to Deluros VIII with five million credits to keep you frozen, and kept the rest."

"He deserved it," said Nighthawk. "He overthrew a government with a force of, what, thirty?"

"There were a few more than that."

"And how many of the enemy were there?"

"Counting the military? Four million, give or take."

"That's a hell of an accomplishment," said Nighthawk. "I know that—and Jeff knew it. I told him about both the clones that came before him." He frowned in puzzlement. "So why the hell wouldn't he believe a man like this?"

A golden-fleeced nurse from the distant world of Karimon entered just then, adjusted various levels of the medications that were being dripped into Newman's system, tinkered with his oxygen supply, and left without a word.

Nighthawk continued staring at the sleeping clone. Finally he spoke again. "Is he all alone?"

"It's a private room."

"I mean, has he got anyone you should contact, anyone who should know he's here?"

"There's a woman, Cassandra Hill. I don't know if they're married, but she'd be the one," said Kinoshita. "The problem is, I don't know his home world, so I don't know how to contact her. He was in no condition to talk when I left Giancola. Maybe I can find out."

"I wouldn't count on it," said Nighthawk. "Look at him. He might go a week or a month without waking up." He went to a communicator and raised the desk. "This is Jefferson Nighthawk. Scan my retina and match it against my ID at the

spaceport. I want all of Jason Newman's medical bills charged
to my account at the Bank of Goldenhue."

"Working...done," replied a mechanical voice.

"And send up a nurse."

"The nurse was just there, and it not due again for another
ninety minutes."

"Send one anyway."

"Is there an emergency?" asked the voice as Nighthawk
deactivated the communicator.

A tripodal Mollutei nurse entered the room a moment later,
walked over to the bed, looked at Newman, then checked all
the machines.

"He seems fine," it said. "What's the problem?"

"Wake him up."

"Why?"

"Because I told you to."

He was a man in his mid-sixties, and he was unarmed.
The nurse was an alien who heard his voice through the trans-
lating mechanism of a T-pack. And yet suddenly he was no
longer Jefferson Nighthawk, but had become the
Widowmaker again, with an air of menace about him that
transcended language and species. The nurse immediately
began fiddling with the various machines that Newman was
attached to, adjusting the flows of oxygen and adrenaline,
and finally stepped back.

"He will awaken shortly."

"Will he be in much pain?" asked Nighthawk.

"Certainly not," said the nurse haughtily. It rattled off a
trio of pain medications that were being dripped into
Newman's body.

"Good. Show my companion how to put him back to sleep
when I'm through talking to him."

"The system will keep him awake for five minutes, no
longer," said the nurse.

"All right, leave us now," said Nighthawk.

The nurse glared at him and walked to the door.

"One more thing," said Nighthawk before the nurse could make its exit.

"Yes?"

"I would be very angry if you were to report this or attempt to hinder me in any way," he said. "Am I making myself clear?"

"Yes, sir," said the nurse, its anger turning to fear. It ducked out before Nighthawk could say anything further.

Nighthawk got to his feet and stood at the foot of the bed. Newman's eyelids flickered in about half a minute. He groaned once, then seemed to make a physical effort to remain silent as he carefully adjusted his position. Finally he opened his eyes.

"Welcome back," said Nighthawk.

Newman stared at him for a long minute with a look of dawning recognition. "Sonuvabitch!" he rasped. Then, "I never thought we'd meet."

"Neither did I," said Nighthawk. "How do you feel?"

"I've been better." Pause. "That kid is *good*."

"That's what I've come to talk to you about."

"I haven't got much to say. I was better at twenty-two or whatever he is than I am at forty-three."

"But not smarter. Jefferson Nighthawks don't shoot Jefferson Nighthawks."

"He's not us," said Newman. Nighthawk looked puzzled. "I was born with your memories and experiences. Every one you ever had, six decades' worth, were crammed into my head before I woke up for the first time. I know every thought you ever had until five years ago; they were *my* thoughts until I started living my own life. Damned near cost me my life, too, because some of those memories were a century out of date. But this kid, he wasn't born with all your memories and thoughts. That was a mistake."

"I didn't want him carrying any extra mental or emotional baggage," said Nighthawk. "And I was around to train him. I'd been frozen when they made you and the other clone."

"I'd have done the same," said Newman. "After all, I'm you—or mostly you, anyway."

"They seem to want to keep you asleep, so I'll try to make this quick," said Nighthawk. "How certain are you that Pickett was innocent?"

"Jubal Pickett never killed anyone. Hell, he was accused of killing a man that I killed myself."

"What about the other eighteen?"

"I knew the man. He couldn't have done it."

"Did you ever tie him in to a Neverlie machine?"

"I didn't have to. Everything he told me checked out."

"Did Jeff talk to you?" persisted Nighthawk. "Ask for proof?"

"The only proof I have is my testimony," said Newman. "That should have been enough for a man who shares my DNA."

Nighthawk was silent for a long minute. Finally he spoke. "I sent him out too soon. I've got to find him."

"And teach him to look for shades of gray?" suggested Kinoshita.

"There are no shades of gray when you're the Widowmaker," said Nighthawk.

"Then I don't understand," said Kinoshita.

"He's not going after the kid because he killed an innocent man," said Newman. "We've probably both killed innocent men along the way."

Kinoshita looked bewildered. "If that's not the reason…?" he began.

"He shot a Jefferson Nighthawk," said Nighthawk. "Whether Jubal Pickett was guilty or not, he had a price on his head and the first three bounty hunters to go after him were dead. That was a judgment call, plain and simple. But right or wrong, you don't shoot another version of yourself. I made this kid the single most efficient killing machine in the galaxy. If he'll shoot his fellow clone, then the day will come when he'll shoot anybody." He paused. "I can't allow that. I'm going to have to find him and make sure he understands."

"And find a way to stop him if he doesn't want to learn," added Newman.

"It shouldn't come to that. He's like a son to me—more than a son. He knows I'm not his enemy. He has no reason not to listen, or to assume I'm misleading him."

"He's been on his own for a couple of years now," said Newman. "That's time enough to form his own opinions."

"He was created to take exactly the kind of man Jubal Pickett was supposed to be," said Nighthawk. "The Inner Frontier still needs the Widowmaker. I just have to make a few adjustments to the current model."

"You're making it sound easier than it's going to be," said Newman. "If you wait a couple of weeks, I'll go with you."

"A couple of weeks?" exclaimed Kinoshita disbelievingly. "You'll be lucky to be out of here in six months!"

Newman looked at Nighthawk. "He's wrong. You know how fast we recover and how much pain we can live with."

"Yeah, he's wrong," agreed Nighthawk. "But it's going to take them more than two weeks to grow you a new liver and spleen. Besides, it doesn't make any difference. I can't let the kid get any farther ahead of me if I'm going to catch up with him before he makes more mistakes. Two weeks, six months, it's all the same. I've got to leave today."

"If you haven't found him by the time I'm out of here…"

"I promise," said Nighthawk.

Newman turned to Kinoshita. "Cassandra's on Murchison III—"

"I'll send her a subspace message the second we get back to the ship," said Kinoshita.

"Let me finish," said Newman, his words starting to slur, his eyelids drooping. "Tell the hospital where she is, and have them contact her after I'm off the pain medication. No sense her coming all this way if all I'm going to do is sleep."

"I'll see to it," said Kinoshita.

"Thanks." He turned to Nighthawk. "I'm glad we finally met."

"So am I."

"When you find the kid, tell him…" Newman lost consciousness, his sentence unfinished.

"Tell him what, I wonder?" said Kinoshita.

"Probably that Jefferson Nighthawks don't shoot each other."

Kinoshita decided not to mention that that was precisely what Nighthawk was going to have to do if reason didn't work.

6.

"SO HOW DO we track him down?" asked Kinoshita as their ship left orbit and sped out of the Giancola system at light speed. "Always assuming you're talking to me again," he added.

Nighthawk chose to ignore the remark about his anger. "You've been traveling with him for the better part of two years," he replied, walking to the galley and ordering the ship to serve him a beer. "You must know something about the way his mind works. Will he go after the biggest target or the closest?"

"Beats the hell out of me," answered Kinoshita, joining him in the galley. "There's no rhyme or reason to it. He goes after whichever one excites his imagination."

"And what excites it?"

"It's *your* imagination," answered Kinoshita defensively. "You tell me."

The older man stared at Kinoshita for a long moment, until the smaller man looked away and ordered a cup of coffee to hide his uneasiness. Nighthawk remained silent, lost in thought, for a long time. Finally, when Kinoshita was sure he had fallen asleep, he spoke.

"There's no sense chasing him all across the Frontier. I have no way of knowing who he's going to go after and in what order, so I'm always going to be a step behind him. And even if I guess right and get to a planet first, what am I going to do—sit around and let some killer murder more victims to make sure Jeff shows up?"

"Then what *are* you going to do?"

"If I'm not going to search the galaxy looking for him, the alternative is to bring him to me."

Kinoshita looked puzzled. "How?"

"I'll send him a message."

"How can he respond if you don't know where to send it?" asked Kinoshita.

"He'll respond to this one," said Nighthawk with absolute certainty.

7.

NIGHT HAD FALLEN on New Barcelona. Five small moons made their way across the cloudless sky at varying speeds, and their light caused the stately minarets and towers of Cataluna, the largest city on the planet, to cast eerie shadows that seemed to be constantly moving. The streets were narrow and twisting, lit only by the ever-changing moonlight.

Cataluna was a beautiful city, but like many other beautiful things its beauty was only skin-deep. And hiding beneath the beauty like a cancer was the District.

The District had begun life, centuries earlier, as the city's red-light district, zoned and mandated by the government so as to keep the less salubrious aspects of life on the Inner Frontier from spreading to the more respectable areas. It wasn't long before the authorities stopped patrolling the District, and shortly thereafter they simply refused to set foot in it. Word got out, of course, and soon the brothels were the least of the enterprises to be found there. Black-marketeers for the entire star cluster set up shop openly. Stolen goods from a thousand worlds were stored and fenced in the shops and cellars of the District. Human and alien drug dens abounded. Anyone on the run from the law could find safe haven in the District. There was nothing you couldn't buy there at competitive prices, from a sexual partner (regardless of gender or even species) to an alphanella seed to a murder.

"Are you sure we have to do this?" asked Kinoshita nervously as they approached the outskirts of the District.

"I'm sure *I* have to," replied Nighthawk calmly. "*You* do what you want."

"But why will he come here?"

"Because it's been two centuries since a policeman or a bounty hunter entered the District. It's off-limits. When he hears what's happening, he'll come. If he's got a wish list of ten men in the cluster, half of them are here at any given time."

"If you know it, he knows it too," said Kinoshita. "And yet he's never been here."

"We have different agendas," said Nighthawk. "And he would have come here sooner or later."

"What makes you think so?"

"Because I was preparing to come here more than a century ago when I contracted the eplasia."

"But he's not you," noted Kinoshita. "Not like Newman is."

"He's the best at what he does," answered Nighthawk. "And that's what the bounty hunter who shows his face here has to be."

"Then what makes you think you'll be alive five minutes after we enter the District?" demanded Kinoshita. "Don't forget—he's forty years younger than you."

"Yeah, but I'm forty years smarter." He stopped to light a smokeless Altairian cigar. "It's like sports. A phenom comes up with all the physical gifts imaginable, so he uses them and excels. After a few years he loses half a step, or he gets slowed by some injuries—but along the way he's studied the game and started using his brain and his experience, and even though his skills have started eroding, he's actually better at his job."

"So you're saying you're better than Jeff?" said Kinoshita dubiously.

Nighthawk shrugged. "Who knows?" Suddenly he smiled. "But it's a damned good analogy, isn't it?"

"How can you joke?" snapped Kinoshita. "You're walking into the most dangerous piece of real estate within five thousand light-years, and if I know you, you're going to seek out the men whose deaths will make the most news."

"Have you got a better way to send him word that we're here? When he hears that a Widowmaker is collecting bounties, he'll have to come."

"It's suicidal!" snapped Kinoshita. "You're an old man, for God's sake!"

"Keep your voice down," said Nighthawk. "No sense getting us shot at before we even arrive."

"You fucking Widowmakers are all alike!" muttered Kinoshita. "You're the worst of them. At least they have some excuse—they get it from you."

"If you're worried, go back to the ship and wait for me. You'll be perfectly safe there."

"You go to hell."

"Make up your mind," said Nighthawk. "Do you serve the Widowmaker or just bitch about him?"

"I serve him," said Kinoshita, lowering his voice. "But there are days I wish I'd never met him."

"Then why *do* you serve us?"

"You know," said Kinoshita, "that's the first time you've ever asked me about myself."

"It stopped you from yelling."

Kinoshita ignored the remark. "When I was a young man, I was a police officer on Deluros VIII, and my given name was Jerome Hayakawa. My first two partners were killed in the line of duty, and I took their names—Ito and Kinoshita. It's a damned silly name for anyone of my ancestry; it would be like calling yourself Jones Smith. But I did it so I'd never forget them. I quit the force when the courts insisted on giving lenient sentences to men who should have been put to death for their crimes. I decided to move to the Inner Frontier and become a bounty hunter, so that when I caught up with a killer the courts would never give him a chance to kill again."

"So how did you get in the clone-training business?" asked Nighthawk.

"I was recovering back on Deluros from some minor wounds and I had some time to kill, so I took the job of training your first clone." He paused and sighed. "I knew five minutes into it that I was lucky to still be alive. His abilities were so far beyond mine—or anyone else's I'd ever seen—that for the first time in my life I became aware of my own mortality. I knew that he would be far better at my chosen mission than I could ever be, and so I made up my mind to serve the Widowmaker, as my samurai ancestors served their feudal lords."

"Interesting" was Nighthawk's only comment.

"But that doesn't mean I have to like it when the Widowmaker behaves like an asshole—either the newest one or the original."

"Do you feel better now?" asked Nighthawk.

Kinoshita sighed. "Yeah, actually I do." He paused. "As long as I've known you and your clones, I've never known how or why you became the Widowmaker in the first place. They were *created* to be the Widowmaker; you *chose* to be. Someday I'd like you to tell me about it."

"Someday," said Nighthawk. He stopped at a street corner. "This is it. We cross the street, we're in the District."

"Then what?"

"Then we find a room."

"I beg your pardon?"

"A room," repeated Nighthawk. "Unless you plan to sleep in the street."

Kinoshita frowned. "I wasn't planning to spend the night here at all. I figured you'd do what you came to do and then we'll get the hell out of here before everyone starts shooting at us."

"You haven't been paying attention, have you?" said Nighthawk. "There's no sense drawing Jeff to New Barcelona if I'm not here to meet him."

"So you're going to kill some butcher or other and then stick around?" demanded Kinoshita.

"Just killing one won't make enough news."

"*Oh, shit!*" muttered Kinoshita. "What are you letting us in for?"

"Shut up," said Nighthawk.

"You're a goddamned lunatic!"

"I said shut up," repeated Nighthawk, and as had happened in the past, Kinoshita realized that Jefferson Nighthawk had disappeared completely, to be replaced by the Widowmaker. "I didn't ask for this. You're the one who got me out here. If you don't like the way I operate, then stay the hell away from me. But there will be no more arguing and no more bitching. Do I make myself clear?"

Kinoshita stared at him, searching futilely for a sign of the Jefferson Nighthawk he had accompanied from the spaceport. Finally he nodded his agreement.

They crossed the street. It didn't feel any different at first. That changed a block into it, when they had to step around a dead man who lay bleeding on the pavement. There were no sidewalks, no slidewalks, just narrow streets filled with foreboding.

Three blocks into the District, Nighthawk stopped and stood perfectly still.

"What's the—?" began Kinoshita.

"Quiet." Then: "We're being followed."

"What are we going to do about it?" asked Kinoshita nervously.

"Nothing. At least I know where they are."

"They?"

"There are two of them. They're just checking to see if we're slumming. You don't have to be a criminal to enter the District. You can come looking for drugs or women or men or half a dozen other things—and if that's the case, it means you've got money in your pockets."

"Pardon a foolish question, but how do they know we're not here to spend our money?"

"They don't."

"Then why shouldn't they shoot us down?"

"Bad for business," answered Nighthawk. "Shoot enough civilians and no one will come here to spend their money anymore."

"Why should they care?"

"Because if they drive business away, what the people who depend on that business will do to them will make a death sentence in a court of law seem infinitely preferable," said Nighthawk. He began walking again, more slowly this time, looking into the windows he passed, while Kinoshita fell into step and spent most of his time trying to spot the men who were trailing them.

Suddenly the street turned in on itself, a cross between a figure eight and a Möbius strip. Buildings met above them, creating narrow passageways on the street level. They could hear music from half a dozen dives, some of it so atonal and discordant that Kinoshita knew it must be coming from taverns that catered to aliens.

"All right," announced Nighthawk a moment later. "We've come far enough. We should be pretty near the center."

"All the buildings are dark, and the closest music's a block away," noted Kinoshita.

"Use your nose."

"My nose?" repeated Kinoshita. He inhaled deeply, and frowned. "I smell something…strange."

"Someone's smoking mexalite." Nighthawk pointed to a grate at the edge of the street, very near where he was standing. "Three sticks of that stuff will fry your brain for a week." Slight smile. "That makes this as good a place to start as any."

Start? thought Kinoshita. *Are you planning to kill your way from here to the edge of the District?*

"It's got to be in the cellar of this building," said Nighthawk, walking to a door. Kinoshita half-expected a tiny panel to slide back and a voice to demand all kinds of identification, but Nighthawk simply stepped forward and the door dilated to let him pass through.

Of course, thought Kinoshita. *Why do they care who you are? After two centuries, the one thing they know you're not is a lawman or a bounty hunter.*

Kinoshita followed Nighthawk into a dimly lit foyer, then to an airlift. They stepped onto a cushion of air and gently descended some fifteen feet below ground level, emerging in a large room illuminated only with indirect red and blue lighting. There were tables scattered around the room. A tripodal Hesporite was playing an instrument that was shaped to accommodate him and was made of an alien alloy, but it emitted a sound that was pure alto sax, smooth and sultry. There were some twenty men and women seated at the tables, and an equal number of aliens, composed of half a dozen different races. A few were drinking, a couple were simply concentrating on the Hesporite's music, most were smoking long thin glowing sticks of mexalite. Kinoshita didn't know what effect it had on aliens—a Canphorite seemed totally unaffected, and a pair of Lodinites looked mildly tipsy—but there was no question that it was sending the human contingent off to secret places that only they could see.

There was no host, no headwaiter, no indication that anyone knew or cared that they had just entered the place. Nighthawk looked around for a moment, then walked off toward an empty table in the far corner of the room.

"Hard to breathe in here with all the smoke," remarked Kinoshita softly. "Can it affect us?"

"It might give you lung cancer," said Nighthawk. "It won't disconnect your neural circuits. I don't know what causes the effect, but I know you can only get it direct from the mexalite. Secondhand smoke will leave you stone cold sober."

"Where are they getting it?"

"I'm sure someone will be along to tell us."

And within a minute a slim human woman, provocatively but not scantily clad, approached them and sat down at their table.

"Hello," she said. "My name is Minx."

"Hello," replied Nighthawk. "Mine isn't."

"Is there anything I can get for you?"

"What did you have in mind?"

"Mister, you name it and we've got it," she said with a smile.

"Let's start with a name."

"I told you. My name is—"

"Not you. This place."

"Horatio's."

"Is Horatio around?"

"He's been dead almost seventy years." She paused. "Now, what can I get you?"

"Nothing at the moment. I've got some business with some men in the District. I need a place to meet them. This'll do as well as any."

"You can't stay here if you're not buying something," insisted Minx.

"Fair enough," said Nighthawk, pulling out a couple of banknotes. "Here's two hundred credits."

"What do you want for it?"

"An hour's worth of silence."

She smiled again. "This will only buy you half an hour."

"Come back when the time's up," said Nighthawk. "Oh, and one more thing."

"Yes?"

"Don't push your luck."

There was something about the way he said it, something ominous. She looked at him, then nodded a quick assent and made a quicker retreat.

"Now what?" asked Kinoshita.

"Now we wait."

"For what?"

"For someone to come along."

"Have you got anyone in mind?"

"I don't even know who's in the District today."

"Well, then?"

"I know who'll be at the top of Jeff's list. Some of them have to be here, and sooner or later one or more of them will walk into Horatio's."

"So you just plan to sit here until one of them shows up?" asked Kinoshita.

"It's easier than going out looking for them," answered Nighthawk. "Only a fool wanders aimlessly at night in the District, and if they were fools they wouldn't have lived long enough to make Jeff's list."

"But we were outside just a few minutes ago."

"Very briefly," replied Nighthawk. "We had a destination in mind. So will they."

"You are the least informative son of a bitch I've ever met," complained Kinoshita.

"You traveled with me from the day I got out of the hospital back on Deluros VIII until the day I sent Jeff out to take my place. You know what I'm like. If it annoys you, you shouldn't have come."

"Let's not go into that again."

"Suit yourself."

It comes back to me now, thought Kinoshita. *Jefferson Nighthawk's not exactly loquacious, but he talks to me. The Widowmaker just concentrates on the business at hand. He tolerates my presence, but he feels no obligation to share any thoughts or plans with me.*

"Are you sure you'll recognize one of the men you want if he walks in here?" asked Kinoshita at last.

"I took the trouble of studying the Wanted lists on the trip here while you were sleeping."

"Of course," said Kinoshita bitterly. "You might have awakened me so I could help spot them before they recognize you."

"They won't recognize me," said Nighthawk. "I quit bounty hunting half a century before any of them were born. To them I'm just an old man visiting the District for a last thrill on the way to the grave."

"I'd forgotten," admitted Kinoshita. "I've seen you in action since they revived you, so I assumed everyone knew you were back."

"I'm not back. I'm just going to make a few minor adjustments to the man I sent out, and then I'm going back to live out my life on Goldenhue."

"I never thought you'd stick it out this long," said Kinoshita. "I just don't picture you as a gardener."

"And a birdwatcher. Don't forget the birding." He paused, then amended: "Well, the avians, anyway. Goldenhue doesn't have any true birds."

Two hard-looking men entered the room, nodded to a couple of others who were already there, and walked to a table.

"They're carrying a lot of firepower," noted Kinoshita softly. "Pulse gun, burner, even a couple of projectile pistols."

"I've always liked projectile weapons," said Nighthawk approvingly. "They're pretty accurate at close range, and they make a hell of a bang. The noise usually freezes your opponent for a second or two. He's mostly used to the humming of a burner or a screecher's whistling."

"So is there paper on these two?"

"I'd be surprised if there wasn't," said Nighthawk. "But they're minnows. I came here to find some whales."

"What's a whale?"

"Big fish. Used to swim in Earth's oceans a few thousand years ago before we killed the last of them. That's what they say, anyway."

Four men and three aliens left in the next fifteen minutes, and two men and seven more aliens entered. Minx was kept busy supplying them with liquor and sticks of mexalite. One Lodinite slipped her a large bill and walked through a door at the side of the room, doubtless on his way to a sexual encounter elsewhere in the building.

She cast an occasional glance at Nighthawk, but never returned to ask for more money.

"So far she's the only person I've seen working the room," noted Kinoshita. "I wonder who runs the place?"

"Ask her who pays her salary," suggested Nighthawk.

"It might be someone we're after."

"*We're* not after anyone," said Nighthawk. "*I* am. And Horatio's won't be owned by anyone I want."

"What makes you so sure?"

"If he's busy running this place and securing his mexalite supply, he hasn't got time to get the kind of price on his head that would bring him to Jeff's attention."

"Maybe he's already got it and is hiding out here," said Kinoshita.

"If he's on that list, he has enough money so he doesn't have to own a dive like this."

Just then a huge man, well over seven feet tall, heavily muscled top to bottom, entered Horatio's. He was totally bald, and when he turned his head Kinoshita saw that he didn't have any eyebrows. His entire face looked smooth as a baby's; there was no indication that he'd ever had to shave. Nevertheless his most striking facial feature wasn't his skin but his eyes— one blue, one brown; obviously he'd been born with one and the other was a replacement.

There was something curious about his hands. It took Kinoshita a minute to figure out what it was: he had no fingernails, nor did it look like he'd ever had any. What he did have was a ragged row of white bone that had been grafted onto the backs of his fingers on each hand, giving his fists the equivalent of a pair of brass knuckles. He carried neither a burner nor a screecher. A pulse gun rested in a small holster on his right hip, and he had a pair of exotic-looking alien weapons tucked in his belt. It had been a few thousand years since men rode horses, and even longer since they wore spurs, but he clearly had something sharp and formidable sticking out of the back of his boots.

"Interesting guy," whispered Kinoshita.

"Very," replied Nighthawk.

"Look at him. He's two and a half men crammed into one package, and armed to the teeth. I sure as hell would never want to face him."

"You won't have to. You're just here as an observer."

Kinoshita suddenly had a sinking feeling in the pit of his stomach. He looked questioningly at his companion.

"He calls himself Hairless Jack Bellamy," continued Nighthawk calmly. "You'd have to hunt far and wide to find a crime he hasn't committed, and he's worth six million credits dead or alive."

8.

KINOSHITA STARED AT the bald man, then whispered to Nighthawk. "Are you going to try taking him right now?"

"No."

"You want to study him first," said Kinoshita knowingly.

"I've already studied him," said Nighthawk.

"Then—?"

"He's not alone."

"You're mistaken, Jefferson," said Kinoshita. "He walked in by himself, and no one has entered after him."

"See that Mollutei sitting all alone across the room?" said Nighthawk. "And the two men drinking beer over there?"

"What about them?"

"They're working for Bellamy. I'll take him outside, when he's alone—or at least where I won't have to turn my back to his bodyguards."

Kinoshita looked at the men and alien Nighthawk had indicated. "How can you tell?" he asked. "They were here when we arrived."

"The men put their mexalite away the second he entered," answered Nighthawk softly. "And the Mollutei checked his holster to make sure the strap was off his pulse gun. They're on duty now."

"They haven't given him a second look."

"They're here to protect him, not shoot him. They've been studying everyone else in the room."

"What if you're wrong?" asked Kinoshita.

"Then he gets to enjoy a few drinks and maybe some mexalite, and live a few hours longer."

Bellamy sat down at a table near the door and signaled to Minx, who brought him a bottle and half a dozen sticks of mexalite without asking what he wanted. He shoved a wad of notes down her neckline and gave her bottom a familiar pat as she walked away.

During the next ten minutes a man and a Canphorite each entered Horatio's, walked directly over to Bellamy's table, sat down and conversed with him in low tones. They handed him various currencies, got up, and walked out.

"This must be his office," observed Kinoshita.

"Makes sense," agreed Nighthawk. "Why let anyone know where he lives? Better to meet them here, where he's got men protecting his back."

"It can't be that hard to find out where he sleeps," said Kinoshita. "You could just follow him back to his hotel, or wherever it is he's staying."

Nighthawk regarded his companion as a teacher would regard a very slow child. "He won't take a direct route to his rooms," he said. "And he'll have three or four more gunmen posted along the way, just in case someone's stupid enough to follow him."

"What makes you so sure?"

"Because he's survived long enough to be worth six million credits," said Nighthawk. "You don't have to be a bounty hunter to claim the reward. Anyone who works for him could stick a bullet in his ear, or burn a hole between his eyes and turn the body in. Most of them wouldn't hesitate for a second if they thought they could get away with it. The fact that he's still alive means he knows how to protect himself."

"Then he'll be protected the second he steps outside," said Kinoshita.

"Probably," agreed Nighthawk.

"We should come up with a course of action, then," said Kinoshita.

"*We* aren't doing anything. *I* am."

"I'm willing to help," protested Kinoshita. "I'm no Widowmaker, but I was pretty good at my work."

"Pretty good won't be enough, not here in the District," said Nighthawk. "I can't face him and whoever's waiting for him if I have to worry about you too."

"You don't have to concern yourself with me. I can take care of myself."

"In most places, against most men, I'm sure you can," said Nighthawk. "But not here, and not now."

"But—"

"If you want to help, stay here after he and I leave, and make sure the two guns and the Mollutei don't come out after me. If they do, they're your responsibility."

"All three?" asked Kinoshita, unable to hide his nervousness.

"If they're here in the District there's paper on them," replied Nighthawk. "Just remember that it's not a sporting contest. Stick a beam or a bullet in each one before he knows you're there."

Kinoshita swallowed hard and nodded his assent.

"Good," said Nighthawk. "Now let's order something before Bellamy notices that we're not drinking or smoking." He signaled to Minx.

"You didn't seem to care about that before," commented Kinoshita.

"Bellamy wasn't here before."

"The others were."

"The others don't matter," said Nighthawk, making no attempt to hide his contempt for them.

Minx approached them, and Nighthawk ordered a bottle of Cygnian cognac. She returned a moment later with the bottle and two glasses.

"Thanks," said Nighthawk, handing her a roll of Maria Theresa dollars.

She counted it, smiled, and handed him two sticks of mexalite.

"I didn't ask for that," he said.

"I know—but you paid too much for the drinks."

She walked away before he could argue.

"She must be the owner," Nighthawk remarked to Kinoshita as he put the mexalite in a pocket. "Or at least living with him. I can't imagine any other reason for her to make sure we didn't feel cheated."

Kinoshita examined the bottle. "This looks like the real stuff." He smiled. "I don't think I've ever had Cygnian cognac before."

"It's just for show. Take tiny sips, and not a lot of them. It's stronger than you think."

They nursed their drinks in silence for the better part of a half hour. The Hesporite took a brief break, then returned and began playing an evocative melody on the sax-like instrument again.

"He could spend the next few hours here," whispered Kinoshita.

"I doubt it."

"Why?"

"When you've got as many men after your head as Bellamy's got, you don't want to be predictable. He's probably got six to ten joints just like this where he makes his contacts and does his business. He'll be leaving soon."

"You're sure?"

Nighthawk didn't even bother to answer him.

Kinoshita dwelled on the comparison Nighthawk had made between the young athlete and the older one. Jeff was simply the best: he didn't plan, didn't analyze, didn't try to stack the odds in his favor. He saw his prey, he confronted it, and he killed it, seemingly without effort. Nighthawk, like the aging athlete, had lost half a step. Maybe he could still take anyone but Jeff, maybe he couldn't, but he saw no reason not to use everything he'd learned, every observation he'd made in his long career, to better the odds. Jeff and Newman had been created to be the Widowmaker, but Nighthawk had had to learn the job from the ground up, step by step, and he never stopped learning.

"There he goes," said Nighthawk as the bald man got up, threw some more money on the table, and walked to the door. "Don't follow me out unless his flunkies do."

Only you would think of skilled bodyguards as flunkies, reflected Kinoshita.

Nighthawk got to his feet, went to the airlift, and reached the street no more then twenty seconds behind Bellamy. He didn't follow the huge man until he'd scanned the area, spotted a man loitering half a block away and a Lexonian sitting in the middle of the street a block in the opposite direction, swaying drunkenly with a bottle in its hands.

Bellamy turned to his left and continued walking. Nighthawk's hand dropped to the butt of his projectile pistol, then moved to his burner. No sense making an identifying bang in enemy territory; the hum of a laser would attract a lot less attention. He drew the burner and aimed it, not at Bellamy, but at the Lexonian. The beam was straight and true, and the alien keeled over without a sound.

For a huge man, Bellamy had incredibly fast reactions. Without seeing the source of the laser beam he hurled himself between two buildings, firing his pulse gun in Nighthawk's general direction as he did so. Nighthawk knew that it would take Bellamy a couple of seconds to right himself and aim his weapon properly, and he used that time to spin and take out the loiterer, who was trying to draw his weapon when the beam burned a black smoking hole in his forehead.

"Who the hell are you?" demanded Bellamy from the darkness.

Nighthawk didn't answer. There was no sense wasting words or letting the huge man home in on their sound. He knew he couldn't wait more than a few seconds for Bellamy to emerge, because there was every chance that he'd follow the narrow corridor between the buildings and escape into the next block.

Taking a deep breath, Nighthawk stepped between the buildings, crouched down in case a pulse of energy was coming toward his head or heart, and put a beam down the middle of the corridor. In the brief instant that it illuminated the area, he was unable to spot Bellamy.

The corridor was about thirty yards long, and he was sure Bellamy couldn't have covered that distance, not with those muscle-bound legs. That meant the bald man had ducked into an alcove while he was planning his next move.

All right, thought Nighthawk. *Let's make sure you don't go out the back.*

He aimed his burner at the path between the buildings and melted the last ten yards of it. It would be an hour before it was cool enough to run across, and he was sure that a man of Bellamy's bulk couldn't jump it.

He considered melting the rest of the corridor, but decided against it. If he made the whole thing too hot to cross, there was no way he could flush Bellamy out or go in after him. He was content to wait; the red-hot molten pavement had to be making Bellamy very uncomfortable.

It took less than a minute. Then Bellamy's voice called out: "Okay, you win—I'm coming out!"

"Toss the pulse gun out first," said Nighthawk.

"I'm in an awkward spot. I can't throw it that far."

"Toss it onto the burning pavement."

The pistol flew out, making a splash of red-hot sparks.

"Now the two weapons you had tucked in your belt."

"I've only got one," called Bellamy.

"Hunt around for the other," said Nighthawk. "I've got all night."

Two more splashes.

"Can I come out now? I'm burning up."

"Hands behind your head, one step every three seconds."

The huge man slowly emerged from the corridor, his massive fingers interlaced behind his head.

"Who the hell are you?" he asked once again.

"Just a morally outraged citizen," said Nighthawk. "Turn around."

Bellamy turned around slowly.

"Okay, I don't see any more weapons," said Nighthawk. "You can put your hands down."

"How did you spot my men?" asked Bellamy.

"The Lexonian had a bottle."

"So?"

"They're desert creatures," answered Nighthawk. "Any liquid, even water, is poison to their systems. And if he wasn't drinking, then he was on duty."

"And the man?"

"I wasn't sure about him. But even if he was working for you, he wasn't going to shoot anyone walking out of Horatio's just for the hell of it, so I took the Lexonian first, and he was so startled I had time to take him too before he even got his weapon out."

"You're not bad for an old man."

"Correction," said Nighthawk. "I'm damned good for an old man."

"Yes you are," admitted Bellamy. "But you'll never get off New Barcelona alive."

"I'm not leaving it at all," said Nighthawk. "But you are. Dead or alive—it's your call."

Suddenly Bellamy smiled. "I don't think so." He took a step forward.

"Your next step's your last one," Nighthawk warned him.

This time Bellamy laughed out loud. He took another step, Nighthawk fired his laser at the huge man's chest—and nothing happened.

"Nice try, old man," he said. "You're every bit as good as you think you are—but this is Hairless Jack Bellamy you're up against."

Nighthawk fired again. Still no effect.

"You think I was born looking like this?" said Bellamy. "This isn't my skin. It's all artificial."

"If it's impervious to pain, why did you run and why did the heat drive you out?"

"I ran because I have good instincts—after all, I wasn't born with this skin—and you should have figured out by now that the heat didn't bother me at all. I just wanted to get a look at you, learn who you are and what you have against me, before I kill you." He smiled. "I'll tell you something else. My new skin is more than impervious to pain—it's invulnerable. Nothing can harm me!"

"Bullshit," said Nighthawk. "I've counted five bodyguards so far. An invulnerable man wouldn't need any."

He pulled his projectile pistol and fired at Bellany's head. He could hear the *thunk!* of the bullet as it hit—but then the misshapen metal simply bounced off.

Bellamy walked toward him, and Nighthawk aimed his laser at the street, turning the pavement a brilliant red-gold in front of the huge man, who laughed and walked right across it.

When Bellamy was six feet away Nighthawk changed the setting on his burner from kill to flash, closed his eyes, and pressed the firing mechanism. The resultant brilliance momentarily blinded the unsuspecting giant, and he staggered off, rubbing his eyes.

Think! Nighthawk told himself. *Use your brain! You've bought yourself fifteen or twenty seconds before he gets his vision back. Don't waste it!*

Nighthawk stared at Bellamy. *There's got to be a way or he wouldn't have bodyguards. So where's his vulnerability? Burners don't hurt him. Bullets don't hurt him. How do you penetrate that artificial skin?*

And suddenly he saw the answer. *You don't penetrate it at all! If you can't hurt him from the outside, you do it from the inside. Quick, now, before he can see again!*

Nighthawk stepped forward, pulled the two sticks of mexalite from his pocket, and crammed them into the giant's nostrils. Bellamy opened his mouth to breathe—and the second he did so, Nighthawk stuck the muzzle of his burner into Bellamy's mouth, past the invulnerable epidermis, and fired. The huge man collapsed without a sound.

Nighthawk was still standing there next to Bellamy's body when Kinoshita finally emerged from Horatio's. The smaller man spotted the dead gunman half a block in one direction, the dead Lexonian a block in the other direction, and the corpse of Hairless Jack Bellamy right in front of him.

Nighthawk looked up as he approached. "I'm really getting a little old for this shit," he said.

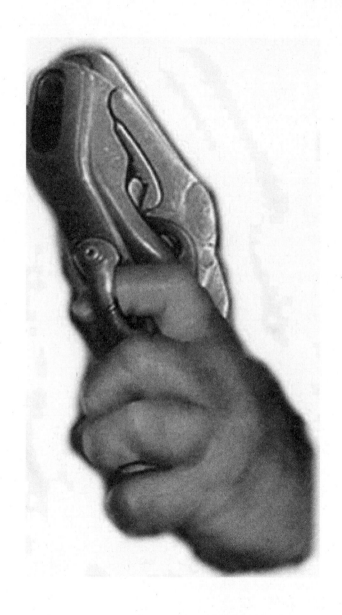

9.

"WHAT DO WE do now?" asked Kinoshita, staring at the three bodies.

"Get some airsleds and cart them off," replied Nighthawk.

"Cart them where? There's no bounty station on New Barcelona."

"We'll get some body bags and ship them to the station on Binder X."

"Right now?"

"I don't plan to leave them on the street all night," said Nighthawk. "Scare up some airsleds. I'll stay here with the bodies. I'm better able to protect them than you are."

"Protect them?" asked Kinoshita, puzzled. "Protect them from what?"

"From claim jumpers," answered Nighthawk.

"All right," said Kinoshita. "I'll be back in a few minutes. I'll try to hunt up some body bags too, or at least get some blankets to cover them up."

"Don't bother. Just bring the airsleds."

"You don't want body bags?"

"I want everyone to see who we've got here, and to know who killed him."

Kinoshita frowned. "Are you sure that's a good idea? You'll be making yourself a target for every killer in the District. Bellamy may not have had any friends, but nobody's going to want word to get out that bounty hunters can come here and live long enough to collect the rewards."

"It'll save me the trouble of hunting for *them*," said Nighthawk. Suddenly the trace of a smile played about his lips. "Besides, I'm an old man. I tire easily."

Kinoshita took another look at the devastation surrounding him and declined to reply. Instead he walked off in search of the sleds.

Nighthawk leaned against a building and lit a smokeless cigar. A woman crossed the street half a block beyond the fallen Lexonian, but paid no attention to it. A moment later two men turned the corner and found themselves confronting Bellamy's huge body.

"Son of a bitch!" muttered one, walking over to it. "Is that who I think it is?"

"It's got to be," said the other. "How many bald seven-footers do you know?"

"Is he dead?"

"Sure as hell looks like."

The first man leaned over the corpse. "I wonder if he was carrying any cash."

"Don't touch him," said Nighthawk.

Both men jumped, startled.

"I didn't see you there," said the first man.

"How the hell did you kill him?" asked the second. "I thought he couldn't be hurt."

"You thought wrong," said Nighthawk. "So did he."

"Did you do the other two?" asked the second man, gesturing toward the other dead human and the Lexonian.

"Yes."

"You must have had one hell of a grudge against them," said the man.

"Can you think of any other reason to kill someone?" replied Nighthawk.

"One."

"Forget it," said the first man. "This is the *District*. There's no law here, no bounty hunters, nothing. Besides, he's an old man."

"He's an old man I've never seen here before, and suddenly Hairless Jack Bellamy is dead. Take a good hard look at him. Have you ever seen him before? Ever see his face on a Wanted poster?"

"I don't give a damn if he's one of us or one of them,"
said the first man. "I just want to know why we can't divide
the spoils."

He reached down toward Bellamy's pocket, then froze
when he heard the click of Nighthawk's pistol.

"Show a little respect for the dead," said Nighthawk.

"You didn't have much respect for him when he was alive,"
said the man.

Nighthawk made no reply but simply stared at him, and
the man slowly straightened up.

"Come on," said his companion. "Let's go."

"He's an old man and there are two of us."

"There were three of *them*," said the second man, indicating the bodies, "and one of them was Jack Bellamy. Let's go."

"All right," said the first man unhappily. He turned to
Nighthawk. "Who the hell are you, anyway?"

"I'm the guy who's not going to let you pick Jack
Bellamy's pockets."

"Have you at least got a name?"

"I've had a lot of names in my life," replied Nighthawk.
"Out here on the Frontier people change names the way they
change clothes."

"You got any I'd know?"

"Maybe one—the Widowmaker."

"The hell you are. I heard there's a new Widowmaker on
the Inner Frontier, and he's a young guy."

"Talking people like you out of suicide has aged me,"
said Nighthawk.

"Suicide?" asked the second man.

"Your friend's inching his hand toward a gun he's got tucked
in the back of his belt," said Nighthawk. "He's got about two
more inches before I have to send for another airsled."

The first man froze.

"We're through talking," said Nighthawk. "Start walking."

"We're on our way," said the second man quickly, keeping
his hands in plain view, well out from his body. "We don't

want any trouble." As he passed Nighthawk, he stopped and added, "If you're smart, you'll get the hell out of the District before anyone knows you were here."

"I've got a little more business to conduct," replied Nighthawk. "As for what happened here, we'll let it be our little secret."

And it would stay their secret, Nighthawk knew, for five minutes at the outside, which was just what he wanted. The more people talked about the Widowmaker being on New Barcelona, the sooner the word would get back to Jeff.

Kinoshita showed up a few minutes later with a trio of airsleds. He and Nighthawk hefted Bellamy's huge body onto one, then loaded the other two sleds.

"Where to now?" asked Kinoshita. "The spaceport?"

"First we'll stop at a police station and have their identities officially confirmed. Then we can apply for the reward. Even if Jeff doesn't hear what happened, he'll be keeping an eye on who's claiming the biggest rewards, if only so he'll know not to go after men who are already dead."

"Yeah, he checks the list every couple of days," confirmed Kinoshita.

"Of course he does. I trained him. And if he sees a few hefty ones claimed on New Barcelona, he'll start looking into it, just as I would."

Nighthawk fastened the three sleds together. They floated some three feet above the ground, and he guided them as he began walking.

"You know," said Kinoshita, walking alongside him, "it occurs to me that the police aren't going to be very happy to see you. They had an unspoken agreement, and you broke it. Some of the residents of the District may even blame them for not stopping you."

"If the killers come out of the District looking for the cops, they're going to have to respond by going into the District looking for anyone with a price on his head. That's not necessarily a bad thing." He paused. "But none of it will happen until long after we've left New Barcelona."

"What makes you think so?"

"If the good guys and the bad guys wanted a war, they've had two hundred years to start one."

"Okay," admitted Kinoshita. "You've got a point."

They attracted some attention after they'd walked two blocks. Bystanders stopped and stared, and began whispering Bellamy's name, but no one made a move to stop them. Two more blocks, and they were out of the District. It was the middle of the night, but word of what they were carrying got out pretty fast, and by the time they came to a police station half a mile from the District they had a curious crowd of perhaps thirty men and aliens following them.

The doors opened to let them through, and the instant the officer on the night desk saw who was on the largest sled he summoned his superiors.

Kinoshita's analysis had been correct. The police were definitely not happy to see a bounty hunter carting Hairless Jack Bellamy's body out of the District, but there wasn't much they could do about it.

"Is there paper on the other two?" asked Nighthawk after they had officially confirmed Bellamy's identity.

"You mean you shot them without knowing?" demanded a captain who was the ranking officer on the premises.

"In self-defense."

"Have you got any witnesses?"

"If there's paper I don't need them," said Nighthawk, "and if there's no paper I'll let you hook me up to a Neverlie machine."

An officer walked over to the Lexonian. "I know this one. He's wanted all the hell over the Frontier, and I think there's paper on him in the Spiral Arm as well. I can't pronounce his name, but he's carrying about two hundred thousand credits on his head."

"The other one's McAllistar Morgan," added the desk officer. "Or at least that's what he's been calling himself lately. He killed two men in a holdup on Benvenuti II, and they're after him for some other stuff as well."

"Well, that's that," said the captain. "Your ass is covered. Now fill out your claim and get the hell off my planet. I hope to hell you haven't caused more problems than you've solved."

"I want the two smaller bounties sent to a hospital on Giancola II, to be applied to Jason Newman's bill," said Nighthawk. "My friend here can give you the exact location and details. Have them send the big bounty here to the station and hold it for me."

"I'll need your name," said the desk officer.

"Jefferson Nighthawk."

"A lot of people have borrowed that name," remarked the captain. "I hear there's a young one out here on the Frontier—one who's actually calling himself the Widowmaker."

"You don't say?"

"You could do a lot worse," said the captain. "Hell, we could use another Widowmaker these days—a legendary hero to clean out the District."

"Well, you know what they say," said Nighthawk with a smile no one but Kinoshita understood. "Be careful what you wish for; you may get it."

10.

"WHAT NOW?" ASKED Kinoshita as they walked back across the street and entered the District.

"Now I go back to Horatio's, and you go around to all the nearby hotels and boarding houses."

Kinoshita looked puzzled. "What do I do there?"

"Take out a room at each," Nighthawk instructed him. "At least ten of them. Twenty if you can find them. Then meet me at Horatio's."

"I assume you want me to take them out in my name, not yours?"

"Right. There's no sense making it too easy for whoever's following you."

"Me?" said Kinoshita nervously. "Who do you think's going to be following me?"

"The same men who are following us right now," answered Nighthawk calmly.

Kinoshita looked around. "I can't see or hear anyone."

"I can."

Kinoshita fingered his screecher nervously.

"Don't worry," said Nighthawk. "There are only two of them, and they don't want you. That's why I took Bellamy out in the street—so everyone would know it was me who did it, not you and not us. I would think by now the word has spread throughout the District."

"Maybe you need me to stick around and watch your back," suggested Kinoshita.

Nighthawk shook his head. "They're going to take their time. After all, I just killed a man who everyone knew couldn't be hurt. They're going to spend a while studying me before they make a move."

"You'd better be right."

"I didn't live this long by being wrong."

"Or being modest," said Kinoshita.

"There's no place in this business for false bravado or false modesty," said Nighthawk. He stood still and closed his eyes for a moment, listening intently. Suddenly he smiled. "One of them's got a prosthetic leg. The right one, I think. He hides it well."

"Shit!" said Kinoshita. "You're *enjoying* this! You can talk all you want about living in peace and raising your goddamned flowers, but you love being the Widowmaker!"

"There's already a Widowmaker," said Nighthawk. "I'm just his coach."

"There's already a Widowmaker," agreed Kinoshita. "And I'm standing next to him."

"That's not the safest place to stand," said Nighthawk. "It's time to start hunting up hotels. I'll see you in an hour or so."

Nighthawk turned and headed off toward Horatio's. He had assumed the two men would split up, and a moment later they did. He could easily have lost the man who was tailing him, or simply waited for him and killed him, but instead he kept on walking, and reached his destination a few minutes later.

"Hi again," said Minx as he stepped out from the airlift and into Horatio's. "I thought we'd seen the last of you for the night."

"I got thirsty," said Nighthawk, sitting down at an empty table. "Bring me a beer, please."

"They say you and Hairless Jack had a little argument out in the street," continued Minx, and Nighthawk became aware that every eye, human and alien alike, was trained on him.

"A little one."

"I hear he's Lifeless Jack now."

"Well, you hear all kinds of rumors in a place like this," said Nighthawk. "How about that beer now?"

She vanished into another room, then returned with a beer in a tall iced glass.

"How'd you do it, mister?" asked a thin man clad all in black who was sitting at the next table.

"Relentless logic wins most arguments," answered Nighthawk.

"They say you carted him off somewhere."

"I was taught to clean up after myself."

The thin man stared at him for a long minute. "You ain't much for giving straight answers, are you?" he said at last.

"I've answered everything you've asked," said Nighthawk.

"All right, how about answering this one: are you the Widowmaker?"

"I've been called that," he acknowledged. "I've been called worse."

"You don't belong here, Widowmaker," said the thin man. "This is the District."

"My money spends as good as yours," said Nighthawk, taking a swallow of his beer. "I figure as long as I'm not breaking any laws I've got as much right to be here as you do."

"You *can't* break any laws in the District!" snapped the man. "We don't have any."

"Then what's your problem?"

"Everyone knows what you do. The District is off-limits to lawmen and bounty hunters."

"I must have missed the Keep Out sign on the door," said Nighthawk.

There was an uneasy murmuring in the room.

"I suggest you all relax," said Nighthawk. "If I wanted any of you, you'd be dead by now."

And with that, they *did* relax.

"Then who *do* you want?" asked a Canphorite from the far side of the room.

"That would be breaking a professional confidence," said Nighthawk with a humorless smile.

"It's got to be the Wizard," said the thin man. "They say he's worth eight million credits dead or alive."

"Nobody wants him alive," added a Lodinite, looking up from the green bubbling stuff he was drinking.

Nighthawk knew the price on the Wizard, of course, but he hadn't known he was in the District until that moment. He decided to see what further information he could elicit without seeming to ask for it.

"I'm after bigger game than the Wizard," he said.

"There isn't any," said a man who was swaying in his chair from the effects of the mexalite he was smoking.

"Sure there is," chimed in another. "The Widowmaker doesn't just go after Men. There's the Younger Brothers, whatever the hell they are."

"Right," said the thin man. "They've got to be worth more than eight million for the lot of them."

"And what about that woman who arrived yesterday?" asked a man from the corner. "What was her name?"

"Cleopatra Rome."

"Right—Cleopatra Rome. She might be worth more than any of them."

They continued to toss names around. Nighthawk was content; there were at least three more, maybe as many as five, that would have to come to Jeff's attention within a day or two of his collecting them.

Curious word, "collecting," he reflected. He never thought of it as *killing* them. The killing was a foregone conclusion. It was finding them, cutting off their escape routes, taking them without collateral damage, and presenting the bodies for the rewards. Collecting. It seemed much more businesslike than killing, and the trick was never to forget that it was a business, that emotion had no place in it. He could be warm and relaxed with Sarah, he could toss off a wry or sardonic line with the best of them—but that was when he was Jefferson Nighthawk. When he was at work—when he was the Widowmaker—humor, love, friendship, tenderness, fear, all of them were locked away into the same closet in his mind that contained Jefferson Nighthawk. From time to time he wondered what a psychiatrist would make of it. Then he reminded himself that at least he'd survived long enough to be of some interest to a psychiatrist.

Kinoshita entered a few minutes later and sat down next to him.

"We're registered at fourteen hotels and rooming houses," said the small man.

"You worked fast," said Nighthawk approvingly.

"They're all within a few blocks of here. I can hunt up more if you want."

"No, fourteen should be enough."

Kinoshita handed him a sheet of paper on which he'd scribbled down the names and addresses of the various hostelries. "Have you got any preference for tonight? I assume we're going to just keep rotating to a new one every day."

"We're staying right here," said Nighthawk, lowering his voice.

"In Horatio's?" said Kinoshita, surprised.

"In the same building. When we leave we'll go to the top floor and see what we can find."

"Then why the hell did you have me rent all those rooms?"

"At least one man, maybe more, followed you to every hotel," said Nighthawk. "If we stay in one, the odds are thirteen-to-one we won't be killed in it. This way the odds are fourteen-to-zero." An amused smile. "There are Men and aliens who want us dead. Let's let 'em stand watch. Why should they have a good night's rest just because we intend to?"

"You know," said Kinoshita, "Jeff would never have thought of that."

"Jeff doesn't have to," said Nighthawk. "He's as good as I used to be. But us old men need our sleep."

"Are you referring to you old men who just killed an invulnerable giant and his henchmen?"

"If I killed him he wasn't invulnerable, was he?"

Minx approached the table. "Can I get your friend anything?" she asked.

"Ask *him*," said Nighthawk.

"I'll have whatever he's drinking," said Kinoshita, indicating Nighthawk. As she walked off, he turned to the older man. "Did you pick up any information?"

"A bit."

"At one of the hotels I heard that Cleopatra Rome just arrived in the District."

"So they say."

"Did she really do everything she's supposed to have done?"

"Probably not," said Nighthawk. "She's too young."

"Does it ever bother you?" asked Kinoshita. "Killing a woman, I mean?"

"Do you think all the killing she's done bothered her?" responded Nighthawk.

"I know. But—"

"Who's more dangerous at ten paces?" asked Nighthawk. "The heavyweight freehand champion of the Oligarchy, or a ninety-pound woman with a burner?"

"Okay, I just asked."

"A woman can kill you as quickly and efficiently as a man can. Your problem is that you haven't overcome your early training."

"How did you learn to overcome yours?" asked Kinoshita.

"Quickly, and under duress," replied Nighthawk. He looked around. "Okay, I think I've been here long enough for word to spread through the District, and they've had time to post men at all fourteen hotels you visited. There's nothing more to be done tonight. We might as well leave."

He laid a few bills on the table, then stood up. Ignoring all the stares, he walked to the airlift, waited for Kinoshita to join him, ascended to ground level, and stepped out.

"I thought we were staying in the building," said Kinoshita.

"We are."

"Then why—?"

"We're supposed to be keeping it a secret. If anyone's watching the airlift mechanism, why let them know? We'll wait here for a couple of minutes, and then go up. If anyone's checking it, they'll think whoever's on it just came in from outside."

You're a remarkable man, thought Kinoshita for the hundredth or the thousandth time. *The kid never plans like this, because he doesn't need to. You were as good as he is, and yet you're always planning three steps ahead. Did it start when you came down with the disease, or when age eroded one percent of your skills, or were you always like this? Someday I'd really like to know a little more about the man I've dedicated my life to serving.*

When Nighthawk decided that enough time had passed, they entered the airlift again and let it take them up to the third floor of the darkened building. Once the rooms had been offices, but that had been two centuries ago. Now those that weren't eaten by decay were storerooms, filled with contraband items, clearly owned by black-marketeers and fences.

Nighthawk walked up and down the corridor, breaking the computer code on each lock and deactivating the various security systems with a skill that surprised Kinoshita, who had thought nothing the Widowmaker did could still surprise him. The older man checked each room and reactivated each security system; after he had surveyed all of them he walked back to the third one he'd examined.

"We'll spend the night here," he announced.

"Why this room as opposed to one of the others?" asked Kinoshita.

"There are no windows, so there's only one way in or out," answered Nighthawk. "And whoever owns it is fencing some delicate Jubarian crystal."

"So?"

"If two pieces of the crystal touch each other, they set up a high-pitched vibration that would wake the dead. I'll lay half a dozen pieces where the door will knock them into each other if it opens. We'll sleep behind that partition, which gives us plenty of time to get ready if someone tries to enter the place."

"You think someone will?"

"If I thought they would, I wouldn't have sent you around to all those hotels," said Nighthawk. "But you have to take enough chances in this business; it just makes sense to avoid the ones you don't have to take."

Nighthawk closed and locked the door behind them, positioned the crystal, and walked over to the alcove behind the partition. He lay down on the hardwood floor, pulled his screecher out, placed it next to his head, and was sound asleep a moment later. *Look at you*, thought Kinoshita. *You killed Hairless Jack Bellamy and two others tonight, and tomorrow you're probably going to go up against Cleopatra Rome, and you're sleeping like it was just another day at the office.*

Then he noticed the screecher. *And you're still the most careful man I know. Even without consciously thinking of it, you never miss even the smallest detail. Anyone else might be sleeping with a burner or a pulse gun out, but you know the building's wood. A laser beam or an energy pulse might set it on fire; a solid burst of sound won't. Young Jeff was the most remarkable specimen I ever saw—but if he ever has to go up against you, I know who I'd put my money on.*

Kinoshita was still comparing all the Widowmakers he had known when he fell into a restless sleep.

11.

KINOSHITA AWOKE WITH a start, and immediately felt Nighthawk's hand over his mouth.

"Quiet!" whispered the older man.

Kinoshita blinked his eyes very rapidly, trying to figure out what had happened. When Nighthawk was sure the smaller man was awake, he took his hand away.

"Someone's out there," he whispered.

"The janitor, maybe?" suggested Kinoshita softly.

"Could be," agreed Nighthawk, screecher in hand. "But he's got a prosthetic leg, and a man with a prosthetic leg followed me to Horatio's."

"How long has he been out there in the corridor?" asked Kinoshita.

"Maybe ten minutes."

Kinoshita checked his timepiece. It wouldn't be dawn for another two hours. "Don't you ever sleep?"

"I slept for a century," replied Nighthawk. "It hasn't got much to recommend it." He paused, listening intently. "There are three of them now, maybe four. It doesn't take that many men to clean a dump like this."

Kinoshita pulled out his pulse gun and positioned himself where he could see the door.

"Why don't they come in?" he whispered nervously.

"They don't know for sure that we're here. My guess is that one of them was stationed outside, and since he didn't see us leave the building they finally figured out that we're holed up here. It took them four hours, so it's safe to say we're not dealing with the brightest men on the planet."

Kinoshita half-expected Nighthawk to step through the doorway and open fire, but the older man stayed where he was, seated on the wood floor, his back propped up against a wall. He was so relaxed that if Kinoshita didn't know better he'd have sworn he was asleep.

Finally Nighthawk turned to his companion. "They've left," he announced. "They're probably searching the rest of the building."

"When they don't find you they'll be back," predicted Kinoshita.

"No they won't," replied Nighthawk. "They don't want to face me. They're just following someone's orders." Kinoshita looked unconvinced, so Nighthawk continued: "We have all the advantages. It's dark, we've had time to take up defensive positions, we know where they are when they enter and they have no idea where we are. They'd be dead meat and they know it. If they were serious about wanting to find us, they'd have opened the door and searched the room."

"So what do we do now?"

"I don't know about you," said Nighthawk, "but I'm going back to sleep."

"But they're still in the building!" protested Kinoshita.

"Not for long. In another five or ten minutes they'll convince themselves that One-Leg was asleep on the job and we walked right out past him. He'll protest like all hell, but the last thing they want to do is learn that he's right, so they'll go back to their boss, put the blame on him, and live to fight—or run away—another day."

"Why didn't you take them out?" asked Kinoshita.

"We're not here to collect all the bad guys," answered Nighthawk. "We're here to make a handful of kills that will draw Jeff to the planet, and killing a bunch of flunkies won't do any good."

"They'd kill you if they could."

"Probably," agreed Nighthawk. "But they can't."

Nighthawk lay back down and was sleeping peacefully in less than a minute, while Kinoshita spent the rest of a very nervous night listening for footsteps that never came. He fell asleep just before dawn.

He'd been asleep less than two hours when Nighthawk shook him awake, gave him a few minutes to gather his wits about him, then went to the airlift. They took it down to Horatio's, then back up to the main floor.

"What was that about?" asked Kinoshita as they stepped into the building's foyer.

"If anyone's watching, let them think we found someplace to hide down in Horatio's," explained Nighthawk. "Why encourage them to look upstairs tonight?"

"Now I'm confused. I thought you said they didn't want to find you."

"Last night's crew didn't. I don't know who's going to come looking for me tonight."

"And in the meantime, who are *you* looking for?"

"There are a few possibilities," said Nighthawk. "But the first thing I'm looking for is breakfast."

He stepped out into the open. There were a few men and aliens on the street, and every last one of them immediately stopped to stare at him—but no one approached or drew a weapon, and after a moment he turned to his right and began walking, Kinoshita at his side.

The street took a pair of sharp turns and seemed to dead-end at an alien temple guarded by a trio of winged, forty-foot-tall stone statues. Suddenly the door vanished and the street continued right through the center of the church, and Kinoshita realized it had only been a holographic projection. The church itself was real, run by an orange-skinned bat-eared race that neither man had ever seen before. There was an incomprehensible service going on, one that seemed to involve screaming, chanting, and ritual flagellation, but the priest and congregation had deactivated their T-packs, the mechanisms that translated most alien language into Terran and vice versa, and all that Nighthawk and Kinoshita could hear was a combination of guttural clicks and high-pitched trilling.

The door at the far side of the church proved also to be a projection, and a moment later they were back on the street. It rose, it dipped, it turned at crazy angles. They passed a number of shops, including a pair of restaurants, and finally Nighthawk stopped walking.

"What is it?" asked Kinoshita, scanning the area for potential killers.

Nighthawk indicated a storefront restaurant. "This looks like as good a place as any."

Kinoshita peered in through the window, then straightened up. "It's for aliens. Look at the tables—there's not a single Man sitting there." The odor of alien food and spices assailed his nostrils. "You passed up two perfectly good human restaurants for *this*?"

"Wait for me out here if you're not hungry," said Nighthawk, entering the restaurant before Kinoshita could respond. The smaller man stood his ground for a minute, then shrugged and followed Nighthawk in.

They took a table near the window and punched in their orders. Kinoshita surveyed the clientele more closely. There were the usual Canphorites and Lodinites, Man's two greatest rivals in the galaxy, plus an Antarean, two Mollutei, a Hesporite, a Drigonsie, and a couple that he couldn't recognize. To his surprise, none of them seemed to be observing him and Nighthawk with open hostility.

"You've been here before, right?" he said at last.

"No, never."

"Well, you sure as hell know something."

"I know a lot of things," said Nighthawk. "For example, I know that one of our fellow diners will approach me before I finish my coffee."

"Which one?"

Nighthawk shrugged. "I don't know. If I were to guess, I'd say it'd be the smallest of the three Lodinites at that table off to the left."

Sure enough, the Lodinite waddled over less than a minute later.

"You are the Widowmaker, are you not?" it said through its T-pack.

"Yes, I am," replied Nighthawk. "Have a seat."

"I am more comfortable standing."

"As you wish. Would you like some coffee?"

"I cannot metabolize it."

"Then I suppose we'd might as well get down to business."

"You know why I have sought you out?" asked the Lodinite.

"Of course."

"I will want something in exchange."

"Five thousand credits now, or one percent of the reward, which will be considerably larger," said Nighthawk.

The two men could see the Lodinite greedily computing the total. "That's ninety thousand credits," it said.

"Your choice."

Suddenly the Lodinite's pudgy little body seemed to sag. "I will take the five thousand now."

"You're sure?"

"I wish it were otherwise, Widowmaker, but you cannot kill her."

"I killed Hairless Jack Bellamy."

"I heard about that," said the Lodinite. "He met you on neutral ground. She will know better."

"Not if you tell me what I want to know," said Nighthawk.

"I will tell you, but it will not help you. The money, please."

Nighthawk pulled a wad of bills out of a pocket, counted off ten five-hundred-credit notes, and laid them on the table. The Lodinite reached a hairy hand for them, but Nighthawk's hand shot out and grabbed what passed for its wrist.

"*After* you tell me," he said.

"Two blocks due south of here is the Royal Ascot Hotel. That is where she can be found."

Nighthawk released its hand and it grabbed the money.

"Lodinites don't all look alike to me," said Nighthawk. "If you lied to me, I'll be back—and I'll find you."

"No one lies to the Widowmaker," said the Lodinite, scurrying off to its table.

"You'd be surprised," muttered Nighthawk as he watched the alien's hasty departure.

"All right," said Kinoshita. "What was that all about?"

"Cleopatra Rome. She's at the Royal Ascot."

"It's hardly royal," said Kinoshita. "That's one of the places where I rented a room. It's a three-century-old dump." He paused. "You knew when we came in here that one of the aliens was going to tell you where she could be found. How?"

Nighthawk turned to his companion. "What do you know about her?"

"Just that she's a notorious killer."

"You know how many aliens she's killed?" asked Nighthawk.

"No."

"More than eighty. Do you know how many Men?"

"No."

"Three," said Nighthawk. "I figured if we went to an alien establishment, at least one of them was going to want her dead even more than he wanted to hinder me."

"So are you going after her now?"

"Is that what Jeff would do?"

"Absolutely," said Kinoshita. He smiled. "Now you're going to tell me he's a young healthy man and you're a sick old one."

Nighthawk shook his head. "No. I'm going to tell you that as good as he is, if he went after her without knowing what he's up against he's a foolish young man and he might not be destined to live to be a sick old one."

"I don't follow you."

"I'm the Widowmaker," said Nighthawk. "I was a legend before any man or alien on the planet was born. Newman and Jeff have kept that legend alive in recent years, and last night I killed a man who everyone believed couldn't be killed." He paused. "The Lodinite knew that, because he knew who I was."

"So?"

"So why did he take five thousand credits now instead of ninety thousand credits after I confront Cleopatra Rome?"

"I don't know," admitted Kinoshita.

"I don't either," said Nighthawk. "But I sure as hell intend to find out before I face her."

12.

NIGHTHAWK SPENT THE next couple of hours walking through the District, trying to learn his way around it. He had Kinoshita point out every hotel and rooming house where he'd paid for rooms, passed them by, and examined a couple that Kinoshita had overlooked.

"This one will do," he announced as they entered a small boardinghouse called the Burnished Moon. "I'm going out into the street now. When I do, see if you can find a back way into this place."

"They followed me to the last fourteen hotels," said Kinoshita. "What makes you think they won't be watching me now?"

"Because they'll be watching *me*," answered Nighthawk. "They only followed you because they didn't know where I was."

"You sure know how to pump up a guy's ego," said Kinoshita.

"You want to be watched? Go shoot a couple of them for the reward." Nighthawk half-smiled, half-grimaced. "I've had people watching me from windows and porches and alleyways for most of my life. It's not as flattering as you seem to think. A lot of them were watching me through telescopic sights."

"Okay, okay, I'm sorry I mentioned it."

Nighthawk walked out into the street, walked to the weapons shop that faced the Burnished Moon, stared at the window for a moment, then entered and browsed for a few minutes. Finally he asked to see a molecular imploder.

"I'm sorry, Mr. Nighthawk," said the elderly woman behind the counter, "but they're illegal even in the District."

"You know who I am?"

"I think almost everybody knows who you are, especially after last night." She paused. "If you're going to be here for, say, a week, I could possibly find an imploder."

"Let me see how long I'm going to be here," said Nighthawk. "I'll get back to you later today if I still think I'll need it."

"There'll be a fifty-percent discount for you," she promised.

"Oh?"

She smiled. "Mr. Nighthawk, there are seventeen weapons shops in the District. If I can advertise that the Widowmaker patronizes mine, it's more than worth the discount to me."

"I'll let you know," he said, walking out into the street, where Kinoshita was waiting for him. "Well?"

"There's a back door, and a service airlift right next to it."

"Good."

"What's this all about?"

"We're never going to get away with sleeping in Horatio's building two nights in a row, and we know they'll have fourteen hotels staked out. We needed another place."

"I could have been spotted out back behind the place."

Nighthawk shook his head. "They weren't watching you."

"What makes you so damned sure?"

"They were watching the Widowmaker, and for the next couple of hours they're going to be busy trying to figure out why I need a molecular imploder. Even if someone saw you back there they'll be too busy to care."

"Why *do* you need an imploder?" asked Kinoshita.

"I don't. But I've always believed in the art of misdirection."

Suddenly Kinoshita smiled. "Wouldn't it be funny if that's what it took to kill Cleopatra Rome?"

"Hilarious," said Nighthawk.

"What now?"

"Now we leave the District long enough to find a subspace radio and pay a visit to the police station."

"The police station?"

"To see if the reward money's been delivered. No sense leaving temptation in their path. It doesn't take much brainpower to figure out that no matter how frugally you live and how much you save, if you're a cop you're never going to get your hands on anything half the size of that reward unless you turn it over to a court as evidence—or steal my reward."

"And the radio?"

"I want to check in with the Giancola II hospital every couple of days to see how Newman's doing."

"I *knew* you felt a bond with him."

Nighthawk observed him the way he might study an exceptionally slow child. "I hope I can reason with Jeff, explain what he did wrong and why he's got to start using his brain. But if I can't, then I'm going to need all the help I can get—and in all immodesty, I can't think of any help I'd feel more comfortable counting on than another Jefferson Nighthawk."

He started walking toward the edge of the District. Kinoshita became aware that every person they passed was staring at them, but Nighthawk paid them no attention at all.

"Aren't you worried?" asked Kinoshita. "Any one of those men or women might take a shot at you."

"They won't."

"How can you be so sure?"

"The ones on the left side of the street are more likely to hit you, and they know they won't get a second shot."

"And the ones on the right side?"

"The sun's in their eyes." Nighthawk paused. "I'm not an egomaniac, but I *am* a realist—and I think it's fair to say that every last one of them knows that if you want to kill the Widowmaker, you'd better take him with your first shot."

"True," agreed Kinoshita. He looked at some of the faces. "But they'd sure *like* to kill you."

"What they'd like isn't my concern. I only care about what they're capable of."

Suddenly a lean, unshaven man stepped out into the street some twenty yards ahead of them. His fingers hovered above the weapon he had tucked into his belt.

"Think very carefully," said Nighthawk with no show of fear or tension. "I haven't come to New Barcelona for you. You can walk away right now."

"You're an old man," said the man. "Maybe you used to be something special, but that was a long time ago."

"I want you to consider three things," said Nighthawk. "First, there's no paper on me; you won't make a credit for killing me."

"I'll be the man who killed the Widowmaker," replied the man. "That's enough."

"Second, this old man killed Hairless Jack Bellamy last night."

The man's eyes widened. He obviously was one of the few residents of the District who hadn't heard the news. "I don't believe it!" he said at last.

"What you believe doesn't interest me," said Nighthawk. "Third, you're not the first or the hundredth fool who thought he could make a reputation by killing me, and I'm still here." Nighthawk came to a stop some six feet from the man and stared into his eyes. "Okay, I'm all through trying to save your life. Make a move, or slink off with your tail between your legs. It makes no difference to me. But make up your mind fast; I'm in a hurry, and I feel no obligation to let you go for your weapon first."

It was Nighthawk's total confidence, his complete lack of concern, that finally got through to the man. He swallowed hard, held his hands well out from his body in plain view, and backed away.

"You're blocking my way," said Nighthawk. "Get off the street."

The man glared at him and did as he was told.

"I'm sure you're thinking about taking a shot at me after I pass you," said Nighthawk. "I wouldn't like that." Suddenly his burner was in his hand, and an instant later, almost faster than the eye could follow, he'd turned, aimed, and melted the handle of the man's weapon. "I wouldn't touch that for a few minutes if I were you."

Without another glance at the man, he began walking again, and Kinoshita joined him.

"Don't tell me," said Nighthawk.

"Tell you what?"

"You were going to tell me there was paper on him and I should have killed him."

"I don't know about the paper—there probably is. But why *didn't* you kill him?"

"Killing him wouldn't make news five feet outside the District," answered Nighthawk. "And I'm not here to kill every man with paper on him. I'm here to attract Jeff's attention. This guy wouldn't even attract the local cops' notice."

In another five minutes they reached the edge of the District, crossed the street that was the dividing line, and headed to a subspace-radio sending station. Nighthawk let the robot clerk read his retina and thumbprint. The clerk checked them against his identity file in the Master Computer on Deluros VIII, cleared his credit with the Cataluna branch of the Bank of Deluros, and finally connected him to the hospital on Giancola II.

"How's Jason Newman doing?" he asked when he'd gotten through to the head of Newman's surgical team.

"The man has remarkable recuperative powers" was the answer. "His cloned organs should be ready to transplant in about six or seven days. Then it's up to him, but I'd say that at the rate he's regaining his strength, he could be out of here in a month, maybe even a little less, as long as he takes it easy."

"He's not the type to take it easy," said Nighthawk.

"Yes, I know. We got the whole story from a Cassandra Hill, who arrived two days ago."

"Thank you," said Nighthawk. "I'll check in again in a few days." He broke the connection and turned to Kinoshita. "Why the hell did you tell Cassandra where he was? I thought he wanted you to wait."

"I didn't tell her anything," replied Kinoshita. "She's a remarkable woman. I don't know if I ever told you the full story of what happened back on Pericles V, but she's the one who actually led the revolt against her father. Newman was really just around for the end of it."

"She sounds like an interesting woman," commented Nighthawk. "I'd like to meet her someday."

"I don't know if that would be a good idea," said Kinoshita.

"Why not?"

"If one Jefferson Nighthawk could fall in love with her, why not another?"

"You've got a point." Nighthawk walked out of the sending station. "Okay, let's see if the reward's been transferred here yet."

They walked another block to the police station, where they learned that all three rewards had been paid. The two smaller ones had been transferred to a holding account on Giancola II that the hospital could draw from to cover Newman's bills. The reward for Bellamy was in the police department's account, awaiting Nighthawk's instructions.

"We've deducted the price of shipping Bellamy's body to the Binder X bounty station," said the officer in charge.

"Didn't they believe you when you vouched for his identity?" asked Nighthawk.

"They took our word for the two others—they were atomized this morning—but for a multimillion-credit reward, they want to run their own tests," answered the officer. "Still, they paid the money even before they checked it, so they're pretty satisfied with the data we forwarded to them." He paused, staring at Nighthawk, as if still trying to figure out how he'd managed to kill Hairless Jack Bellamy. "I assume you don't want your money in cash?"

"No," replied Nighthawk. He scribbled down a twelve-digit number and handed it to the officer. "Just transfer it to this account at the local branch of the Bank of Deluros and tell them to route it to Deluros VIII."

"You live in the Deluros system?" asked the officer, surprised. "I always figured you lived on the Inner Frontier."

Nighthawk shook his head. "I do."

"We could send it direct to your home world."

"My home world has a branch of the Bank of Deluros," said Nighthawk. "I can get my hands on the money whenever I want, once you've deposited it."

And, thought Kinoshita, *this way no one knows where his home world is.*

"Well," said the officer, "we haven't had bombs in the building or riots in the street yet. Who are you going to bring us next?"

"I was thinking of Cleopatra Rome."

"Cleopatra Rome!" exclaimed the officer. "You don't believe in making things easy for yourself, do you?"

"What can you tell me about her?"

"I can tell you this: she's going to make killing Bellamy seem like child's play."

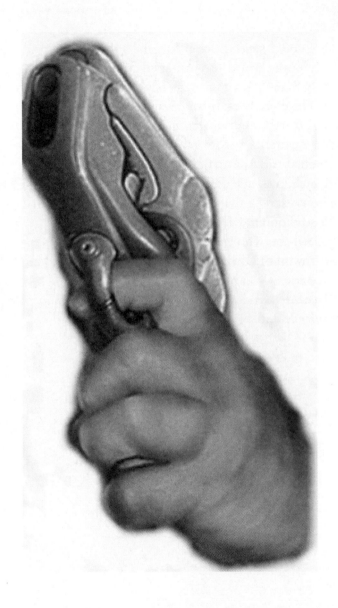

13.

NIGHTHAWK DECIDED THAT as long as they were out of the District, they might as well eat at one of Cataluna's better restaurants before returning. The establishment, modestly named the Apex of the World, was atop one of the city's tallest buildings, and from their table by a window they could look down across the District.

"You wonder why they haven't simply dropped a bomb and wiped the whole place out," commented Kinoshita, gesturing toward the District as they sipped their drinks and waited for their meals to arrive.

"Because they're not fools," answered Nighthawk.

"I don't think I follow you."

"The District looks to be about a mile square, give or take a couple of blocks," said Nighthawk. "New Barcelona's probably got ten million square miles, maybe more. But that little piece of turf, distasteful as its residents may be, unquestionably generates more money than the rest of the planet—hell, the rest of the system—put together."

"They can't tax it, so what good does it do?" said Kinoshita. "It's strictly an underground economy."

"Doesn't matter. Every single thing they buy in the District, from food to weapons to clothing, has to be imported, and the tariff rate is usurious—or it would be under normal circumstances. And the few legitimate businesses that have set up shop in the district just pass the cost along."

"*Are* there any legitimate businesses?" asked Kinoshita.

"Of course there are," answered Nighthawk. "There are the gun shops, the hotels, the restaurants, the bars. Even the drug dens have to buy couches from the furniture dealers who supply them; the same applies to the hotels and the whorehouses. You're making the mistake of looking at the clientele; try looking at the business owners. They were probably starving in the part of the city we're in now, so they moved to the District. They face a lot more risk, but the rewards are commensurate with the risk. A sandwich at that alien restaurant we ate at costs more than a six-course meal on the roof here—and you wouldn't believe the prices that weapons shop was charging for burners and screechers." He paused. "No, if you want to send New Barcelona spiraling into a permanent economic depression, bomb the District."

Their meal arrived at that point. Kinoshita had ordered a mutated shellfish in a cream sauce, while Nighthawk had a steak imported from Pollux IV.

"I hadn't realized how tired I was of soya products," remarked Kinoshita as he dug into his shellfish.

"I know, but your body is used to them. If anything's going to put you in the sick bay it's a rich meal like this when you haven't had one in months—especially with that alien lobster or whatever the hell it is."

"It'd be worth it," said Kinoshita, taking another bite.

"Did Jeff sample a lot of foods or stick to the safe stuff?" asked Nighthawk.

"I never paid much attention," said Kinoshita. "I do know that nothing ever made him sick. You had a hell of a constitution when you were a young man. Hell, you still do."

"It didn't stop me from coming down with eplasia."

"When did you first notice it?"

Nighthawk shrugged. "I don't know. When I was about in my mid-fifties, I suppose, though there might have been earlier signs of it. At first I thought it was just a rash of some kind, something I'd picked up on some alien world I'd visited. When it didn't go away I went to a doctor. He'd never seen eplasia, so he prescribed some ointment. I applied it religiously, and all that happened was that the rash got worse. After another year, and two more doctors who at least admitted they didn't know what the hell I had, I went into the Democracy to find a clinic that specialized in skin diseases." The muscles in his jaw tightened noticeably. "That was when they laid the death sentence on me."

"How long did they give you to live?"

"They didn't know. A year. Ten years. It didn't make any difference. They assured me that long before the end I'd kill myself—and once they learned who I was, they suggested that the day would come that I'd purposely lose a gunfight rather than keep on living."

"They didn't know Jefferson Nighthawk," said Kinoshita.

"It got pretty bad," continued Nighthawk. "There came a day when I'd look in the mirror, and there was more bone showing than flesh. My knuckles stuck up through the skin on my hands. I didn't have any hair, because there wasn't enough skin on my head to hold it in place. I gave anyone who saw me nightmares—not just kids, but grown men and women too. And there was a smell of rot and decay I couldn't get away from." He winced at the memory. "The smell was me."

"And still you didn't kill yourself."

"I was never afraid to die. You can't work in my business if you *are* afraid. But something inside me wouldn't let me just give up and kill myself—and purposely losing a fight would have been suicide. Maybe the onlookers and coroner wouldn't recognize it as such, but I would." He was silent for a long minute, and Kinoshita could tell he was reliving those final days with the disease, days when he had to force himself to look into the mirror or step outside where people could gape at him—or turn away from him in horror and disgust. "Then I heard about a very private, very expensive facility on Deluros VIII, at the center of the Oligarchy, where they were cryogenically freezing any man or woman with a terminal disease who could afford to stay frozen until a cure was discovered. The cost was better than a million credits a year, but I'd stockpiled twenty million credits, and I locked them in at eight percent interest."

"Seemed reasonable," said Kinoshita.

"It was," replied Nighthawk. "How the hell could I know that it would take them more than a century to effect a cure, or that the economy would go through an inflationary spiral for more than a decade? I was still locked it at eight percent, but suddenly it was costing five million credits a year to stay frozen. It didn't take me long to run through most of my principal."

"That's when they created the first clone?"

Nighthawk nodded. "They had to wake me up and get my authorization. I still remember it. I was too weak to sit up on my own, and when I saw my hand in front of me I knew I hadn't been cured. I thought they were about to tell me that they'd decided they could never come up with a cure." He smiled bitterly. "What they told me was just as bad. I was almost broke, and they were going to have to wake me and toss me out. The only alternative was to create a clone for some guy on the Inner Frontier who'd heard the Widowmaker was still alive and was willing to pay enough for a replica to do a job for him that I'd be able to stay frozen for a few more years."

"That was the first clone—and my first experience with the Widowmaker," said Kinoshita. "He had all of Jeff's skills— all of *your* skills—but he had none of your experiences or memories or judgment. He fell in love with the first girl he met, a girl who was didn't give a damn about him and was working for men who wanted him dead. He let his heart rule his head—or maybe it was his gonads that ruled both of them. At any rate, it's something I never saw happen to you or Jason, and in the end it got him killed. But at least he accomplished his mission, and brought in some money."

"Half of what he was promised, from what I've been told," said Nighthawk.

"There was more than enough corruption to go around," answered Kinoshita. "His friends, his enemies, your barristers. Still, it was enough to keep you going for two more years, and by then they were on the way to curing eplasia. But they hadn't cured it before you ran out of money again, and that's when a second clone was created."

"Jason Newman."

"Yes, though I'm still not used to calling him that. He was Jefferson Nighthawk when I traveled with him and we took Pericles V. They'd made a breakthrough in the science of cloning, and he was born with all of your memories. In fact, I'm told they had quite a job convincing him that he was a clone, because he *knew* he was you."

"I never thought about that," admitted Nighthawk. "Yeah, I can see where that would be a problem."

"Anyway, his mission paid enough to keep you alive and give you a nest egg when they revived you." He paused and looked across the table at Nighthawk. "I still remember the first day I saw you in the hospital. I'd have almost bet money you'd never wind up looking like a normal man. What was the toughest adjustment you had to make after being frozen for a century?"

"Seriously?" said Nighthawk. "It wasn't the new technology. Technology is just another word for machines. You learn how they work, and you adjust to them or you don't bother with them. The biggest problem I had was being attacked by enemies the two clones made, men and women I'd never seen before and couldn't recognize. Hell, you were with me—you can remember. Every time I thought I'd found a planet where I could settle down and live out my life in peace, someone with a grudge against the Widowmaker, someone who'd been born sixty or seventy years after I was frozen, would come hunting for me. That's why I finally went back to Deluros VIII and had them clone Jeff."

"Well, I'm glad things worked out and that you didn't end it all when you came down with the disease," said Kinoshita. "Though I'm not leading quite the life I had in mind when I was a young man just starting out." He paused and stared at Nighthawk. "How about you?"

"I'm glad I didn't end it all too."

"I meant, is this the life you had in mind when you were a young man?"

"No," said Nighthawk. "I confidently expected to be dead almost a century ago."

"Damn it, you know what I'm asking!" said Kinoshita. "What made you become the Widowmaker?"

"Because I could."

"What kind of answer is that?"

"The best you're going to get," said Nighthawk. "Now decide what you want for dessert, or else I'll pay the tab and we'll get going."

"Are you *ever* going to tell me about it?" persisted Kinoshita.

"It's history," replied Nighthawk. "And evidently it's not even very good history. At least, whenever I see one of those holos they make about the Widowmaker, they're never the way it happened."

"Maybe someday you should dictate your memoirs so there'll be an accurate record."

"There's a record. Just follow the trail of bounties I've collected."

"There's got to be more than just that."

"That's what made me the Widowmaker," said Nighthawk. "If you want to know every meal I've eaten, every planet I've been to, every woman I've slept with, then you want the Nighthawk Laundry Lists, not the record of what made me different." He turned and signaled to the human waiter. "Make up your mind. Do you want dessert and coffee, or not?"

"Not," said Kinoshita. "You're ruining my appetite."

Nighthawk paid the bill, and the two men went back down to the ground level. Nighthawk stopped at a shop in the lobby specializing in alien tobaccos and picked up a small box of smokeless Greenveldt cigars.

"How much?" he asked.

"Sixteen credits, five Maria Theresa dollars, or six Far London pounds," said the robot clerk. "I cannot accept New Punjab rupees."

Suddenly a woman came out from the back of the store and approached Nighthawk. "For the man who killed Hairless Jack, no charge," she said.

"I pay my way," said Nighthawk.

"Your money's no good here," she said. "I won't accept so much as a credit."

Then he remembered his talk with the owner of the weapons shop inside the District and asked for a piece of paper. When she gave it to him, he wrote a glowing endorsement of the shop, proclaimed that he would buy his cigars from no other establishment on New Barcelona, and signed his name with a flourish.

"Will you accept this?" he asked.

She read it and a huge smile spread across her face. "I'll put it in the front window, Mr. Nighthawk."

"We're square now?" he asked, preparing to leave.

"Far from it," she said. "I'm in your debt." She stared at him for a moment, as if trying to make up her mind about something. "Maybe I can even the score. Lean over." Nighthawk bent down and she whispered in his ear.

"You're sure?" he said, straightening up.

"Absolutely."

"Thanks." He lit a cigar and walked out, followed by Kinoshita.

"That was a very generous thing you just did," said the smaller man.

"I'd be like that all the time if I could."

"But?" said Kinoshita. "There's always a but."

"But as hard as I try to avoid it, the path I travel puts me in contact with a lot more Jack Bellamys and Cleopatra Romes than law-abiding cigar-store proprietors."

"It must be something in your character."

"It wasn't anything in my character that caused me to leave my wife and my home and come to a cesspool like the District," said Nighthawk. "It was a would-be samurai named Kinoshita, who asks too damned many questions."

"If that's the way you feel, I'm all through asking them," said Kinoshita in hurt tones.

"Where have I heard *that* before?"

They rode the slidewalk for half a block when Kinoshita spoke up again. "I have one more question, and then I'll be quiet," he said.

"That didn't last very long, did it?" said Nighthawk, more amused than annoyed. "All right, go ahead and ask."

"Where are we going now?"

"Off to find Cleopatra Rome."

"I thought you wanted to learn what her particular skills and abilities were."

"I haven't got time."

"What are you talking about?"

"The lady in the cigar store," said Nighthawk. "What she whispered to me was that if I had any intention of going after Cleopatra Rome, I'd better do it quick. The guy she's living with works at the spaceport, and Cleopatra Rome has booked passage out tomorrow morning."

Suddenly the shellfish began doing flip-flops in Kinoshita's stomach.

14.

THEY CAME TO the building that housed Horatio's and entered it, but instead of going to the airlift Nighthawk walked straight through the large lobby to the dilapidated men's room that was off in a corner.

"That's not a bad idea," said Kinoshita. "I think I'll join you."

The room was quite large, the remnant of better and more lucrative days. While Kinoshita sought out a urinal, Nighthawk walked over to the row of sinks and began carefully removing his weapons and laying them on long counter just above the sinks.

He tested the battery on his burner, drew it out of his holster a few times to make sure it moved swiftly and smoothly, that there was no hidden grit on either the surface of the weapon or the leather of the holster.

Next came the screecher. Nighthawk usually kept it tucked in the back of his belt, so the only thing he checked was the battery. He didn't like what he found, so he removed the coin-sized power source, tossed it in a trash atomizer, and inserted another.

After that came the projectile pistol. He cocked and uncocked it a few times, made sure it was fully loaded, and checked the spare clip he kept in a pocket.

He withdrew a knife from each boot. The one in his left boot had a serrated edge for close-in hand-to-hand fighting. The one in his right boot was a perfectly balanced throwing weapon, and Nighthawk could throw it with remarkable accuracy.

When he was satisfied that all his weapons were in perfect working order, he put them back, each in its place, and removed a small pouch from a pocket.

"What's that?" asked Kinoshita.

"Contact lenses," said Nighthawk.

Kinoshita looked puzzled. "I didn't know you had any trouble with your eyes."

"I don't."

"Then why—?"

"The left one sees into the infrared spectrum, the right into the ultraviolet."

"Still why?"

"Because I don't know what to expect, and it's best to be prepared for anything. I probably won't have time to make adjustments once I confront her."

"Isn't this a little premature?" asked Kinoshita. "You don't even know where she is."

"It's better to prepare in advance than after the fact," replied Nighthawk. "And I've got a pretty good idea of where she is. I just don't know what she's capable of doing."

"Where do you think she is?"

"Everyone else knows I'm on the planet, so she must know it too. And she knows I killed Bellamy and I'm still here. Bellamy didn't work for anyone, so she'll conclude that I'm not after one particular gang, but rather the biggest bounties—and she's as big as they come. If she wanted to confront me, she'd have been looking for me last night and this morning, and I haven't been that hard to find, so it figures that she'd rather avoid me. We know she's leaving New Barcelona tomorrow morning, and she can't count on the fact that someone wouldn't have told me or sold me the information by now, not with the price she's carrying around on her head. So she's going to want to get to the spaceport as quietly and unobtrusively as possible. There's a bullet shuttle that goes nonstop from the District to the spaceport every four hours. We're heading for the spot where it picks up its passengers from the District. That's where she's going to show up sooner or later."

"You're just going to stand there for hours and hope she doesn't know what you look like or that no one will point you out to her?" demanded Kinoshita.

"Don't say foolish things; it's unbecoming," replied Nighthawk. "I've never yet seen a shuttle stop that didn't have a couple of restaurants nearby. We'll set up shop at a table where I can keep an eye on things and wait for her."

"If she wants to avoid you, she'll just take some other route to the spaceport."

"No she won't," said Nighthawk. "She's worth nine million credits dead or alive, and any other route to the spaceport requires her to set foot outside the District, where she's fair game to any sniper—and I saw a number of them when we walked to the police station this morning."

"You did?" said Kinoshita, surprised. "I never saw a single one."

"You weren't looking for them."

"True," admitted Kinoshita. Then: "When do you think she'll show up?"

"The first time? Maybe a couple of hours."

"The first time?"

Nighthawk nodded. "I figure she'll disguise herself as anything from a beggar to a whore and check out the shuttle stop to make sure no one's lying in wait for her. Nine million credits is a lot of money; there are lots of Men and aliens in the District who would like to claim it. Even those with prices on their own heads—or what passes for their heads."

"And you're sure she's going to behave the way you say, even though you've never met her and know nothing about her?" said Kinoshita.

"I know one thing about her," said Nighthawk. "She's still alive, when everyone wants her dead. That bespeaks a certain intelligence, or at least a high level of cunning, and a well-developed sense of self-preservation. She'll do what I said."

"And if she spots you?"

"She probably will."

"What then?"

"I'll be curious to see her reaction," said Nighthawk. "Either she'll try to kill me before I know it's her, or she'll leave and hope I never know how close I was to her." He paused. "It's up to me to spot her before she either leaves or attacks."

"That's a tall order," said Kinoshita. "How will you be able to know who she is?"

"There are ways," said Nighthawk. He came to a stop. "See that little island surrounded by all the slidewalks? That's the shuttle stop."

"How do you know?" asked Kinoshita. "We've never been here before."

"I've got good eyes. I can read the sign."

"*Good* eyes?" exclaimed Kinoshita. "If you could read that little sign from a block away, you've got eyes like a goddamned devilhawk!"

"Anyway, that's the shuttle stop." Nighthawk looked around, spotted three restaurants, and finally walked to the one that would afford him the best view of the area. When he asked for a booth by the window that faced the shuttle stop, he was told that they were all full.

"We'll wait in the bar," he replied. Then he slipped a couple of bills to the manager. "Bring us two beers and let me know as soon as a booth opens up."

He and Kinoshita walked to the long polished bar, made of some dark alien hardwood. There were no stools, but rather cushions and footrests, each hovering above the floor.

"Interesting sensation," remarked Kinoshita after their beers had been delivered. "I keep feeling I'm going to fall off."

"Try not to think about it and you'll be okay," said Nighthawk.

"What if she shows up right now, before you can spot her?" asked Kinoshita.

"Then she won't be able to spot me, and that'll make her nervous. She'll be back."

"I'm always amazed at how you cover every angle," said Kinoshita. "It's been a while. I'd almost forgotten just how thorough you are."

"Isn't Jeff?" asked Nighthawk. "I taught him to be."

"Jeff assumes that he can handle any foe or any situation, and so far he hasn't been wrong. To use your analogy, he's the young athlete who's relying totally on his speed and strength. You're the aging athlete who's using his brain and his experience to make up for the step he's lost."

"It sounds good," said Nighthawk. "But I was always like this. This isn't a profession where you can say, 'I lost the last three gunfights. I think I'd better start relying more on my intelligence in the future.'"

"But when you were young, you were as good as Jeff. You didn't need your brain then."

"I *always* used it," replied Nighthawk. "It came with the rest of me."

"Then why doesn't *he*? It's *your* brain, after all; we know it works."

"Probably because he knew from the outset that he was the Widowmaker, created with all the abilities I possessed in my physical prime. There wasn't any Widowmaker when I started out, and I didn't have the benefit of another Jefferson Nighthawk who'd been through it all and could teach me the ropes or tell me how good I was."

"How old were you when you killed your first man?" asked Kinoshita.

"Not very."

"*How* old?" persisted Kinoshita.

"I just told you," said Nighthawk.

A booth emptied out just then and Nighthawk headed over to it before the servo-mech had a chance to clean it. He sat down and let the robot work around him. Kinoshita stood back until the robot left, then sat down opposite Nighthawk.

"Do you see anyone who might be her?" he asked.

"I can't tell yet."

"I see three women. If she's here, she's got to be one of them."

"What makes you think so?" said Nighthawk.

Kinoshita blinked rapidly. "You're right," he admitted. "I wasn't thinking. If she's just scouting out the area, of course she could disguise herself as a man." He paused, studying the passersby. "Jeff would just stand out there and dare her to face him."

"I hope I trained him better than that," said Nighthawk. Kinoshita looked at him questioningly. "She doesn't have to take the shuttle. All she has to do is show up at the spaceport in time for her flight. If he felt he *had* to force the issue, the place to wait for her is there, not here." He sipped his beer. "I may wind up having to do that myself, but I've got about twelve or fourteen hours to spot her here first."

"If you do spot her, will you try to take her now?" asked Kinoshita.

"Depends."

"On what?"

Nighthawk shrugged. "Instinct. I'll know what to do when I finally see her."

Kinoshita finished his beer. He pressed his thumb on a small red circle on the table, and instantly a holographic drink menu popped into existence, rotating slowly just above the surface of the table.

"They've got quite a selection," he commented. Nighthawk didn't answer, and he kept on reading. "I think I'll have a Dust Whore. They tell me that it was actually created back when we were still Earthbound. Some country called Chicago, as I recall. Or maybe it was an independent city-state." He looked across the table at Nighthawk, who was looking off to his left and smiling. "What's so funny?" asked Kinoshita. "I wasn't making a joke."

"I wasn't laughing at one," said Nighthawk, staring out the window.

"Well, then??"

"She's one smart lady."

"Who are you talking about?"

"Cleopatra Rome," he said.

"You see her?"

Nighthawk nodded.

"Where is she?" demanded Kinoshita, peering out through the window.

"You'd have to be blind to miss her."

Kinoshita scanned the area, and finally his gaze fell on a gorgeous young woman riding in a rickshaw-like contraption. She was clad entirely in well-worn leather, loaded top to bottom with weapons, her keen purple eyes coolly surveying her surroundings.

"Boy, she really looks the part, doesn't she?" said Kinoshita.

"She sure does," said Nighthawk, still smiling.

"What's the joke?" demanded Kinoshita. "What do you know that I don't know?"

"Don't give me straight lines like that," said Nighthawk. "I could write a shelf of books about what I know and you don't."

"What's this got to do with Cleopatra Rome, and why do you think she's so damned smart?"

"Because you were a pretty fair-to-middling lawman, and yet she fooled *you* completely," said Nighthawk in amused tones.

"What are you talking about?"

"See the woman pulling the cart?" said Nighthawk.

Kinoshita stared at the tall, lean woman with the square jaw and almost alien eyes that seemed to see everything, the scar running from the edge of her ear all the way down her cheek and onto her neck, the wide belt that had a pair of telltale bulges over the hips, the calf-high boot that held more than her muscular leg.

"Are you trying to tell me—?"

"Right," said Nighthawk, getting up from the booth and heading toward the front door. "That's Cleopatra Rome."

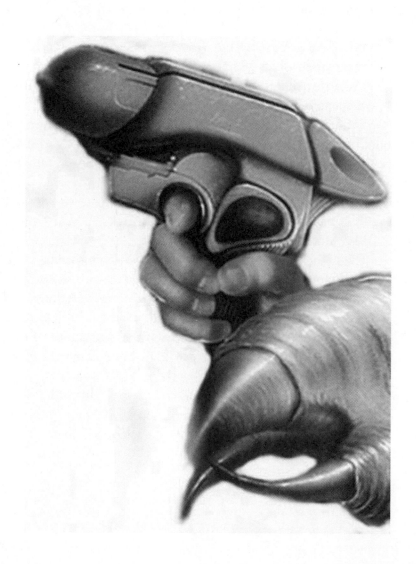

15.

NIGHTHAWK WALKED OUT onto the street to better study his quarry. Kinoshita was a step behind him.

"Widowmaker!" yelled the girl in leather, pointing to him. "Come a step closer and I'll kill you!"

Suddenly the street became totally silent. There was no talk, no music, none of the normal hustle and bustle. Most people froze where they were, not wanting to get close to either the Widowmaker or his prey; a few raced for shelter.

"Spare me your threats," he replied with no show of concern.

"Go back where you came from and leave me alone!"

"I'm not here for you," said Nighthawk.

Even the girl seemed surprised. "Then go away!" she finally managed.

But Nighthawk was no longer paying any attention to her. His concentration was focused on Cleopatra Rome, who stared at him emotionlessly, sizing him up as much as he was doing to her.

"I'm warning you!" said the leather-clad girl.

"Do you see this man by my side?" said Nighthawk. Without waiting for an answer he continued: "I have no interest in you, but if you try to involve yourself in what's about to happen, he'll kill you. There's no need for you to die. If there's paper on you, I don't know about it and I don't care about it. If you walk away right now, nothing will happen to you. If you stay, you're putting yourself at risk for no reason." The girl looked flustered and indecisive. "You're in over your head. Walk away now and nothing will happen to you."

The girl seemed unable to move or speak for a moment. Then she jumped out of the rickshaw and raced off into an alley.

"Nice try," said Nighthawk to Cleopatra Rome.

"She served her purpose," said Cleopatra Rome.

"Oh? Just what *was* her purpose?"

"To attract your attention. I like to look upon the face of my enemy before I dispatch him to the next plane of existence." She smiled a cold, passionless smile. "Now I've seen it."

"Do you always speak like that?" asked Nighthawk.

"Do you have a problem with the poetry of language?"

"Use some and I'll let you know."

She looked up at the sun, then back at Nighthawk. "It's a hot day, Jefferson Nighthawk, and only one of us will live to see the end of it. There's no reason why either of us should die thirsty. Let's go inside for a drink."

Whatever Nighthawk was expecting her to say or do, that wasn't it. "Why not?" he replied, forcing a shrug to show that he wasn't surprised. "I'm new to the District. Have you got any place in mind?"

"Anywhere but Horatio's," she said. "I disapprove of their clientele."

"You're well informed."

Another cold smile. "I'm alive."

Nighthawk indicated a tavern across the street. "How about that one?"

"That will be fine."

The second the words left her mouth, the tavern emptied out. By the time they'd crossed the street even the bartender had raced out the door.

Nighthawk turned to Kinoshita. "You wait here."

"But—"

"Do *you* want to go up against her? Just say the word and I'll wait out here for you."

"Damn it, Jefferson!"

"Let's try again," said Nighthawk. "You wait here."

Kinoshita nodded his agreement and kept his mouth shut, and Nighthawk followed Cleopatra Rome into the tavern. She walked behind the bar, examined the stock, and pulled out a bottle of Alphard brandy.

"Three-century-old stuff," she said approvingly as she studied the label. "Have you ever had any?"

"More than a century ago," said Nighthawk. "It was pretty good drinking when it was only two hundred years old."

"Yes, I heard about you," said Cleopatra Rome. "They say you came down with some disease and froze yourself for a hundred years or so."

"Essentially."

"What does that mean?"

"It means I didn't freeze myself. I had help." He smiled. "I thought you were the stickler for language."

"My error," she said. "I also heard that you got some kind of rejuvenation treatment, that suddenly you were twenty-two or twenty-three years old and back in business. I guess the treatment wasn't permanent."

"I guess not," said Nighthawk. If she was good enough to kill him, he wanted it to end right there. He saw no reason to tell her that there were two more versions of him abroad in the galaxy.

"Too bad," she said with no show of sympathy. "You're an old man, Jefferson Nighthawk. How much longer do you think you can keep on being the Widowmaker?"

"Long enough."

"To kill me, you mean?"

He saw no reason to answer such an obvious question, so he simply took the bottle from her, uncorked it, and took a swallow before handing it back.

"Why don't you hire me instead?" said Cleopatra Rome.

This time he couldn't hide his surprise. "You want to say that again?"

"You heard me."

"Why would I want to hire you?"

"Why not?" she replied. "We're both in the same business."

"The hell we are."

"Think about it. I kill people for money. You kill people for money. The only difference is that I'm a private contractor and you work for the Oligarchy."

"I work for *me*."

"Oh?" she said, arching an eyebrow. "Who do you collect your bounties from?"

"The Oligarchy."

"Well, then?"

"They're not my employer," said Nighthawk. "They're my bank."

"You're splitting hairs," she said. "We're both killers, and we both get well paid for what we do. No one forces us to kill. We choose to—and if we don't like the price, we choose not to."

"There are differences. I don't break the law. You break it every time you work."

"Some of the men and aliens I kill are very bad," she said. "Some of the ones you kill are very good."

"It's possible," he acknowledged. "But under the right conditions even good men can do terrible things."

"So you kill some good men and *I* kill some good men," she said. "I told you we were the same."

"We're not the same, and we're not in the same business. This is a galaxy of laws. You break them. I don't."

"This is a galaxy of meat eaters and meat," replied Cleopatra Rome. "And you and I are at the top of the food chain. We shouldn't be fighting each other when there's enough raw meat for both of us."

"Are you enjoying yourself?" asked Nighthawk.

"Why do you ask?"

"Because if I was about to die, I sure as hell wouldn't waste my last few minutes having a philosophical debate with the guy who's going to kill me."

"Actually, I *was* rather enjoying it," said Cleopatra Rome. Nighthawk shrugged. "To each his own."

"Still, I've got enough," she said. "I suppose we can stop now."

"Enough *what?*" he asked.

"Enough Jefferson Nighthawk."

"I don't know what the hell you're talking about."

"You will," she said with a predatory smile. "You will."

His fingers inched down toward his burner. "Promises, promises," he said sardonically.

"Why do you suppose I came in here with you?" said Cleopatra Rome. "Your talents are well known. I can't outfight you. I'm not as accomplished with my weapons as you. Why should I put myself at your mercy?"

"It was a stupid decision," said Nighthawk. "My mercy is in short supply these days."

"How do you think I killed all those Men and aliens?" she continued. "By shooting them?"

"I assume you're going to tell me," said Nighthawk.

"No," she said, still smiling. "I'm going to *show* you."

And suddenly she wasn't Cleopatra Rome any longer. She was Sarah, her binoculars slung over her shoulder, a bird guide in her hand.

"Look!" she said, pointing to a tree that suddenly seemed to spring into existence. "A silver-throated sunbird!"

"This is wrong," said Nighthawk, frowning.

"Okay," said Sarah. "What do *you* think it is?"

Nighthawk felt uncomfortable. Something was bothering him, but he couldn't put his finger on it. He looked at the avian sitting on the end of the branch.

"It's a blue-crested sunbird," he said, wondering why he felt such uneasiness.

"You're right," she said, peering through the binoculars. "You always had the most remarkable vision."

"How did we get here?" asked Nighthawk. "I was in a bar on New Barcelona."

"You had a dream," said Sarah. "You told me about it at breakfast, don't you remember? We're on Goldenhue."

"Goldenhue," he said, nodding. "We're on Goldenhue."

"I'm getting tired, Jefferson. Will you take the book from me? It's very heavy."

"Sure," he said, reaching out and taking the book. Suddenly he frowned. "That's funny."

"What is?"

"I thought books were supposed to be flat. This one is round."

"It's a new style," said Sarah. "I picked it up Roosevelt III."

Nighthawk blinked, shook his head vigorously, and suddenly threw the book through a window on the side of the tavern. A moment later there was a small explosion. He drew his burner and pointed it at Sarah, who was once again Cleopatra Rome.

"Where'd you learn to do that?" he asked.

"You don't *learn* something like that," she replied, unfazed by his weapon. "You're born with it, and over the years you learn to refine it. Where did I make my mistake? The bomb?"

"No, I believed it was a book."

"Then what?"

"Sarah's never been to the Roosevelt system."

She sighed and shook her head. "It's my own fault for improvising."

"Improvising?"

"I pulled Sarah's face and figure and speech patterns out of your mind, but I improvised the bit about the Roosevelt system. It just seemed like a good answer at the time. Stupid of me. Once you spot anything wrong, however slight, the whole illusion vanishes. I guess I'll have to try one that you don't know as well."

And as quickly as the words left her mouth, she was a lovely young girl, still in her teens, with auburn hair that cascaded down almost to her waist, clear blue eyes, a delicate nose and chin, a small bustline, narrow waist, slender legs.

"Hello, Jeff," she said in a melodic voice. "It's been a long time."

Nighthawk simply stared at her without answering.

"Why won't you speak to me, Jeff? I waited and waited for you for all these years. I even stayed young for you, exactly the way I was the day you left. Aren't you glad to see me?"

"Belinda," he said. It sounded more like a croak.

"Look at you, Jeff," she said sadly. "You've become an old man. You used to be so handsome. Now you're all gnarled and twisted. What happened to you?"

"Life did. Eplasia did." He suddenly felt the burden of his years. "Life did."

"You never wrote. You never left a subspace message. You never came back, and I waited for so long. Why?"

"I had things to do."

"Were they more important than me?"

"No," he admitted. "But they seemed more important at the time."

"It's not too late, Jeff," she said. "You still have a few years left. We can still be together."

"It's tempting," he said.

"All you have to do is come back to me," said Belinda. "I'll be waiting."

"But you're here right now," said Nighthawk, a puzzled look on his face.

"I have to go back home and tell my parents that all my hopes and prayers weren't in vain. It would be cruel to leave with you and not let them know. They love me very much."

"Send them a message."

She shook her head. "I have to say good-bye properly. After all, they cared for me all these years that you've been away. Give me a day to break the news to them, and then come for me."

"Whatever you say." Then: "I don't know where you live."

"Where I've always lived," said Belinda. "On Rasputin. Do you remember the address?"

Nighthawk stared at her.

"The address, Jeff—do you remember it?"

"No."

"I'll write it down for you," she said, withdrawing a long, gleaming stylus from her belt. "Do you have any paper with you?"

Nighthawk shook his head.

"I'll write it on your shirt," she said. "You can copy it onto a computer when you get back to your ship."

She had reached forward, preparing to write an address on his chest, when his hand shot out and slapped the stylus out of her hand. It clattered across the floor, a shining knife with an eight-inch blade.

He had completely forgotten the burner in his hand. The flat of his other hand smashed into her neck. There was a cracking noise, and she careened into a wall and collapsed. As the light of life began vanishing from her eyes, she stared at him, the question written across her face.

"There was never a Belinda," he said. "She was my idealized woman—at least, she was a century and a half ago, when I was maybe fourteen years old. She seemed so real to me that you plucked her out of my mind and didn't know the difference. And," he admitted, "neither did I. But in my fantasy, I imagined she lived on a world named Rasputin, a crazy man I read about when I was a kid, and the world was never as real to me as the girl."

Her eyes had clouded over, and he wasn't sure she'd lived to the end of his explanation.

He took another swallow of the Alphard brandy, put it back on its shelf, and then, because he was every bit as thorough as Kinoshita believed, he sat down and tried to comprehend exactly what he had experienced so that he could be better prepared if he ever met another person with the same ability.

He tried to figure out how she'd managed to pull meaningful memories and images out of alien minds, how she'd been able to read or interpret them at all. This was a remarkable woman he had just dispatched, and he found himself actually wondering what kind of team they might have made if her offer to join him had been legitimate.

This is ridiculous, he told himself harshly. *She was right. I'm an old man, surviving by luck and instinct. I don't need any partners. I don't even know what the hell I'm doing here. I should be back with Sarah on Goldenhue, watching birds, trying to make those goddamned roses grow, and reading my books.*

And because he was nothing if not honest, he added: *Still, this is the most alive I've felt in a long, long time. Maybe you can only truly appreciate life when it's forcibly impressed on you just how ephemeral it really is.*

After a few minutes he walked to the door and stepped out into the street.

"What happened?" asked Kinoshita. "I didn't hear a sound."

"It's over. Get an airsled."

Kinoshita stuck his head through the doorway. "What weapon did you use on her?"

"Her ignorance and her carelessness."

"Ignorance and carelessness?"

"Yes," said Nighthawk. "When you stop and think about it, they're the best weapons in anyone's arsenal."

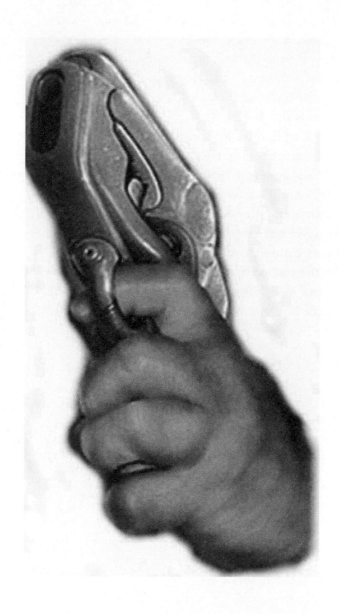

16.

KINOSHITA WENT OFF to find an airsled. When he returned he found Nighthawk sitting at a table in the still-deserted tavern, sipping his Alphard brandy.

"This is expensive stuff," said Nighthawk. "Pour some for yourself before we leave. It'll be a long time before you get another opportunity to drink it for free."

Kinoshita went behind the bar, found an empty brandy snifter, poured in a few ounces from the bottle that was still on the bar, and walked over to join Nighthawk.

"They already know she's dead," he said, nodding toward the street.

"Of course they do. They knew when you came out alive and brought back an airsled."

"Well, if anything catches Jeff's attention, it has to be taking Bellamy and Cleopatra Rome in two days' time." Kinoshita paused. "I got a lot of dirty looks when I came back here with the airsled. Maybe we should warn Jeff that the Widowmaker's not too popular on New Barcelona."

"If we knew how to contact him, I wouldn't be here shooting bad guys," said Nighthawk. "Besides, no one's going to bother him."

"But—"

"They hate the Widowmaker. And after two days here, they know he's a wrinkled, gray-haired old man. Jeff's a kid in his early twenties. They won't give him a second glance."

"I hadn't thought of that," admitted Kinoshita.

"No reason why you should have," said Nighthawk. "It's not you they want to kill."

Kinoshita took a sip of his brandy. "This is awfully good, maybe the best I've ever had. I can see why it costs a couple of hundred credits for a glass."

"You can take the bottle back to the ship if you want," said Nighthawk. Suddenly he smiled. "I don't think anyone will try to stop you."

Kinoshita considered it, then shook his head. "No. Just about the time I got used to it it'd be gone, and I can't afford to drink it on a regular basis."

"We just made close to twenty million credits in two days," said Nighthawk. "It's not *that* expensive."

"That's *your* money, not *ours*. You killed them, you get the reward."

"We'll worry about whose money it is when we see what's left after we pay Jason Newman's hospital bills." He paused. "You know, I almost felt like I was talking to myself back on Giancola. A younger version, with a different face, but *me*. I never once felt that way with Jeff."

"Jason knows every thought you ever had until five years ago, and has experienced—or *thinks* he has experienced—everything you ever did up until that day," said Kinoshita. "Jeff was a blank slate that you tried to mold into your successor, but Jason was *you*."

"It gets confusing," said Nighthawk.

"It's probably more confusing for Jason than for you or Jeff. Your memories are real, and Jeff doesn't have any. But Jason knows that everything he remembers from more than five years ago is false, that all his dreams and thoughts are on permanent loan to him."

"He seems to have adjusted."

"Of course he has," said Kinoshita. "He's Jefferson Nighthawk too."

"Spare me the hero worship, and if you're through drinking, let's get the body loaded and onto the sled."

"Do you want me to find a blanket, something to cover her?" asked Kinoshita.

"No," replied Nighthawk. "The more people who know she's dead, the more people will talk about it. Who knows what it takes to get word out to wherever the hell Jeff is?"

"So we're just going to walk her right through the District and up to the police station, the same as we did with Hairless Jack?"

"That's right," said Nighthawk, getting to his feet and walking over to Cleopatra Rome's corpse.

"Did it ever occur to you that we'll make pretty easy targets doing that?" asked Kinoshita, helping to heft the body onto the airsled.

"No one will bother us."

"I admire your confidence," said Kinoshita. "But can I ask what makes you so sure?"

"Killing Hairless Jack Bellamy might have been luck," said Nighthawk, "but taking Bellamy and Cleopatra Rome in two days' time means that I'm really not someone you want to mess with." He smiled at Kinoshita. "I know it's difficult for you to believe, but you'll be safer today than you were yesterday."

"I hope you're right," said Kinoshita. "What were her skills? All I see is a knife."

"It's all she needed," said Nighthawk. "She wasn't an alien, but given her abilities she must have been a mutant. She could create the most believable illusions."

"What kind of illusions?"

"Comforting ones."

"That doesn't tell me much."

"She could appear to be someone you trusted, could make you believe you were somewhere else, somewhere safe with an old friend or an old lover—or a current one."

"How the hell did you beat someone like that?" asked Kinoshita as they walked out the door and stepped onto the street.

"Did you ever have a dream, and at some point you realized it was a dream because something was wrong?"

"Yes."

"Same thing."

"She'd made close to one hundred kills," said Kinoshita. "You must have been the first guy who was able to pierce the illusion she created."

"I doubt it," said Nighthawk. "But I was the first one to pierce it in time to save myself."

They turned in the direction of the police station. Most passersby avoided them, a few refused even to meet their gaze. But a handful walked up and stared at the body, just to convince themselves that the notorious Cleopatra Rome was truly dead. As they neared the edge of the district, a familiar-looking Lodinite waddled over to them.

"I see that you have killed her," it said.

"That's right."

"But you did not seek her out at the Royal Ascot," continued the Lodinite.

"Why face her in her lair?" asked Nighthawk. "It figured to be very well protected. Besides, I knew she'd be at the shuttle stop."

"I risked my life telling you where she lived."

"I risked *my* life facing her," said Nighthawk. "Put your hand down."

"My hand?" said the Lodinite, puzzled. "I do not understand."

"An expression," said Nighthawk. "Roughly translated, it means thanks for the help and the good wishes, but since I already paid you five thousand credits and didn't even use your information about the Royal Ascot, you're not getting one credit more."

The Lodinite looked at the body again. "At least she will kill no more of my people," it said at last.

"Or mine," agreed Nighthawk.

"You are absolutely sure you do not wish to thank me in a meaningful way for my advice and support?"

"I killed her," said Nighthawk. "That should be thanks enough."

The alien walked off without another word.

"He's going to tell everyone that you refuse to pay for information," said Kinoshita. "He'll conveniently forget about the five thousand credits."

"Just as well," said Nighthawk. "If word gets out that I'm paying for information, every resident of the District is going to try selling out his best friend, his partner, his boss, and his bedmate. I don't need that kind of hassle. I'm just here to force Jeff to pay us a little visit."

"You mean you really wouldn't kill another notorious murderer if you didn't think it would help bring Jeff here?" asked Kinoshita disbelievingly.

"No, I really wouldn't." Nighthawk paused to light a smokeless cigar, then grabbed the sled as it started drifting away. "Do you know how many men and aliens I've killed in my life?"

"Not precisely."

"Believe me, there were a lot, more than I think you can imagine," said Nighthawk. "Now look around you at the District. Nothing's changed."

"But this is the District. It's a tiny area that's set aside for criminals like these."

"So you're saying that if I leave the planet I won't find any more killers, that Jason and Jeff are wasting their time looking for bad guys on every world they touch down on?"

"No," admitted Kinoshita. "No, of course I'm not saying that."

"Argument ended."

"But if you've felt this way all along, why did you remain the Widowmaker?"

"Because I was the best at my job, and because things would have been worse if I'd quit, or if I hadn't created Jeff."

"And that's the only reason?" said Kinoshita. "You did it because you *could* do it?"

"Have you got a better reason?" asked Nighthawk as they crossed out of the District and headed toward the police station. They stopped for a moment when they came to the cigar shop. Nighthawk left Kinoshita outside with the airsled and a growing crowd of awestruck children while he entered, bought a Greenveldt cigar, and told the woman behind the counter that Cleopatra Rome would not be making her flight connections after all.

Then he rejoined Kinoshita and the two walked to the police station.

"I don't suppose you'd consider joining the force, Mr. Nighthawk?" said the captain as they brought the airsled inside.

Nighthawk smiled and shook his head. "Just have the money transferred here, and then place it in my account."

"We'll do it," said the captain, "but it may take an extra day or two."

"Oh?"

"Yeah" was the answer. "There's been a killing at the bank. We've shut it down until we get everything we need from the crime scene."

"Robbery?"

"Not that we can tell."

"Who got killed?"

"One of the vice-presidents. He seems to have been shot trying to stop the thieves from doing something—but we don't know what. They could have incinerated one of the robot clerks and run off with some money, but they apparently weren't interested in that."

"Safe-deposit boxes, perhaps?" suggested Kinoshita.

The officer shook his head. "They didn't go near them."

"What the hell else does a bank have besides money and lockboxes?" asked Nighthawk.

"We're still trying to find out."

"Well, I wish you luck," said Nighthawk. "Let me fill out the paperwork and we'll get out of your way."

He spent a few minutes describing the death of Cleopatra Rome to a computer and had just finished letting it register his retina and thumbprint in lieu of a signature when another officer approached the captain.

"We've got it, sir," he announced.

"Good," said the captain. "Let's have a look at it."

Suddenly a life-size holo of two men appeared. They stepped over the lifeless body of the bank's vice-president and began working on his computer. After a moment one of them inserted a small glowing cube in it—a "code buster," the captain called it—and suddenly the area above the computer was alive with holographs of data streams.

"Well, that's obviously what they were after," commented the captain.

"They look vaguely familiar," said Nighthawk, staring at the two men.

"They ought to," replied the captain. "You know the man you killed the night you killed Jack Bellamy? The one you say was about to fire at you from down the street?"

"Yes?"

"They're his brothers."

Nighthawk tensed noticeably. "Zoom in on those data streams!" he commanded.

The screens got larger and Nighthawk studied them as hundreds of figures raced past. Then suddenly the figures froze.

"Shit!" he muttered. "I thought so!" He turned to the captain. "How long ago did this take place?"

"Maybe four hours. Why?"

"They didn't want money," said Nighthawk. "They wanted my account number." He pointed to the holograph of the bank's computer, where a long number was displayed on the screen. "Part of the code gives my home planet." He turned to Kinoshita. "You stay here on New Barcelona and wait for Jeff. Keep out of the District until he shows up; it's not safe for you to go there alone."

"And what about you?" asked Kinoshita.

"I'm going to the spaceport," said Nighthawk. "Sarah's all alone, and they've got a four-hour head start on me."

17.

NIGHTHAWK CAME OUT of the Deepsleep pod an hour before his ship reached Goldenhue. He methodically checked each weapon, then checked them again. He had the galley serve him a sandwich and smiled as he imagined Kinoshita's surprise that he could sleep and eat at a time like this.

As he entered the atmosphere, his ship's radio came to life.

"Ship's registry and name of commander, please," said a mechanical voice.

"BPM11216, Jefferson Nighthawk commanding."

"Business on Goldenhue?"

"I live here," said Nighthawk. "Put me through to a human supervisor, please."

"Checking…matching voiceprint…you are Jefferson Nighthawk, resident of Goldenhue. I will patch you through to my supervisor."

An instant later a holograph of a balding man with a carefully manicured goatee flashed into existence in front of the ship's computer.

"Hi, Jefferson. What can I do for you?"

"Hi, Max," replied Nighthawk. "I need to know if any ship with a New Barcelona registry has landed in the past day."

"Let me check," said the man, looking at a spot that seemed to be just beyond Nighthawk's left shoulder. "Yes, one touched down a little more than three hours ago. It's registered to James Mendes."

"Thanks, Max," said Nighthawk. "Now I need one more favor."

"What's that?"

"Quarantine the ship for ninety minutes, and don't let anyone put Sarah on it."

"I don't know if I can do that, Jefferson."

"Trust me—if there wasn't paper on both men before yesterday, I guarantee there is now."

"Both?"

"Yeah, there are two of them. Both named Mendes, though neither of them are James."

"What's going on?" asked Max.

"I'll catch you up on all the details later," promised Nighthawk.

"What do I do after ninety minutes?"

"Keep the ship, auction it, whatever you want. They won't be using it."

"Is Sarah all right?"

"I hope so. I just want it quarantined in case they're going to the spaceport while I'm heading to the house—but I don't think they will. It's me they want, not her."

"I can have a shuttle waiting for you," offered Max. "It'll get you to your house a lot quicker than anything else you could use."

"Thanks," said Nighthawk. "I'll take you up on that."

He broke the connection as the ship entered the atmosphere and let the automatic pilot set it down at his reserved landing spot. The shuttle was waiting for him, and he got right into it, fed the coordinates of his house into the navigational computer, and ordered it to take off. It immediately began racing toward his home.

He figured it would take him five minutes to reach his destination. Any ground conveyance would have taken the Mendes brothers close to forty minutes, maybe longer. And they would have had to clear Customs and Immigration, purchase visas, and find a vehicle, so he figured that they would reach the house less than an hour ahead of him.

He brought the shuttle to a halt a little more than half a mile from the house, in a clearing that couldn't be seen from any of the windows. If they had come to kill Sarah she was already dead, and they would pay dearly for it; but if she was still alive, he had the element of surprise on his side. He was pretty sure they didn't know he'd been following them, and he saw no reason to warn them of his presence.

He approached the house, walking among the trees and foliage that went up to the edge of his property. He looked up at the sky: there were still at least five hours of daylight left, possibly six, and he had no intention of waiting until nightfall to enter the house.

He saw their hovercar anchored to the ground in front, so he knew they were still there. As far as he was concerned, that meant they'd die there.

Nighthawk circled the house, trying to spot where they were and whether Sarah was still alive. He muttered a curse; they had commanded the windows to polarize, and no light escaped their opacity.

He paused to consider his next move. He was loath to burst in. Not that he was worried about himself, but until he knew where Sarah was he didn't want any shooting. Still, he couldn't just stand out here and hope they'd try to transport her back to their spaceship while he picked them off from the safety of the trees. For all he knew they were content to wait for him to kill off all their rivals in the District before getting word to him that they'd taken control of his house and his wife.

All right, he thought, *the first thing I need to do it figure out where to enter.* There was no sense trying the windows. He couldn't open them from the outside, and whatever weapon he used to shatter or melt them would alert the Mendes brothers to his presence.

So it's got to be a door. Now, do I want the front, side, or back? He considered the situation. *It doesn't matter unless I know she's not anywhere near the door I come in through. How do I do that?*

He studied the house and the property. There was a small stand of trees about eighty feet from the front door.

Okay, I can set the trees on fire with my burner, which should get them to the front of the house—but with the windows all polarized they'll never know. What can I do to alert them? I can't just melt a window. They'd figure out that I was trying to divert their attention from the other doors.

He analyzed the problem, and finally hit upon a solution. It wasn't one he especially liked, but it was the only one he could come up with on short order.

He turned and walked back into the woods, pulled his screecher, aimed it at the upper branches of a nearby tree, and fired. Three colorful birds immediately fell to the ground, dead. He walked over and picked up the largest of them.

Next, he approached the house, drew his burner, and set fire to the stand of trees out front. Then he pulled a dagger out of his left boot, slit the dead bird's throat, and hurled it against the front window with all his strength, where it hit with a loud *thud!*.

Nighthawk flattened himself against the side of the house and waited. A few seconds later someone on the inside ordered the window to become transparent again. He couldn't see what happened next without being seen himself, but he could picture it in his mind's eye. One of the Mendes brothers would look to see what had happened. He'd notice the blood on the window, walk over, look down, see the dead bird, and assume it had flown into the window and killed itself. It was something that probably happened on every world that had avians—and before he could wonder why a sighted bird would fly headfirst into an opaque window, he'd notice the fire. That would make him curious and a little nervous. After all, suddenly there were two unusual events occurring seconds apart, and the first thing he'd do was have his brother take a look and consult with him. Did it mean Nighthawk was here—and if so, what should they do about it? One would surely go to Sarah and put a gun to her head or a knife to her throat to hold Nighthawk at bay if it was really him and he entered the house.

That meant there'd be only one guarding all three doors, and he'd be concentrating on the front of the house, because that's where the bird and fire were.

Nighthawk walked around to the back door and ordered it to open. It was locked, but he uttered the code that overrode the locking mechanism, and an instant later he was standing in the kitchen, burner in hand. There was a sudden motion off to his right. It was one of the brothers, and Nighthawk turned and fired, scorching the man's hand and melting his weapon.

"Where is she?" he demanded.

The man cursed at him while clutching his blackened hand.

"I'm only going to ask once more," said Nighthawk.

"She's right here," said a voice, and he saw Sarah, a gag over her mouth, being pushed into the room by the other Mendes brother, who held a wicked-looking knife at her throat. "Take his weapons."

The wounded brother approached Nighthawk to remove his weapons. As he reached out, Nighthawk grabbed his wrist, whirled him around, and wrapped an arm around his throat.

"Let him go or I'll kill her!" said the man holding Sarah.

"If I let him go you'll kill us both," said Nighthawk. "You'd never let her live now that she can identify you."

"You don't have a choice, Widowmaker."

"*You* do, though," said Nighthawk, tightening his grip on the wounded brother. "You can die slow or fast—and that's the only choice left to you."

"What the hell are you talking about?" demanded the man with the knife. "I've got your wife!"

"I don't give a damn what you did that made you move to the District, and I don't care that you killed a bank officer in Cataluna," said Nighthawk. "But you've invaded my house and threatened my wife, and you're a pair of walking dead men. I'm going to kill your brother now"—a quick twist, a loud *crack!*, and the man dropped like a stone—"and if that knife so much as breaks her skin, I promise that you'll take a month to die."

Suddenly a look of panic spread across the remaining brother's face. *This isn't the way it was supposed to happen!* it seemed to say.

"We can deal!" he said at last.

"No deals," said Nighthawk. "You threatened my wife."

"You killed my two brothers!" said the man. "Let me walk, and we'll call it even."

"No deals," repeated Nighthawk coldly.

Sarah could feel the hesitancy, the uncertainty in her captor, and she suddenly twisted free and flung herself to the floor. Nighthawk put a laser beam between the man's eyes an instant later.

"Are you all right?" he said, walking over, kneeling down next to her, and gently removing her gag.

She nodded. "What was that all about?"

"I'll tell you all about it later," said Nighthawk, helping her to her feet. "Let's get a drink into you first, or a tranquilizer, or whatever you think you need."

"I don't need anything," said Sarah. "When they didn't kill me immediately, I knew they were just planning on using me as bait. After that I wasn't worried anymore."

"Why the hell not?" asked Nighthawk. "They had all the advantage—numbers, the house, a hostage."

"Yes," she agreed, reaching out and taking hold of his hand. "But I had the Widowmaker."

18.

KINOSHITA TOSSED UNEASILY on his bed, then suddenly sat up. Something was wrong, but it took his sleep-laden senses another moment to figure out what it was. That was when he saw the young man sitting on a chair in the corner of the room.

"How the hell did you get in?" he demanded.

"Hello to you too," said Jeff.

Kinoshita shook his head vigorously. "You cracked the code on the lock."

"It's one of the things I do really well."

"I never heard you enter the room."

"I didn't want to wake you," said Jeff. "But now that you're up, put on your pants and let's get some breakfast." He smiled. "I'll avert my eyes if you're feeling shy."

Kinoshita swung his feet onto the floor, rubbed his eyes, stood up, walked to the wooden chair where he'd tossed his clothes the night before, and began dressing.

"How did you find me?" he asked.

"I didn't know you were hiding," said Jeff. "In fact, I got the distinct impression that you *wanted* to be found."

Kinoshita slid his feet into his shoes. "Okay, let's go," he said, and commanded the door to iris.

Jeff followed him to the airlift, and they descended to the hotel's shopworn lobby. The walls needed a paint job, the metal trim was showing signs of rust, a few of the floor tiles were miscolored and one was cracked.

"You can afford better than this," commented Jeff.

"It's temporary."

"All hotels are temporary—and you can still afford better."

"I'm not trying to draw any extra attention," said Kinoshita. "There are a lot of people on this planet who'd like to see me dead."

"But they're probably all in the District," said Jeff. "As long as you don't go in and they don't come out, you're safe." He looked into the hotel's restaurant, which was about half full. "Is this place any good?"

"There are better."

"Lead the way," said Jeff. "It's my treat."

Kinoshita walked out onto the slidewalk, accompanied by Jeff, and rode it two blocks to a little eatery he'd discovered the day before. When they got there he stepped off and entered the place, nodded to the robot cashier, which gave no indication of recognizing or even seeing him, and walked to a table along the back wall.

"What do you recommend?" asked Jeff.

"The coffee's good. The food's palatable."

Jeff studied the menu, then ordered an omelet made from the imported eggs of a half-avian, half-reptile creature with an unpronounceable name that lived in New Barcelona's arid equatorial desert. Kinoshita settled for some coffee imported from Pollux IV and a plain muffin.

"Very good," said Jeff, taking a tentative sip as their coffee appeared almost instantly. "Nice strong flavor." Then: "Where is he?"

"I beg your pardon?"

"He sent for me. Here I am."

"He's on Goldenhue," said Kinoshita.

"Are you trying to tell me you took Hairless Jack Bellamy and Cleopatra Rome yourself?" said Jeff with a smile. "Because if you are..."

"Of course not," replied Kinoshita. "*He* killed them. You knew that before you came to New Barcelona. In fact, it's *why* you came, isn't it?"

"It was as clear a signal as he could send," agreed Jeff. "He had to know I'd be curious about what another Widowmaker was doing here, especially after he killed two of the people at the top of my list."

"That's what he figured."

"If he wants to talk, why didn't he just send me a subspace message?"

"We didn't know where you were," answered Kinoshita.

"Working," said Jeff noncommittally. "What's he doing on Goldenhue after he went to all the trouble of drawing me to New Barcelona?"

"A couple of men from the District, men with a grudge against him, found out he lived there."

"Sarah," said Jeff.

"That's why he went," said Kinoshita. "He should be back before long."

"I hope so. But he's an old man, and everyone who's not dead is unbeaten in mortal combat."

"He's an old man who killed Bellamy and Cleopatra Rome," replied Kinoshita.

"Okay, he's a formidable old man," said Jeff. "Now, let's get down to business: what does he want with me?"

"He wants to talk to you."

"What about?"

"I'll leave it to him to tell you."

"It's got to be about the clone that calls himself Jason Newman," said Jeff. "I mean, hell, he's had close to two years to talk to me if he wanted to, and he acted like he couldn't care less that I was alive until you told him about Newman." He paused. "That *is* where you went after you took Newman to the hospital, isn't it?"

"Yes," said Kinoshita, as their food was transported to their table.

"How *is* Newman?" asked Jeff, starting in on his omelet.

"He's alive."

"I know he's alive," said Jeff irritably. "If I'd wanted to kill him, I would have. How is he recovering?"

"Slowly," said Kinoshita. "They're cloning a new spleen and liver for him, and he needs a prosthetic arm."

"I'm sorry," replied Jeff sincerely. "But I couldn't take any chances, not with him. It was hard enough to beat him without killing him."

You could have just believed him, thought Kinoshita bitterly— but he elected not to say it. It would be argumentative coming from him, whereas hopefully it would be authoritative coming from Nighthawk.

"When did he leave?" asked Jeff when it became apparent that Kinoshita wasn't going to pursue the subject of his fight with Jason Newman.

"Two days ago."

"Figure at least a day to get to Goldenhue, maybe a day and a half. Give him a couple of hours to take care of business. No way Sarah lets him leave right away. So he's probably still there, or just taking off. That means we've got another day, maybe more, before he gets back to New Barcelona."

"Yes, I suppose so," said Kinoshita. "Why?"

"No sense letting all that time go to waste," replied Jeff. "We might as well make the galaxy a little safer while we're waiting for him to return."

"I don't do your bidding anymore," said Kinoshita.

Jeff stared at him for a long moment, and even though he had an unlined, youthful face, it was a stare that made Kinoshita increasingly uneasy. He'd seen it before, and usually it presaged someone's death. Then, as quickly as it came, it vanished, and Jeff shrugged. "That's up to you," he said. "Are you going to make me tie in to my ship's computer, or are you going to tell me who's worth taking in the District?"

"Jefferson said there were three people who were big enough to attract your attention. He killed two of them. The third is the Wizard."

Jeff nodded thoughtfully. "Yeah, he'd draw anybody's attention. What do you know about him?"

"Just that he's carrying a four-million-credit bounty," answered Kinoshita.

"There's more than that—a lot more."

"Oh? What?"

"That's not a dead-or-alive bounty," said Jeff. "They only pay off if he's dead." He smiled. "Which figures."

"Why do you say that?"

"Because he's the Wizard."

"I don't follow you," said Kinoshita.

"He spent twenty years as a stage magician, using the Wizard as his stage name. From everything I've been able to find out, he was pretty damned good at his job. There's probably not a cell door lock he can't pick, not a force field he can't deactivate, not a pair of tightly bonded manacles he can't slip in half a minute's time."

"Okay, it makes more sense now," said Kinoshita.

"Let me finish my coffee and I'll see if I can come up with a spell or two of my own," said Jeff.

"You're going into the District after him?" said Kinoshita. "Just like that?"

"It's what I do. You know that."

"But you don't even know your way around there," protested Kinoshita.

"I don't know my way around any planet until I land on it," said Jeff.

"A lot of people in the District are looking to kill the Widowmaker."

"I don't doubt it," answered Jeff with no show of concern. "And they all know that he looks pretty much the way I'll look in another forty years or so."

"But—"

"Suppose you stop raising objections that you know I'm going to ignore and tell me what your real problem is."

"I can't do it!" said Kinoshita unhappily.

"What is it you can't do?" asked Jeff.

"I can't let you go into the District alone."

Jeff looked amused. "You're going to stop me?"

"No one can stop you from doing something you want to do," answered Kinoshita. "We both know that."

"Ah," said Jeff. "You're going to tag along and *save* me from the denizens of the District."

"Stop it!" said Kinoshita angrily.

"You're under no obligation to come with me," said Jeff. "We no longer travel together, in case it's escaped your notice."

"I'm coming."

"Suit yourself."

Kinoshita looked his annoyance. "It doesn't suit me at all."

"Then why bother?"

"Because I serve the Widowmaker—and until Jefferson Nighthawk comes back or Jason Newman gets out of the hospital, you're the only Widowmaker I've got."

"Thanks for that ringing endorsement."

"Would you rather I lie to you?"

"Much," said Jeff, getting to his feet and tossing a couple of platinum coins on the table. "Time to go to work."

Kinoshita grabbed his half-eaten muffin and carried it out to the slidewalk. They rode the walk north for half a mile, transferred to a westerly walk for two blocks, and then crossed the street that marked the border of the District.

"I'd always meant to get by here sooner or later," commented Jeff, looking around at his surroundings. "I don't subscribe to law-free zones."

"Somehow I'm not surprised," said Kinoshita.

"Where do they all congregate?" asked Jeff. "I might as well start asking around until someone can tell me where to find the Wizard."

"What makes you think anyone will tell you?"

"They usually do," replied Jeff, and for just a second Kinoshita thought the tone and tenor were those of Nighthawk's voice.

Kinoshita turned to his right. "The heart of the District's about five blocks ahead," he announced.

"The District doesn't have a heart," said Jeff. "Just a groin and a couple of veins covered with puncture marks."

"And a Wizard."

"Temporarily," said Jeff, increasing his pace. "Very temporarily."

19.

THEY WALKED TO the center of the District. Then Jeff entered a nearby drug den. There were two men and a woman there, all semi-catatonic after chewing alphanella seeds, and a Canphorite whose large eyes couldn't focus.

"Can I help you?" asked the proprietor, a burly woman with a deep voice and too much make-up. Her fingers were still recovering from having the prints removed, and her eyes still showed the tiny scars that came with a change of retina patterns.

"Just looking for a friend," said Jeff. "But he doesn't seem to be here."

"Perhaps he comes in from time to time," said the woman. "What's his name?"

"Beats me," said Jeff. "But he calls himself the Wizard."

"I didn't know he *had* any friends."

"Well, actually we're not really friends," amended Jeff. "I just owe him money."

"And you're going out of your way to find him and pay off your debt?" she said dubiously.

"He's the Wizard. Would you want him mad at *you*?"

"You have a point," admitted the woman. "I can't help you, though. He's never come to my place."

"Have you got any idea where I can find him?"

"I know he's somewhere inside the District," she said. "That's enough. Once he knows you're looking for him, *he'll* find *you*."

"Thanks for your time," said Jeff. "Perhaps I'll make use of your services next time I'm on New Barcelona." He turned and walked back out onto the street, where Kinoshita was waiting for him.

"Any luck?" asked Kinoshita.

"It's early yet."

Jeff walked into half a dozen bars and a pair of drug dens with the same question and the same story. No one seemed to know where the Wizard could be found. When he walked out of the last bar, he joined Kinoshita once again.

"Okay," he said. "I've laid the groundwork. Now it's up to him."

"I don't think I follow you."

"About three hundred residents of the District know I'm looking for the Wizard. At least a few of them have to know where to find him—and since he knows I don't owe him any money, he should be curious enough to come looking for me."

"After the way Nighthawk took care of Bellamy and Cleopatra Rome, he'll probably come looking to kill you," suggested Kinoshita.

"I doubt it. Everyone got a good look at me, and the ones who are sober and clearheaded enough to find the Wizard will be able to tell him I'm not the man who's been collecting bounties in the District. I think he'll be curious to find out who I am and what I want."

"So what do we do now?" asked Kinoshita.

"We stay on public display so he knows I'm not laying a trap for him," said Jeff. "If he shows up after the old gentleman gets back, I'll step aside and let him take another bounty. But if the Wizard makes contact before then, he's mine."

"And if he shows up with some friends?"

"Then their life expectancy can be measured in hours," said Jeff with no more passion than if he were discussing the weather. A brief pause. "You know, I've never seen a magician," he continued with youthful enthusiasm.

"There aren't any magicians."

"All right, then—an illusionist. Oh, I've heard about them and seen them in holos. But I've never seen one in person. I think it would have been interesting to see if I could spot how they do their tricks."

"From what I hear, you may get your chance sooner than you think," said Kinoshita.

"I certainly hope so." He paused. "Let's go get a drink."

"I'm not thirsty."

"Neither am I," replied Jeff. "But I'm pretty sure you can't tell me where the Wizard is. Maybe I'll meet someone in the bar who can."

"They won't," said Kinoshita. "After all, he's the Wizard, and no one knows that you've been the Widowmaker for the past couple of years."

"Maybe they'll just tell me about him, then," said Jeff, heading for a tavern he hadn't been to yet. "What his favorite weapon is, whether he travels alone. You wouldn't believe how little information there is on him in the computer—just that he was a performer for about twenty years. Evidently he took the full force of a screecher in a dispute over a woman, and came back a thief and a killer." He paused thoughtfully. "I wonder what Jefferson would be like if someone killed Sarah?"

"That's a morbid thought," said Kinoshita distastefully.

"I love her like a mother," said Jeff. "But when you're the Widowmaker, you know better than to get emotionally involved with anyone. The second your attachment becomes known you've put them as risk." He frowned. "*He* taught me that. What the hell did he come back for after he married her?"

"I'm sure he'll be happy to discuss it with you when he gets back to New Barcelona."

"I got the distinct impression that nothing made him happy except digging in that damned garden and spying on birds," continued Jeff.

"Sarah makes him happy," said Kinoshita. Then: "*You* made him happy."

"Thanks for the compliment—but I just made him happy because it meant he'd have more time to nag his flowers and his birds."

"You don't understand him."

"Of course I do. I *am* him."

To which Kinoshita had no reply.

They entered the spacious tavern. Kinoshita headed for an empty table, then noticed that Jeff had walked up to the bar, so he reversed course and joined the young man.

"I'll have some Corvus crystalblue," said Jeff to the human bartender. "Another for my friend here, and one for yourself."

"Thank you, sir," said the bartender, pouring the blue liquor into a trio of oddly shaped glasses.

Jeff turned to face the twenty humans and dozen aliens who were seated about the room. "I'm buying for the house, if any one of you can take a message to the Wizard."

"What message?" croaked a tripodal Mollutei.

"Just tell him his friend Jeff is here in the District with the money I owe him. I've got to leave for the Roosevelt system in the morning, so I'd like to take care of my debt tonight."

"Where are you staying?"

"I don't know yet," said Jeff. "But if he's half as good as he says he is, he won't have any trouble finding me." He waited for the Mollutei to reply, but it said nothing further. At last he downed his drink, looked directly at the little alien, and said, "Well?"

"Well what?"

"Well, am I buying everyone a drink or not?"

A momentary pause as the Mollutei considered.

"You are."

"You heard him," said Jeff to the bartender, handing him a few bills. "If anything's left over, keep it for yourself."

As the bartender carried the blue liquor from table to table, filling and refilling glasses, Jeff nodded to Kinoshita and slowly walked back out into the street.

"What now?" asked Kinoshita.

"It's boring as hell, but we do the same thing in three or four more bars. No sense making the same offer in the drug dens. Most of them wouldn't remember their names, let alone my message, by the time they walked out the door."

"None of you," noted Kinoshita, "not you, not Jason, not Nighthawk, not even that ill-fated first clone, had any use for drugs or addicts, yet you don't mind alcohol. To me they seem to be one and the same."

"There's a difference in degree," answered Jeff. "The old gentleman taught me how to hold my liquor, and even how to hold a few of the lesser drugs, because he knew that a lot of the information the Widowmaker seeks is to be found in such places. But I don't especially like hard liquor, and I won't use drugs unless I'm traveling incognito and need information in a drug den. Most men are still rational after a few drinks; most drug addicts are totally useless to themselves and anyone else after the first dose. I don't like depending on either, but if I have to count on one or the other for information or anything else, I'll take the drinker every time."

"I know a lot of drug users who would disagree."

"Only when they're cogent enough to form an argument, which means when they're not high on drugs. And people always rationalize their weaknesses. I know a lot of faithless husbands and wives who will swear that monogamy is against Man's nature and that it doesn't really cause their spouses emotional pain. And I've heard more than one swindler say that if God didn't want them fleeced, He wouldn't have made them sheep." Suddenly he smiled. "I'll bet there are even would-be samurai who think they can justify leaving the lord they've sworn to serve."

Kinoshita considered answering him, but kept silent. Anything he said he was sure Nighthawk could say better and with far more authority. "All right," he replied at last, "you've made your point. Let's hit those bars and get this thing rolling."

"Consider it done," said Jeff, and in less than an hour it *was* done.

"What now?" asked Kinoshita.

"Now we wait."

"Where and for how long?"

"Where it's easy to find us, and for however long it takes." He looked around. "It's a little early for dinner, but I want to keep on display as long as I can. He'll have a tougher time checking me out in a hotel room."

"You *want* him to study you?"

"Someone's collecting all the big bounties in the District," replied Jeff. "He's not going to show himself until he knows I'm not setting a trap for him. You've spent a few days here. Which restaurant has the biggest windows?"

"There's an alien restaurant a few blocks from here that Jefferson and I ate in, but…"

"Fine. Lead the way."

Kinoshita took a couple of steps, then stopped. "This is crazy!" he said. "You'll be a sitting duck!"

"That's the point of the exercise," said Jeff. "There are two ways to go about this. I can root about in every cellar and attic and dark corner until I find him, and hope he hasn't rigged the place with a couple of dozen defensive mechanisms—or I can draw him to me. And he won't approach me until he's sure I'm not a threat to him."

"He's never seen you in action."

"An *overt* threat," amended Jeff. "He knows I want to meet him. He knows I don't owe him money. He doesn't know for a fact that I don't want to kill him, so the easiest way to assuage his fears is to make a target of myself."

"You'll never know what hit you," predicted Kinoshita.

"If I'm willing to be a target, he'll have no reason to kill me," said Jeff. "Eventually he'll show himself, or arrange a meeting—and once he does that, he's mine."

"Just like that?"

"It's always just like that."

"You're the boss," said Kinoshita, setting off for the restaurant.

"I always was," said Jeff. "Some of us just forget it from time to time."

They reached the restaurant in a few minutes. Jeff asked for a chair by the window, and Kinoshita nervously seated himself opposite the young man. Humans and aliens walked by in a constant stream. Some looked in, most didn't.

They ordered cold drinks and sandwiches, and while they were waiting for their orders to arrive, Jeff stopped observing the passersby in the street and turned back to Kinoshita.

"Tell me about him," he said.

"As far as I can tell he was happy on Goldenhue," answered Kinoshita. "He had his garden, and…"

"Not the old gentleman," said Jeff. "I know all about him. He trained me. Tell me about the one I shot on Giancola, the one who calls himself Jason Newman."

"He was something to behold," said Kinoshita admiringly. "He had your physical gifts and Jefferson's experience. When he decided that he was going to turn on the man who'd paid to create him and overthrow his government with a handful of men, I thought he didn't have a chance in hell. It was a hundred, maybe a hundred and fifty men and aliens against a standing army of millions and the best-protected structure in the cluster. But he pulled it off. He killed Cassius Hill and got enough money to keep the original Jefferson Nighthawk alive for another three years, which was all the time he needed. By then medical science could finally cure his eplasia."

"If he was that good, how did he lose his hand?"

"He was betrayed."

"By whom?"

"By his memory," said Kinoshita. "Remember, it was Jefferson Nighthawk's memory. And when he brought it to bear against Hill's defenses, it was a century out of date. He did something that would have been perfectly safe at the time Jefferson Nighthawk was frozen, when his memories were set— but it almost cost him his life a century later, and it *did* cost him a hand. It wasn't Newman's fault. Hell, it wasn't anyone's. Without those memories and experiences, he'd have been…"

"Me?" suggested Jeff with a sardonic smile.

"Sometimes physical ability isn't always enough," said Kinoshita. "Sometimes the most important weapon you have is your experience."

"Perhaps," said Jeff. "But right now I've got less than two years' worth of experiences in my entire life, so I hope you won't mind if I depend on my ability."

The sandwiches arrived. Kinoshita wasn't especially hungry, so while Jeff ate, the smaller man looked around the restaurant, observing the meals the various aliens had ordered. One looked like green sludge, another like thousands of tiny purple pellets, and one orange-furred Tormalindi had what looked like a plate of linguini, except that each piece squealed when he stabbed it with his equivalent of a fork and squirmed desperately as he noisily sucked it into his mouth.

There was a time, reflected Kinoshita, when he would have found such a display disgusting. That was before traveling to so many worlds with so many Jefferson Nighthawks. Now it was merely interesting, and he could foresee the day when it would no longer even attract his attention.

"That was good," announced Jeff a moment later, as he finished his sandwich. He looked across the table. "You haven't touched yours."

"I'm just here to keep you company," said Kinoshita. "I'm not really hungry."

"Do you mind, then?"

"Help yourself."

Jeff ate the sandwich, and, not for the first time, Kinoshita marveled at how none of the Widowmakers ever missed a meal or lost a moment's sleep preparing for whatever conflict lay ahead.

Of course, why should you? he thought. *You've never lost.*

Then he remembered that that wasn't exactly right. Jason Newman had lost a hand on Pericles, and damned near lost his life on Giancola II. Nighthawk had lost his health for a century. And the first clone had lost his life before he'd had a chance to begin living it.

No, for all your skills, Widowmakers aren't immune to pain and defeat. I hope Jeff will keep that in mind when he finally faces the Wizard.

But Kinoshita knew he wouldn't.

Jeff looked out the window and frowned. "I wonder how the hell much longer I have to sit here before he gets his fill and decides to meet with me."

"You think he's been observing you?"

"If he's any good he has, and that dead-only bounty implies that he's good."

"Maybe he'll just walk in and see what you're after," said Kinoshita hopefully.

"Not a chance," replied Jeff. "He knows I want to meet him, but he doesn't know *why*, so he's going to be damned sure we meet on his turf, where he's got all the advantages."

"I wonder where that is?"

"We'll find out soon enough," said Jeff. "I just hope he makes contact before the old gentleman gets back from Goldenhue." He took one last look out the window. "I guess we might as well be going."

"Where?"

"A couple of more bars, I suppose," said Jeff without much enthusiasm. "Then, if I still haven't heard from him, we might as well rent a couple of rooms for the night."

Kinoshita took a last sip of his drink, picked up a napkin, and wiped his mouth off.

"Well, I'll be damned!" said Jeff, looking at him and smiling.

"What is it?"

"This guy's as tricky as he's supposed to be."

"I don't know what you're talking about."

"Go to the men's room. You will."

Still puzzled, Kinoshita got up and went to the rest room. The moment he entered it he walked up to the mirror to see what had so amused Jeff. There, on his upper lip and cheek, where he'd applied the napkin, were the words MARIEMONT THEATER, *9:00 TONIGHT.*

Kinoshita washed his face off, dried it, and returned to the table.

"You saw it?" asked Jeff.

"Yes. Are you sure it's from the Wizard?"

"Who do *you* think it's from?"

"I don't know. Maybe it's an ad for a play."

"Look around the restaurant," said Jeff. "Do you see anyone else wearing ads on their faces?"

"No," admitted Kinoshita.

"I'll bet that if you check you'll find that if the Mariemont Theater isn't totally shuttered, it's at least dark tonight." Jeff stood up. "Now we can go."

"What are you going to do until nine o'clock?"

"There's not much to do in a place like this," replied Jeff. "I think maybe I'll rent that room after all. You can wake me at eight thirty."

"Don't you want to make any preparations at all?" asked Kinoshita.

"I'm the Widowmaker. Let *him* make the preparations."

20.

TRUE TO HIS word Jeff fell into an untroubled sleep, and Kinoshita woke him at the time he'd requested. Like all the other Nighthawks, he came to his senses instantly. There was no grogginess, no taking a moment to focus his eyes or remember where he was and what he had to do next. He stood up, walked to a sink, muttered "Cold!," held his hands under the faucet as the cold water flowed out, and splashed some on his face.

"I checked a map while you were asleep," said Kinoshita. "The Mariemont's about three blocks from here."

"Shuttered?"

Kinoshita nodded. "It hasn't been used for the last five years."

"Figures."

"Maybe we should call this off," said Kinoshita. "He's had months, maybe years, to rig the theater to his needs. There could be a death trap every step."

"There could be," said Jeff, showing no concern. "But if he wanted to kill me, he'd have tried when I was sitting next to the window in that restaurant, or when we were standing out in the street. He wants to know why I'm interested in him."

"Why is anyone interested in a man with a four-million-credit price on his head?"

"You know it and I know it—but he could probably give you a hundred reasons why someone he's never met before should want to see him. They'd all be wrong, but if he wasn't an egomaniac he wouldn't be seeing me."

"I tried to gather some data about him from the computer," said Kinoshita, gesturing to the desk computer that the hotel supplied with every room. "I even paid the fee to tie in to the Master Computer on Deluros VIII. All of his crimes have been codified, but there's almost nothing about *him* personally."

"That's probably why he's still free," said Jeff.

"Still, there should be *some*thing about him. All I have are a couple of twenty-year-old holos."

"The ones where he looks like Merlin, with that silly cap and all the zodiac signs on his robe?" said Jeff.

"Yes."

"It just means he's been careful of late," said Jeff. He sat down on the edge of the bed and began pulling on his boots. "What's the time?"

"Eight forty-five. It's about a five-minute walk to the theater."

"Let's go down to what passes for the hotel's restaurant and grab some coffee."

"It's eight forty-five!" repeated Kinoshita urgently.

Jeff smiled. "You prefer tea?"

"You'll be late!"

"I plan to be."

"Why?"

"Because he wants me there at nine. Let's make him sweat for a few minutes."

"Maybe he'll think you're not coming."

"He'll know better," Jeff assured him. "He's got spies all the hell over."

"What makes you think so?" asked Kinoshita.

Jeff smiled again. "How do you think that napkin got to the right person?" he replied. "Someone's been watching us every step of the way." He opened the door and stepped out into the corridor. "Let's give them something to look at."

Kinoshita followed him to the airlift, and a moment later they were sitting in the lobby restaurant. Neither really wanted their coffee, and they nursed it slowly until Kinoshita announced that it was five after nine.

"Okay," said Jeff. "I suppose we might as well get going. You're sure you know where it is?"

"Yes."

"Okay, lead the way."

They walked out into the street, turned right, and right again at the next cross street. They then proceeded for two more blocks, and finally came to a stop in front of a darkened building with a marquee that had once told passersby that this was the famed Mariemont Theater, Home to the Greatest Entertainment on the Planet.

Jeff turned to Kinoshita. "Are you sure you want to come in with me?"

"I serve the—"

"Yeah, I know, I know," interrupted the young man. "Okay, keep behind me, and don't try to be a hero. That's *my* job."

Kinoshita nodded his agreement, and Jeff tested the door to the theater. It was locked. Then he placed a hand against it and pushed—and the door irised around his hand. He stepped slowly toward the door, and passed right through it.

"The man's showing off" was his only comment as Kinoshita followed him into the darkened lobby. Jeff walked to a door leading to one of the aisles and opened it.

The stage was empty, as were the six hundred seats. Jeff walked down the aisle, looking neither right nor left, and came to a stop when he was about fifty feet from the stage.

"Any time," he said in a loud voice.

Suddenly there was a blinding flash of light, a huge puff of smoke, and a clap of thunder in quick succession—and then, standing on the stage facing them, was the Wizard. He was a man of medium height and weight, with a white beard and white shoulder-length hair. He wore a glistening blue robe made of some metallic fiber and covered with the signs of the zodiac. His tall conical hat was made of the same material and bore the same signs. He carried a strange-looking black wand in his right hand.

"No dancing girls?" asked Jeff.

"They're in the second act," said the Wizard with a smile. Suddenly he produced a bouquet of flowers and tossed them to Jeff. "You're late, young man."

"I'm in no hurry," answered Jeff. "I've got my whole life ahead of me."

"A fine answer," said the Wizard. "Now let us consider just how long or short its duration might be. You have told everyone you've met that you owe me money. Before we go any further, I want it."

Jeff reached into a pocket, pulled out a coin, and tossed it to the Wizard.

"Keep the change," he said.

"I shall," said the Wizard. "Now suppose you tell me the real reason you wish to see me, and why you are accompanied by the Widowmaker's lackey."

"I'm nobody's lackey!" snapped Kinoshita.

The Wizard ignored him and continued looking at Jeff. "My question stands. Why are you here?"

"I'm four million credits behind on my rent," said Jeff.

The Wizard laughed. "You should have quit while you still had your one-credit piece, young man. You could have gone home a winner. Now, alas, you will go home a corpse."

"Anything's possible," said Jeff. "But I doubt it."

Suddenly his burner was in his hand, and he fired a lethal blast between the Wizard's eyes.

"Warm," said the Wizard, showing no effect, not even a scorch mark. "Not hot, but definitely warm."

Jeff drew his pistol and fired five quick shots into the Wizard's chest.

"If you've damaged my tattoo, I'm going to be very cross with you," said the Wizard, his voice heavy with mock anger, his eyes filled with amusement.

"It's an illusion!" said Kinoshita. "It's some kind of projection! He's not there at all."

"Very good, little lackey!" said the Wizard. He pointed a finger at Kinoshita. "Now ask yourself if an illusion can do *this!*"

A bolt of force shot out of his finger—not electric, not laser, not nuclear, but sheer, almost solid, almost primal *force*—

and knocked Kinoshita a good twenty feet through the air. He landed heavily on his back. The air gushed out of him, leaving him gasping for breath.

Jeff had pulled his screecher out from the back of his belt, where he kept it hidden, but before he could fire it the Wizard turned to him. "O ye of little faith!" he said. "Abracadabra!"

And suddenly the screecher vanished from Jeff's hand. It didn't melt, it didn't turn to powder, it didn't drop to the floor—it simply vanished. One instant he was holding it and the next it was gone, never to return.

"I wouldn't spend that four million credits just yet if I were you, young man," said the Wizard. "In fact, I'll bet you'd be happy to pay five million to get out of here in one piece, a consummation devoutly to be wished."

Jeff pulled a dagger out of a boot and hurled it all in one fluid motion. As it approached the Wizard it lost all its momentum and seemed to freeze in space, inches from the magician's chest. He reached out, grabbed it by its hilt, and threw it back. Jeff ducked, and it buried itself in the back of a padded seat.

"I'm feeling mighty spry for an illusion," said the Wizard with a chuckle. "Or does your friend think I did *that* with mirrors?"

Jeff didn't waste any words. He aimed his burner at the Wizard and fired again. The Wizard seemed to flinch and turn a shoulder toward him, but once again the weapon had no discernible effect. Jeff followed up with more bullets, firing until his gun was empty.

"All right, you've had your fun," said the Wizard. "Now it's my turn."

He grinned, and suddenly the young clone was frozen into immobility. He couldn't move a finger, couldn't even blink an eye.

The Wizard walked to the edge of the stage and leaned over Jeff. "I like you, young man," he said. "You're absolutely fearless, and you have a fine sense of humor. I'm going to ask you a question. I want you to consider your answer very carefully, because it may be the last thing you ever do. Are you ready?"

Jeff remained totally motionless.

"Well, at least you didn't say you *weren't* ready," continued the Wizard easily. "Here is my question: if I allow you to live, will you swear your fealty to me and promise to do my bidding, even to the point of sacrificing your life to save mine?"

Jeff suddenly found that he could speak, though the rest of his body was still immobilized.

"Well, young man? The galaxy is waiting."

"You go to hell," said Jeff.

"Foolish," said the Wizard, shaking his head sadly. "Not unexpected, but foolish."

"I take it you've made this offer before?"

"Every single time."

"Did anyone ever take you up on it?" asked Jeff.

"Far more than you'd suspect."

"And they're working for you now?"

The Wizard shook his head again. "They're all dead. May they rest in peace."

"You killed them." It was not a question.

"Of course," said the Wizard. "How can I trust a man who will swear fealty to me just to stay alive? Do you appreciate the paradox, young man? The handful of you who really belong in my service, who would add immeasurably to my wealth and reputation, are precisely those who answer as you did, so of course I must kill them. And those who give me the answer they think I want to hear are untrustworthy, so I must kill them as well."

"The end result is that you kill everyone."

"Wouldn't you?" replied the Wizard. "When everyone is either an enemy or a fool, what alternative is there?"

"You could let him live," said a voice at the back of the theater. "It might even start a trend."

The Wizard squinted into the darkness, curious but unperturbed. "Another party heard from," he said. "Would you care to show yourself, sir?"

Jefferson Nighthawk walked up the aisle toward the stage.

"The Widowmaker himself!" said the Wizard. "Do you know this young man that I am about to dispatch?"

"You're not killing anyone," said Nighthawk. "But I may send him to bed without his supper for letting you live this long. I thought I trained him better than that."

"You're being too harsh on the young man, sir," said the Wizard. "He has already tried a variety of weapons. Nothing can kill me."

"One thing can."

"Oh?" said the Wizard sarcastically. "And what is that?"

"Me," said Nighthawk.

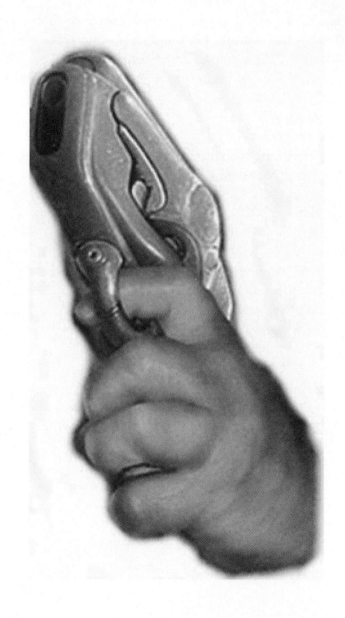

21.

THE WIZARD THREW back his head and laughed.

"Didn't you see what happened to this young man?"

"Of course I saw," said Nighthawk. "I was watching from the back of the theater."

"Let me guess," said the Wizard. "You were hoping he would kill me, and then you would step in and claim the credit and the reward."

"I don't give a damn about either," replied Nighthawk truthfully.

"Then why did you hang back?"

"I was pretty sure he couldn't kill you, but I was willing to give him the chance."

"And you think you can?"

"No," said Nighthawk. "I *know* I can."

"You're an old man, Widowmaker," said the Wizard. "Your reactions are slow, your joints are stiff, your vision is fading, your stamina is gone. Do you really think you can succeed when this young man failed?"

"If I didn't, I wouldn't be facing you."

"*He* faced me," said the Wizard, nodding toward Jeff. "Look at the good it did him."

"He's the most efficient killer on the Inner Frontier," said Nighthawk. "Gun or knife, hands or feet, you couldn't find a better one." He paused and looked at Jeff. "But he doesn't always use his brain."

"One of the symptoms of youth," agreed the Wizard. "But meaningless in this particular case. As I keep explaining to you, I cannot be killed."

"Everyone can be killed," replied Nighthawk calmly. "Even you."

"I don't believe I'm going to bother making you the same offer I made your friend. I already know what your answer will be. Prepare to die, Widowmaker."

"You talk too much," said Nighthawk, drawing his burner and firing it not at the Wizard, but at the thick black wand he held in his left hand.

Suddenly an inhuman squeal of pain rang out through the empty theater.

"*No!*" screamed the Wizard.

Nighthawk walked the rest of the way up the aisle while the Wizard watched him, transfixed. He climbed the stairs onto the stage, took the charred wand away from the magician, and broke it in half. There was one final agonized scream, and then all was silent.

"What the hell did you do?" asked Jeff, suddenly able to move again.

"What you should have done," said Nighthawk. "You fired your burner at him, and it didn't do any good. Then you fired bullets. Then a knife. Were you going to throw one of the seats at him next?"

"But why fire at the weapon, rather than the man who was wielding it?" asked Kinoshita.

"It wasn't a weapon at all," said Nighthawk. "Tell them, Wizard."

The Wizard, who had seemed almost paralyzed with shock, suddenly came to life and hurled himself at Nighthawk with an incoherent guttural growl. The older man sidestepped gracefully and brought his hand down sharply on the back of the magician's neck. There was a cracking sound, and the Wizard fell motionless to the stage.

"It wasn't a wand," continued Nighthawk as if nothing had happened. "It was a symbiote, an alien being that protected him and attacked his enemies in exchange for whatever service the Wizard provided it."

"Are you saying that the damned wand was alive?" demanded Jeff, clambering up onto the stage.

"It could throw a protective shield around the Wizard, and could freeze you where you stood," said Nighthawk. "You should have figured it out yourself."

"How?"

"He gave you the only hint you needed," said Nighthawk. "He never aimed it at you, never treated it like a weapon. No projectiles or rays came out of it. But he never once put it down, and when you fired your weapons at him, he turned a shoulder toward you. It may have looked like he was protecting his face, but you already knew your weapons couldn't hurt him, so it stood to reason that he was protecting something you *could* hurt—and what else was there besides the wand?"

Jeff considered what he'd heard and slowly nodded his head. "Yes, I see it now."

"Now's a little late," said Nighthawk.

"You're the only man in the galaxy who would have figured it out before he could kill you," said Jeff with open admiration.

"There's one other," replied Nighthawk.

"Who is he?" asked Jeff curiously.

"You almost killed him."

"Jason Newman?"

"That's right."

"But I didn't kill him," said Jeff. "I could have, but I didn't."

"That's what we have to talk about," said Nighthawk. "That's why I sent for you."

"If you wanted to talk to me, why didn't you just contact me by subspace radio?"

"Kinoshita didn't know where you were," answered Nighthawk. "No one did. So I decided to draw you to New Barcelona rather than waste my time tracking you all over the Inner Frontier."

"That was a hell of a way to attract my attention," said Jeff.

"Would any other way have worked?"

Jeff considered the question. "No," he admitted. "Probably not." He paused. "By the way, thanks for saving my life."

"You're welcome," said Nighthawk. "But Kinoshita was right. I sent you out too soon."

"I think you're overstating the case," said Jeff defensively. "That's the first time in my life I was ever in any serious danger."

"It only takes once."

"I've taken some of the most dangerous men and aliens on the Inner Frontier," said Jeff. "Terrible men, men who deserved to die a dozen times over. I've never gone after an easy target, not once. I only tackle the ones nobody else is willing to face. I'm doing what you created me to do, what you trained me to do." He made no attempt to hide his emotional distress. "You're the only man I've ever wanted to please. I had hoped you'd be proud of what I've accomplished."

"I *am*," said Nighthawk.

"You sure as hell don't sound it," said Jeff, clearly unconvinced.

"A father can be proud of his child and still know that he needs more training," said Nighthawk. "I'm very proud of you, Jeff. You're everything I was, maybe better—but in the past month you've made three mistakes in a business that doesn't tolerate errors."

"Three?" said Jeff disbelievingly. "What were they?"

"You made one of them tonight. You rushed in before you'd analyzed your enemy and pinpointed his weaknesses— and at this level, the level the Widowmaker operates at, that's usually fatal."

"Okay," acknowledged Jeff. "I admit that was a blunder. What were the other two?"

"You killed a man who was probably innocent."

"I don't know that," said Jeff defensively. "There were warrants all the hell over the galaxy for him, and just one man said he was innocent."

"It was a man that you, of all people, should have trusted," said Nighthawk.

"Aren't you the person who taught me that the Widowmaker doesn't sit in judgment?" said Jeff. "He doesn't pass sentences, he merely executes them."

"Yes."

"There was paper on Jubal Pickett."

Nighthawk sighed. "There's been paper on innocent men before. There will be again."

"Are you trying to tell me that you examined the evidence on every man you ever went after, and if you thought they were innocent you'd give them a pass?" demanded Jeff.

"No, of course I'm not."

"Well, then?"

"I never had an unimpeachable source tell me a man I was about to kill was innocent."

"I'll grant you the first mistake, the one I made here tonight," said Jeff. "But I don't agree that killing Jubal Pickett was one. To this day I don't know for a fact that he was innocent, and neither do you."

"They were both mistakes, and they were both as much my fault as yours," said Nighthawk. "I didn't prepare you properly for these situations. I should have spent more time with you before I sent you out." He paused. "But you made a third mistake of far greater magnitude, one that made it imperative that we meet."

"And what was that?"

"You shot a Jefferson Nighthawk—a man who was closer to you than a father or a brother."

"*You're* closer to me," said Jeff. "I don't even know Jason Newman."

"I told you who he was," said Kinoshita, who had been listening silently to that point.

"All right, you told me who he was," said Jeff. "I never laid eyes on him before, and he got between me and my prey. He drew on me!"

"He got between you and your prey because he thought I'd trained you better than I did," said Nighthawk. "He knew you'd never fire on a Jefferson Nighthawk."

"He went for his weapon!" protested Jeff.

"You went for yours."

"Damn it!" said Jeff. "What was I supposed to do? You're the one who trained me. You taught me everything I know, and then you turned me loose, pointed me at the Inner Frontier, and said 'Kill the bad guys.' That's what I was *doing*—and he tried to stop me!"

"Calm down, Jeff," said Nighthawk. "I'm here to fix a problem, not exacerbate it."

"I am calm!"

"Then stop shouting."

"I'm sorry," said Jeff, lowering his voice. "But I'm the Widowmaker, and you're making me feel like a petulant schoolboy."

"I don't mean to," said Nighthawk. "Look at me. Have I ever lied to you?"

"No, of course not."

"Do you trust me?"

"You're even closer to me than a father," replied Jeff. "Of course I trust you."

"Then believe me when I tell you that I'm not angry at you," said Nighthawk. "I wanted to live out my remaining years in peace, and I was so anxious to start that I sent you out sooner than I should have."

"I was ready!" said Jeff. "Look at what I've accomplished!"

"As you said, I taught you everything you know—but if you feel you were right to kill Jubal Pickett and fire on Jason Newman, then I haven't taught you everything you *need* to know. It's not your fault. It's probably not even mine. I'm new to the parenting business. I never had a son or a daughter. I've never been close to anything or anyone—at least until I met Sarah."

"I thought *we* were close," said Jeff, unable to keep the pain from his voice.

"I'm working at it," said Nighthawk. "Everyone has faults. That's one of mine. Until I came down with that damned disease, all I knew was killing—and then all I knew was suffering. I've been alone most of my life, so forming emotional bonds is as new to me as the Widowmaker business was to you."

He paused uncomfortably, then continued. "I risk my life every time I go up against an enemy. It's second nature to me; I don't even think about it—and I never face an opponent expecting to die. Dying is not in the Widowmaker's lexicon— yet the first clone died for me, and Jason Newman was willing to die so that I could live. That's a very uncomfortable concept for me, because it implies that there are people I should be willing to die for."

"What about Sarah?"

"I don't know," said Nighthawk. "I know I'd *risk* my life for her. I'd risk it for you, or for Kinoshita. But I don't know if I'd sacrifice it for anyone. I fought too damned hard to keep it when the disease hit." He took a deep breath and let it out slowly. "I'm still working it out. One of the good things about living as long as I have is that you find you can still learn." A tight, pained smile. "And one of the bad things is that you find you still have a lot *to* learn."

"Why are you telling me this?" asked Jeff.

"Because if I can't love you like a son yet, I can at least be honest with you, and let you know that you're not the only Widowmaker who still has things to learn and faults to overcome," said Nighthawk.

"This is a side of you I've never seen before," said Jeff. "I don't know what to say."

"You don't have to say anything," replied Nighthawk. "Just listen. Kinoshita and I were so busy teaching you how to kill and to protect yourself that I didn't spend enough time teaching you how to use your judgment, and in truth you probably never needed it until you touched down on Giancola II. I happen to be in a position to know that you've got a pretty practical mind."

"I've always thought so," replied Jeff with feigned lightness.

Nighthawk stared at him for a long moment. "Whatever it takes, we'll get things straightened out."

"I'm willing to try," said Jeff. "I want you to be proud of me."

"I always was," said Nighthawk. "Though as long as *you* know how good you are at your work, I don't know why you care what anyone else thinks."

"Because I'm me and not you," answered Jeff. "You chose not to have any emotional commitments. I never chose not to have a father."

"I didn't choose to be like this," said Nighthawk. "It's just the way I'm made. And our father died a hundred and sixty-three years ago."

"*Your* father did."

"All right," conceded Nighthawk. "Mine did." Suddenly an ironic smile crossed his face. "I guess we're going to train each other."

"I guess."

Nighthawk looked down at the bodies of the Wizard and the wand-shaped alien. "I suppose we might as well hunt up an airsled and turn the body over to the police. And on the way out, we'll toss what's left of the symbiote into the trash atomizer I saw in the lobby."

"Why?"

"I think we'll start your higher education right here and now," said Nighthawk. "*You* tell *me* why."

Jeff stared at the small, cylindrical alien for a moment, frowning. Then he looked up. "Of course."

"Well?"

"If we deliver the alien's body, sooner or later someone's going to figure out that it was the key to the Wizard's power, and they're going to search the galaxy looking for more of them. Better to let everyone think the Wizard was a mutant or a true magician."

Nighthawk nodded his approval. "Okay, you passed the first test."

"How many more are there?"

"As many as it takes."

"Well, let's go find an airsled," said Jeff, walking over, picking up the symbiote's body. "Where do we go after we leave the body with the police?"

"Right back here," said Nighthawk.

"You mean the District?" asked Jeff, surprised.

"Can you think of a better classroom?"

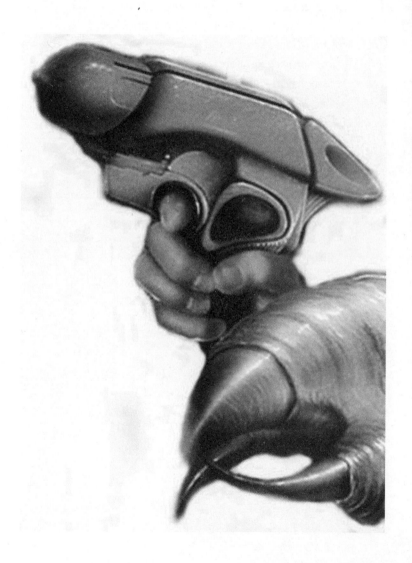

22.

THE TWO MEN, who looked like father and son but were actually even more closely related, walked slowly down the street. It was midmorning, and Nighthawk had left Kinoshita at the police station with orders to stay there until the bounty money had been approved.

Nighthawk pointed out various individuals of different alien races, questioning Jeff about them: where would they hide their weapons, what were their vital spots, what method of attack were they likely to choose, what tiny signs would indicate that an attack was imminent?

Finally, after almost two hours had passed, he stopped in front of a tavern.

"It's a warm day," he said. "I'll buy you a beer."

"Thanks," replied Jeff. "Deciding how to kill every alien I see is thirsty work. I could do with a break—*and* a beer."

"It's more than a break," said Nighthawk. "We're finished."

"I don't understand."

"I just realized that I've been going about this the wrong way," explained Nighthawk. "In the two years you've been around, the Wizard was the first man who gave you any trouble at all. The only reason I could beat him when you couldn't is that I've got decades of experience to draw upon. I can't give you that experience; you're going to have to acquire it a piece at a time and figure out how best to use it."

"I have a question," said Jeff. "When you were my age, could you have taken him?"

Nighthawk signaled the robot bartender to bring two beers.

"Probably," he said.

"Why? You'd have had no more reason to believe he was in a symbiosis with an alien than I did. You were at the peak of your physical powers, you knew no one could beat you—so what was the difference?"

"The difference is that the instant you were born you were the Widowmaker, with unequaled skills and a reputation that's been building for a century and a half—and never underestimate the effect that reputation has on someone who finds himself forced to face you." Nighthawk paused long enough to take a swallow of the beer the robot just delivered. "But there wasn't any Widowmaker when I was a kid. The people I saw, the deaths I witnessed, the corruption I encountered, all of that led me to my calling. If I'm a little more cautious than you, it's because I've seen too damned many people die, so I know it can happen."

"I know I can be killed," said Jeff defensively.

Nighthawk shook his head. "You know it academically, but have you felt the need to go one step out of your way to protect yourself, to push the odds in your favor?"

"No," admitted Jeff. "No, I haven't."

"It's nothing to feel guilty about," said Nighthawk. "You're the best. I saw to that. And until last night, you never needed an advantage. For all I know, you never will again."

"Then that's it?" asked Jeff. "You've got nothing more to teach me, and we go our separate ways?"

"I've got things to teach you, and you have things to learn," replied Nighthawk. "They just don't have much to do with the art of killing. How you apply them to the Widowmaker business is up to you."

"May I ask you a question?"

"Go ahead. I have no secrets from you."

"I'd like to know how and why you became the Widowmaker," said Jeff. "Kinoshita's been curious about it since the day he started teaming up with Widowmakers. The one who died didn't know, and of course I don't either. And he tells me that you and Jason Newman never talked about it."

"It's none of his business," said Nighthawk. "It's no one's business except ours—Jason's, mine, and now yours." He was silent for a moment, ordering his thoughts. "I never planned to be a bounty hunter. I grew up on a farm on Phalaris II. I was twelve years old when a gang of thirty men and aliens robbed the bank and the businesses there. My father was in town on business; he was an innocent bystander. He'd never even owned a weapon in his life. They killed him anyway. And they paid off the planetary police, so no one arrested them or followed up on any leads. They didn't even question the survivors. When I saw that, I stole a couple of burners and went after them on my own. One by one I picked them off—but by the time I'd killed the thirteenth, I was spotted and identified. They came out to our house to kill me. I wasn't there, but they killed my mother and my sister."

The muscles in Nighthawk's jaw twitched, and he continued. "That was a little more killing than the police had bargained for—or at least more than they'd been paid to ignore—and the remaining gang members fled to the Preteep system. I followed them there and killed all but three of them. They grabbed some hostages and escaped. Later they killed the hostages—a woman and her two daughters. I tracked them down and killed them, face-to-face."

"At twelve years of age?" said Jeff, clearly impressed.

"Thirteen," answered Nighthawk. "It took some time to hunt them all down." He paused. "My parents and sister were buried on our farm, but of course no one had kept up the payments, and I heard that it was going up for auction. I wanted to buy it back, if only to plant proper headstones on their graves. I knew there was paper on most of the gang members, so I took the last three to the bounty station on Daedalus IV and asked how to claim the reward, which would have come to four hundred thousand credits, more than enough to buy the farm. A kindly white-haired old gentleman helped me fill out the forms, and even bought me a couple of meals. I stopped by every day to see if the money had arrived—and on the fifth day the old man was gone, and so was my money."

"Is *that* when you became the Widowmaker?" asked Jeff.

"It was years before they began calling me that," said Nighthawk. "Anyway, I became a bounty hunter after I tracked the old man down and took back my money."

"*After?*" repeated Jeff. "You didn't kill him?"

Nighthawk shook his head. "I knew even then that if I killed every lawbreaker on the Inner Frontier, there weren't going to be too many people left alive. People come out here to get *away* from the Oligarchy and its laws. So I created a code I've tried to live by: I will kill only those who themselves have killed—or, if the occasion demands, I'll kill in self-defense. As I got more skilled, I limited myself to the men and aliens that normal lawmen and bounty hunters couldn't take. It's the same code I taught you when I was training you."

"I know," said Jeff. "And I've lived by it. I fired on Jason Newman in self-defense."

"Did you?"

"You sound like you don't think so," said Jeff.

"Let me suggest that he stood between you and Pickett precisely because he knew you *wouldn't* shoot him, that you lived by the same code he and I do, that if he didn't pull a weapon on you you wouldn't draw first. Think hard, Jeff—did he go for his weapon before you did?"

Jeff closed his eyes, trying to relive the scene. Finally he opened them. "I don't know."

"Well, it's an honest answer."

"We're both so fast."

"I know," said Nighthawk. "Now let me ask you a question, just one, and then the subject is closed. With everything I've told you, with everything you know, do you think Jason would have fired at you if you hadn't gone for your weapon?"

"No," said Jeff slowly. "No, he wouldn't have."

"Good," said Nighthawk, placing a hand on Jeff's shoulder and squeezing it gently. "You're learning."

"Learning what?" asked Jeff bitterly. "Not to shoot Nighthawks?"

"No, you're learning to believe me when I tell you something you'd rather not hear."

Jeff looked at him, surprised. "I guess I am," he said.

"And I'm learning to confront things I'd rather not think about," continued Nighthawk.

"Such as?"

"You didn't ask to be born. The fact that I feel an obligation to you, that I trained you and will keep working with you, doesn't absolve me from other things I owe you. As you pointed out, you don't have a father. It's not enough to tell you that genetically you and I share the same one; he's been dead for a century and a half. You don't have a mother. You never had a childhood. By the time you were a week old Kinoshita and I were teaching you how to handle weapons. You're actually better-adjusted than you have any right to be—but as I said, that doesn't absolve me. I wanted to retire, to live out my life with Sarah, to never hold a weapon in my hand again."

"There's nothing wrong with that," said Jeff. "You were the Widowmaker for a long time."

"There's nothing wrong with *wanting* that. What was wrong was the way I went about it." He looked at the young man. "I created you to be a lightning rod. I wanted them to stop shooting at me and start shooting at someone else—at you. You never had a choice. It was a shitty thing to do, and I'm sorry."

"I'm not," said Jeff firmly. "I enjoy being the Widowmaker. I'm proud of what I've accomplished. I like the fact that kids look at me with awe when I walk down the street, and that killers fear my name." He paused. "I just wish I knew that there was one person in the whole damned galaxy who cared about me—not about the Widowmaker and what he can do for them, but about Jeff Nighthawk."

"I'm working on it," said Nighthawk.

"Did you ever feel this way?" asked Jeff.

"No. Every person who ever cared about me wound up dead. That was last thing I wanted. The closer people got to me, the sooner they died. Do you know why I wasn't on New Barcelona when you arrived here?"

"Kinoshita told me a couple of men found out that you lived on Goldenhue, and you had to go back there to make sure Sarah was all right."

"She wasn't all right. They were using her as bait for me, but they never planned to let her live whether I showed up or not. And the reason they were there was because they didn't have the guts to face me, so they went after someone I cared for. It wasn't the first time."

"They've gone after Sarah before?"

"I've been the Widowmaker for a long time," said Nighthawk wearily. "They've gone after *everyone* I ever cared for."

"That explains a lot."

"You can take care of yourself better than any man alive, maybe better than any man who's ever lived," said Nighthawk. "Intellectually I know that. But I've got a gut feeling that says if I get too close to you you're a dead man."

"I suppose telling you that you're wrong wouldn't matter," said Jeff.

"How do you argue with an instinct?"

"I don't know."

"Neither do I," said Nighthawk. "But I'm trying."

"You know, I came here with a lot of built-up resentment," said Jeff. "It's all gone now. I don't envy you."

"It could be worse."

"You meant you could be me?" suggested Jeff with a smile.

"I could be Jason Newman."

"Why do you say that?" asked Jeff curiously.

"He'll never be the original Widowmaker or Jefferson Nighthawk; that's reserved for me. And he'll never be the best; that's reserved for you. He tried so hard not to be a shadow of the Widowmaker that he changed his name and even his face. And where is he now? Tied in to a bunch of machines in a hospital tens of thousands of light-years from his home world, put there by a Widowmaker."

"When he's better, I plan to go out to Giancola," said Jeff.

"And do what?"

"Apologize," said Jeff. "And ask him to forgive me."

Nighthawk stared at him silently for a moment. "Have another beer," he said at last. "My treat."

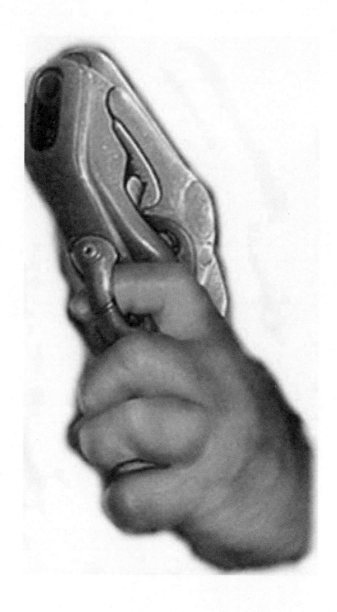

23.

NIGHTHAWK AND JEFF wandered over to Horatio's in midafternoon.

"Welcome back," said Minx to Nighthawk as they entered. "I hear you've been a busy Widowmaker."

"We're going to grab a table in the back," said Nighthawk. "When my friend arrives, send him over."

He and Jeff had been seated about ten minutes when Kinoshita stepped out of the airlift and looked around. Minx pointed to Nighthawk's table, and the little man walked across the room to join them.

"The money arrived," he reported, pulling up a chair.

"Good," said Nighthawk. "Did you arrange for the new routing?"

"Transfered it to the Cataluna branch of the Bank of Spica II, from there to the Andrican Savings and Loan, then the First Planetary Bank of Far London, then route it through Binder X and Roosevelt III to Goldenhue, where it's waiting in the numbered account you had me set up this morning."

"That money's doing a lot of traveling," commented Nighthawk. "You know, back when I was a young man, I heard of more than one speculator getting rich by moving his money every eight or ten hours and drawing interest three times a day. With a million worlds in the Oligarchy, they could always find some with twenty-five-percent inflation, and that meant that, compounded daily, they doubled their money every year without ever doing anything but depositing it in banks—until the economies crashed, anyway. The Oligarchy finally outlawed it; it was taking too much money away from the fundamentally sound banks."

"I thought you were sending all the bounties you earned in the District to the hospital at Giancola to pay for Jason Newman's medical bills," said Jeff.

"I've already sent them more than ten million credits," replied Nighthawk. "They could clone a dozen spleens and livers and buy him two dozen new arms with that, and still have plenty left over."

"Now that it's en route to Goldenhue, what do you plan to do with the bounty on the Wizard?" asked Jeff.

Nighthawk shrugged. "I haven't given it much thought." Suddenly he smiled. "Maybe I'll spend it all trying to create a rose that grows in that damned soil." He turned to Kinoshita. "Did you reserve the rooms?"

"Yes."

"What rooms?" asked Jeff.

"We're targets wherever we go," said Nighthawk. "But we're bigger targets in the District than in the rest of the city. I had Kinoshita get us some rooms at..." His voice trailed off. "Where the hell *did* you get them?"

"The Golden Palace," said Kinoshita. "Three suites, including the Presidential. I figured the man who's keeping the Wizard's bounty can afford it."

"Cancel two of them and keep the Presidential," said Nighthawk. "It's got to have four or five bedrooms, and we'll take turns standing guard."

"You expect someone to come after us?" asked Kinoshita.

"We broke tradition and started collecting bounties in the District," answered Nighthawk. "The residents can't be too thrilled with us right about now. Once we're ensconced in the suite, we'll decide what to do next."

"I thought we were staying here," said Jeff.

"I thought so too, and maybe we will," said Nighthawk. "But I've been out of touch with the rest of the galaxy for a few days. Let's see what's going on. There may be more interesting situations elsewhere."

"Why bother?" asked Kinoshita. "Half the Men and aliens walking around the District have some kind of paper on them."

"He already knows how to kill people," said Nighthawk. "We took the three who needed taking, the only three who could provide the Widowmaker with a real challenge."

"Correction," said Jeff. "*You* took them."

"The Widowmaker took them," said Nighthawk. "Eventually that will accrue to your benefit." He stood up. "Ready to leave?" His two companions stood up. "I can't say I'm going to miss this joint."

"I can't say I blame you," remarked Jeff.

"Just a minute." Nighthawk walked over to Minx, leaned over and said something to her in low tones, then shoved a bill into her hand.

"What was that about?" asked Kinoshita as they took the airlift to the main floor and stepped out of it.

"Tell him, Jeff."

Jeff looked blank for a moment, then suddenly smiled. "Of course! You told her we were staying at some place in the District, and tipped her to keep her mouth shut."

"Then what was the point?" asked Kinoshita.

"Go ahead," Nighthawk said to Jeff.

"He only gave her one bill, probably a small one," replied Jeff. "She knows what kind of bounties he's earned since he got here, and now she knows that ten or twenty credits is the most she's going to get for keeping his whereabouts a secret. So she's got information to sell, and she'll probably be selling it in the next ten or fifteen minutes."

"And that means no one will come looking for us in the Golden Palace," added Nighthawk. "Or less people, anyway."

They walked out into the street.

"Ugly place," remarked Nighthawk. "I won't be sorry to see the last of it."

"What's Goldenhue like?" asked Jeff.

"A little agricultural world, nothing special," said Nighthawk. "We were thinking of moving to the Spiral Arm, but Sarah's got family on the Inner Frontier, and her son works on Roosevelt III, so…"

"I didn't know she had a son," said Jeff.

"I've never met him," said Nighthawk. "He was at college when I teamed up with Sarah, and as long as we send him money from time to time, he's content to keep his distance." He smiled. "I don't talk about him much with Sarah. My best guess is that he's got some kind of business scam going, and he's scared to death I'll find out and turn him in for the reward."

"Would that be before or after Sarah staves your head in for even thinking about it?" asked Kinoshita.

Nighthawk chuckled. "She's a tough lady. I suppose that's why we get along. Sooner or later, when the chips are down, every other woman I've known, and almost every man, is afraid of me. Not that I'll do them any harm, but rather that I have the ability to do it and if I choose to exercise that ability there is nothing anyone could do to prevent it."

"I know," said Jeff. "Even the ones I risk my life for breathe a little easier when I leave."

"Doesn't that bother you?" said Kinoshita.

Nighthawk shrugged. "You get used to it."

"That's comforting," said Jeff. "I was starting to wonder if it would ever stop bothering me."

"It will," replied Nighthawk. "But there are disadvantages. No one expects you to care about the people who want to kill you. Eventually you'll discover that it's just as hard to care about the people who view you with fear or barely disguised repugnance, who definitely want you out there on the front lines defending them but don't want you getting close. In the long run it probably makes you a better killer, but when you stop caring it makes you a poorer human being."

"That's some admission," said Kinoshita.

"It's no surprise to you," said Nighthawk. "You complained about my cold-bloodedness the whole time we traveled together."

"The surprise is not that it's true," said Kinoshita, "but that you admitted it."

They were now half a block from the street that marked the dividing line between the District and the rest of Cataluna, and suddenly two small boys burst out of an alley, aiming toy guns at them.

"*Down!*" yelled Jeff. Nighthawk threw himself to the ground instantly. Kinoshita was a second slower, and received a laser burn on his arm.

Jeff fired a bullet in the air. The explosion startled the two boys.

"Freeze!" he snapped, pointing the gun at them.

The boys stood stock-still, terrified, and Jeff approached them cautiously. He looked briefly at the first boy's toy weapon, then took the other boy's from him.

Nighthawk made sure that Kinoshita's wound was superficial, then joined Jeff. "Who gave you this?" he asked the boy with the burner.

The boy was so frightened he couldn't answer. Jeff knelt down next to him so that he would appear less imposing.

"You didn't know the burner was real," he said. "It wasn't your fault. Nobody's mad at you." He waited until the boy calmed down a bit. "You know this man is the Widowmaker, don't you?" The boy nodded his head. "He's the one the man who gave you the pistol told you to aim at, right?"

"It was a woman," said the boy.

"I'll tell you what," said Jeff. "The Widowmaker will give you one of his very own bullets to keep if you'll tell us who the woman is."

"We never saw her before," said the other boy. "She gave us each a gun and told us to pretend to shoot the Widowmaker —that he'd think it was funny."

"What did she look like?"

The boy shrugged. "Kind of average."

"Height? Weight? Hair color?"

"Medium," said the other boy.

Nighthawk smiled grimly. "So she was average, except for the parts that were medium."

"That's right," said one of the boys earnestly.

"Do you know where she is now?" asked Jeff.

The boys both shook their heads.

"All right," said Jeff, standing up as Nighthawk handed a bullet to the boy with the burner.

"Can I have one too?" said the other boy.

Nighthawk tossed a bullet to the boy. "If you see that woman again…" he began.

"Yes?" said the boy.

"Tell her I've got a bullet for her too."

"You could give it to me, and I'll give it to her if I see her," suggested the boy.

"No, I don't think so," said Nighthawk. "Tell her I'll deliver it myself."

The two boys thanked him for the bullets and ran back into the alley from which they'd emerged.

"How are you holding up?" asked Jeff as he and Nighthawk returned to Kinoshita, who was on one knee, grasping his upper arm.

"I'll be okay," he said. "It hurts like hell, though."

"I seem to remember that there's a medical clinic a block or two from the Golden Palace," said Nighthawk. "We'll stop there and get you attended to."

"I can go myself."

"Did you plan to pay for it yourself?" asked Nighthawk.

"If I have to."

"Well, then, isn't it fortunate that you don't have to?" said Nighthawk. "Can you walk or do you want an aircar?"

"Of course I can walk," said Kinoshita irritably. "I think of Jason Newman on Giancola and everything he's gone through there and on Pericles, and I'd feel guilty as hell riding to the clinic in an aircar for a little flesh wound."

"Are you really coming back to find the woman who gave the burner to those kids?" asked Jeff as they crossed out of the District and into Cataluna proper.

"No," said Nighthawk. "But there's no reason not to make her look into every shadow she passes for the next couple of weeks."

"The only way she'll get your message is if one of the boys sees her again," said Jeff. "What if she holds it against them for telling you about her?"

Nighthawk's face tensed. "I never thought of that." He stopped walking. "Take Kinoshita to the clinic, and check into the Golden Palace when they're done with him."

"You're going back after her?"

"I'm going back after the boys. They're the only ones who know what she looks like."

"They could be anywhere," said Kinoshita.

"I'll find them," said Nighthawk with absolute certainty. He turned and headed back into the District.

An hour passed. Kinoshita had the burn treated and painted with a pain deadener. Next they went to the Golden Palace and claimed their suite. Two more hours passed, and Jeff checked on the resting Kinoshita, then suggested that they go up to the elegant rooftop restaurant for dinner. Neither of them mentioned Nighthawk in the course of their dinner; both thought of very little else.

After they'd finished eating, Kinoshita announced that he was thirsty. The roof had a well-stocked bar and wine cellar, but Kinoshita decided that he felt more comfortable in the lobby bar. He never mentioned that it afforded an unobstructed view of the hotel's entrance, but he never had to. Jeff joined him, and they passed the time, each nursing a single drink, until the bar closed.

They moved to the lobby. Finally Kinoshita's various medications for his wound and his pain made him too drowsy to remain, and he reluctantly went up to the suite. Jeff remained where he was, seated in a chair covered with the blue-and-gold spotted pelt of some alien animal, his gaze glued on the front door.

Then, just as the sun was rising, Nighthawk entered the Golden Palace. Jeff stood up and approached him.

"You found her?"

"I found her."

Jeff didn't bother to ask if the woman was dead. The answer was obvious.

"If you're getting hungry, they opened for breakfast about twenty minutes ago."

"I don't want anything to eat," said Nighthawk. "I could do with some coffee, though."

They entered the informal lobby restaurant and sat down at a table, the only two customers in the establishment.

"You were right, Jeff," said Nighthawk after they'd punched in their orders.

"About what?"

"She'd have killed them. I should have thought of that before I told them what to say." He grimaced. "Like I said, you're not the only one who makes mistakes and has a lot to learn."

"We'll learn it," said Jeff. "We're two sides of the same coin. I'll learn from you, you'll learn from me."

"I wonder if Jason Newman isn't the best off of the three of us," said Nighthawk with a wry smile. "Most of my experience, most of your physical skills."

"Or you could say that he's the worst off, because he's got less experience than you and less skills than me," replied Jeff.

"Well, whichever way you look at it, you're here and I'm here and that poor son of a bitch is in a hospital bed, tied in to a dozen machines."

But he wasn't.

24.

THEY HAD JUST finished their breakfast and were about to go up to the Presidential suite and finally get some sleep when Kinoshita rushed into the restaurant in an agitated state.

"What's the problem?" asked Nighthawk.

"I've got to leave New Barcelona," said Kinoshita.

"When?"

"This morning. Now."

"You want to calm down and tell us what this is about?"

Kinoshita sat down, and Nighthawk shoved his untouched coffee in front of the smaller man. Kinoshita picked up the cup, took a sip, then put it back down.

"I just got a subspace message on my private channel," said Kinoshita. "Only four people in the galaxy know my code. You're two of them."

"I assume Jason Newman is the third?" said Jeff.

Kinoshita nodded. "And Cassandra Hill is the fourth."

"Cassandra Hill," repeated Jeff. "Isn't that the woman he's living with—the one he rescued from her father?"

"He didn't rescue her," Kinoshita corrected him. "She was actually leading a revolution. Jason was hired to kill her, and when he took a look at both sides, he chose to go to war against his employer—her father—instead."

"Okay, so she contacted you," said Nighthawk. Kinoshita looked questioningly at him. "It couldn't have been Jason. He's still tied in to all those machines. And it sure as hell wasn't Jeff or me."

"It was Cassandra," confirmed Kinoshita. "She said I was the only person she could turn to, the only person Jason ever worked with and trusted." He nervously lit a smokeless ciga-rette. "I can't tell you how many times he saved my life. I've got to go; I don't have any choice."

"What is it?" asked Nighthawk. "Has she got wind of some threat against him at the hospital?"

"He's not *in* the hospital," said Kinoshita. "They gave him his new organs two days ago. He checked himself out this morning."

"Remarkable man," said Nighthawk. "I'd have bet he couldn't stand up without help for another ten days." He paused. "So he checked himself out. What's the problem? Does she need help getting him home?"

An ironic smile crossed Kinoshita's face. "He's a Widowmaker. What do *you* think?"

Nighthawk considered the question for a moment. "Oh, shit!" he said at last.

"He's gone out after someone," said Jeff. "But why? Why not just ask us?"

"Would you ask for help?" replied Kinoshita.

"No," admitted Jeff. "No, I wouldn't."

"You want to give us the whole story?" said Nighthawk.

"He got a message—a plea for help—from Pallas Athene," said Kinoshita.

"Who the hell is Pallas Athene?"

"Jason took a little more than one hundred men, women, and aliens to Pericles V. We won, which is to say we overthrew Cassius Hill and his government—but we had only five survi-vors: Jason, Cassandra Hill, me, an alien called Friday, and Pallas Athene."

"Was she human?" asked Jeff.

Kinoshita nodded. "As brave and skilled as any Man or alien I've ever encountered. Well," he amended, "anyone who isn't named Nighthawk. Somehow you knew that what-ever happened in that charnel house, Jason and Athene would survive it."

"She sounds formidable," commented Nighthawk.

"And then some," said Kinoshita.

"And she called for help?" continued Nighthawk. "From what you say, she must be in one hell of a jam."

"She must be," agreed Kinoshita. "Anyway, he got her message and announced that he was leaving the hospital. The details are a little hazy—Cassandra was very upset—but I gather the doctors told him he couldn't leave, so he ripped every tube and monitoring device out of his body, got dressed, and started walking out. When an orderly—a six-hundred-pound Torqual—tried to stop him, Jason cut him up pretty badly with a scalpel he'd managed to get hold of. Then he put tourniquets on the wound, stopped at the front desk long enough to tell them where the Torqual was and to send an emergency medical team up to him, and left."

"One day after major surgery?" said Jeff.

"Yes."

"Does Cassandra have any idea where Jason's gone?"

Kinoshita shook his head. "They met Pallas Athene on Sylene IV, but she hasn't lived there for three years."

"It shouldn't be that hard to find her," said Nighthawk. "The message had to come to him at the hospital. They'll keep it on file, and we can run a trace on it."

"We?" repeated Kinoshita.

"He's a Jefferson Nighthawk," said Nighthawk.

"And he wouldn't have been in the hospital in the first place if it hadn't been for me," said Jeff. "I'm coming too."

"I appreciate the help…" began Kinoshita.

"With no insult intended" said Nighthawk, "we're not helping *you*. We're helping *him*."

"And he's going to need it," added Jeff. "If Pallas Athene is everything you say she is, and she can't handle the problem herself…"

"You'd be surprised what Jason can do under duress," said Kinoshita.

"Two days ago they cut him open and performed a pair of major organ transplants," said Nighthawk, "and today he's flying off to face somebody that Pallas Athene can't handle alone. I'd say that in this case *duress* is an understatement." He got to his feet. "We're wasting time here. Let's get to the ship."

The other two men followed him out the door. They summoned an aircar, and half an hour later Jeff's ship, which was larger than Nighthawk's, was reaching light speed and heading for Giancola II. Jeff and Kinoshita elected to enter Deepsleep pods for the journey, but Nighthawk remained awake, speaking to the computer, learning what he could about the death of Cassius Hill, studying the fall of Hill's government. Jason had hidden his tracks well; there was no mention of Jefferson Nighthawk or the Widowmaker, no mention of Kinoshita or of anyone named Friday or Pallas Athene, only a passing mention of Cassandra Hill.

He was still seeking details when the ship began approaching the Giancola system and Jeff and Kinoshita awakened. Both were hungry—the Deepsleep pods slowed the metabolism but didn't stop it, and one usually awoke with an empty stomach and a ravenous appetite. By the time they'd eaten and returned to the control room, the navigational computer was receiving landing instructions from the spaceport.

There was a delay at the Customs and Immigration booth when two Jefferson Nighthawks with identical fingerprints and retinagrams presented their passports, but while such an occurrence was beyond the robot agent's experience and programming, Nighthawk pointed out that it wasn't illegal, and finally it gave them each a twenty-four-hour visa.

They took a shuttle to the hospital, got out, and entered the lobby. A slim, dark-haired woman ran up to Kinoshita and threw her arms around him.

"I'm so glad you came, Ito!" said Cassandra Hill. "I just didn't know what to do!"

Suddenly she seemed to notice his companions for the first time. "You're the original," she said, studying Nighthawk's face. "He was going to look just like you in another twenty years,

before his cosmetic surgery." She turned to Jeff and her whole
demeanor changed. "*You're* the one who put him here."

"I made a mistake," said Jeff. "I'm here to make amends."

"You practically kill a man who's closer to you than a brother,
and all you can say is that it's a mistake?" demanded Cassandra.

"I was wrong, and I'm sorry," said Jeff.

"That's not much of a comfort."

"I know."

There was an awkward silence.

"Let's go sit in a corner where we won't be overheard,"
said Nighthawk, walking off to the farthest set of chairs and
sofas he could find. The other three followed him.

"Do you have any idea where he is?" asked Kinoshita,
when they were all seated.

She shook her head. "He wiped the message so that no
one could follow him. He knew you'd be keeping tabs on him,
and he didn't want anyone else risking their lives." She grimaced in frustration. "Damn it! I fought side by side with him
against my father! We've made a life together! I had a right to
go with him!" Suddenly the anger vanished, to be replaced by
concern. "The doctors say that the first major shock to his
system—even a blow to the stomach—will probably kill him.
And of course he left without his medications."

"We'll find him," said Kinoshita soothingly.

"Do you mind if I ask a couple of questions?" interjected
Nighthawk.

Cassandra nodded. "Go ahead. I'll try my best to answer them."

"What was the nature of this threat that Pallas Athene
couldn't handle it by herself?"

"I don't know—but I know *her*. She wouldn't have asked
if there was any chance she could face it alone."

"Did she say whether it was coming from a single source?"
continued Nighthawk.

"I don't know."

Nighthawk signaled them to silence as a pair of doctors
walked by, then spoke when they were out of earshot. "Do

you know what weapons he took with him? Anything exotic, like a molecular imploder?"

"Just what was on his ship," she said. "The usual. He didn't use exotic weaponry."

"One last question," said Nighthawk. "What race did the alien called Friday belong to?"

"Friday?" she repeated, surprised. "I haven't thought of him in years. He was a Projasti."

"Never heard of them," said Nighthawk. "What planet do they come from?"

"Marius II."

"If Jason thought he'd need help, would he have approached Friday?"

"They didn't like each other," said Kinoshita.

"That wasn't my question." Nighthawk turned back to Cassandra. "Well?"

"He might have," said Cassandra slowly.

"All right," said Nighthawk. "We'll find him."

"How?" blurted Kinoshita.

"The spaceport will have a record of how much fuel he had in his ship," said Nighthawk, "and we'll compute how far he could go with it. We'll run a quick trace on his ship's registry, and if it doesn't show up at any fueling station, we'll be able to figure out the maximum distance he could have gone. He may be crazy to go out in that condition, but he's not suicidal, so I think we can eliminate any high-gravity worlds; they'd practically rip him open." He turned to Jeff. "While Kinoshita is getting the information we need from the spaceport, I want you to find out if Friday is on Marius II."

There was a brief commotion as a team of doctors and nurses raced to the emergency room.

"I don't think he'd been back to the Marius system in decades," said Cassandra when they had passed through the lobby. "And I don't know his real name. Jason couldn't pronounce it, so he just dubbed him Friday."

"All right, let me think for a moment," said Nighthawk, closing his eyes. Suddenly he opened them. "Remember you were asking about that last bounty, Jeff—the one on the Wizard? Your fingerprint and retinagram are the same as mine." He pulled a disk out of his pocket and handed it to the young man. "Take as much money out of my account as you need and spend whatever it takes to have some underpaid and mildly corrupt civil servant track Friday down for us. Same with Pallas Athene. Go up to a million credits for each of them if you have to."

"How?" asked Jeff. "We don't even know his real name."

"We know that a Projasti was on Sylene IV five years ago. So was she. That will show up on their passports, and you'll find out his real name as well. Start there and follow them forward."

"That could take a while."

"Tell whoever you're dealing with that part of the fee depends on speed. When you're done, we'll know if Jeff enlisted Friday's aid, and we'll have a pretty good idea where Pallas Athene is."

"Where will you be?" asked Jeff.

"Right here. Now get going. Take Kinoshita to the bank with you and give him enough cash to encourage someone at the spaceport to tell us what we want to know."

As the two men left, Cassandra turned to Nighthawk. "I want to thank you for coming," she said. "When I found out Jason was gone, all I could think of was to contact the one man who knew him best. I never even thought of asking you. I suppose, in a way, you know him better than anyone."

"I suppose," said Nighthawk. "Tell me about—"

"About Jason?"

He shook his head. "About Pallas Athene."

"She was absolutely fearless and totally humorless. I think she enjoyed proving she was better than anyone else—well, anyone but Jason. She was a deadly shot with any weapon, and I don't think even Jason was better with a knife." She stared at him. "Why do you ask?"

"Because I'd like to know just what kind of threat would make her call for help—and especially to call for a man who'd changed his name and face, a man who'd moved to the Outer Frontier expressly to get away from the kind of conflict she was trying to involve him in."

"I don't know. I never saw her back down from a fight or ask for help before. Something very dangerous must be threatening her."

"Probably," agreed Nighthawk. "But I promise you one thing: anyone who has to face a trio of Widowmakers is going to learn what *dangerous* really means."

25.

KINOSHITA WAS THE first to report back to the hospital.

"He filed a flight plan that would take him straight into the heart of the Oligarchy," said Kinoshita. "I assume that's to throw anyone who's following him off the track, and that he plans to stay on the Inner Frontier."

"Why not the Spiral Arm or the Outer Frontier?" asked Cassandra. "Or even the Rim?"

"He could eventually wind up there," acknowledged Kinoshita. "But he'd have to refresh his ship's nuclear pile, and we both know he's too careful to do that. Before he'd let us trace him through the ship's registry, he'd steal another one."

"He's in no condition to steal a ship," said Nighthawk. "He'll be getting stronger every day, but he's pretty weak right now. Besides, if the situation wasn't urgent he wouldn't have left, and that means he doesn't have time to steal ships and avoid pursuit."

"So we've limited him to a fifth of the galaxy," said Kinoshita. "What do we do now?"

"We wait," said Nighthawk.

"He's getting farther away every minute!" said Cassandra. "And he's traveling at light speed!"

"We don't have enough information yet. It's a big galaxy out there."

"You're just like him!" she snapped. "Never worried, never flustered, never anxious! We normal people aren't like you!" There was an uncomfortable silence. "I'm sorry," she said. "I'm just so damned worried about him! You're all Jefferson Nighthawk. Why is he the one who always gets the worst of it?"

"Because I wasn't around to help him."

"I'd forgotten," she said. "That horrible disease. I guess you've both done your share of suffering."

"I never asked for sympathy," said Nighthawk. "I'm sure Jason hasn't either."

"That doesn't mean he doesn't deserve it," she said. "He never had a choice about being the Widowmaker, and as soon as he could, he put the name, the face, and the job behind him."

"So did I," said Nighthawk. "Well, the job, anyway. But when you're the only person who can do it, and it has to be done…"

She looked at him irritably. "You even use the same words he would use."

"Why not? He's more like me than the other two. I gather the medics had a hell of a time convincing him he *wasn't* me when they first woke him up."

"I find this a very frustrating situation, Mr. Nighthawk," said Cassandra. "I want to be angry with you, but if there was no you there'd be no him—and that terrible calm of yours is precisely what's kept him alive in all the encounters he had on Pericles and since then."

Nighthawk laid a hand on her shoulder. "He kept me alive until they could cure me. I promise you I'm not going to let him die if there's any way to save him."

"I know," she said. "I just wish I knew why he has to keep going up against impossible odds."

"Because he can," said Nighthawk.

She was about to reply, but realized she had no answer and remained silent.

Jeff showed up a few minutes later.

"Well?" said Nighthawk.

"I came up blank on Pallas Athene," he said. "But I've pinpointed Friday." He grinned. "He must not have much to hide, because he's actually using Friday on his passport. I had them run a check on it, and he was on Sylene IV and

Cellestra four years ago. He's got to be the same Friday we're looking for."

"Where is he now?"

"Renaissance V."

"Never heard of it."

"It was opened while you were…incapacitated," said Jeff. "The interesting thing is that it's only about two hundred and twenty light-years from here."

"If he went to enlist Friday's help, they're probably both gone by now."

Jeff grinned. "I don't think so."

"What do you know that you'd like to share with us?" said Nighthawk.

"Friday's in a maximum-security prison awaiting execution," replied Jeff.

"Still?"

"Still. I checked; he was in his cell twenty minutes ago. But I learned something interesting: he had a visitor yesterday."

"Was it Jason?" asked Cassandra.

"He gave his name as Xavier MacDonald, but who else could it have been?"

"It was Jason, all right," said Nighthawk. "Xavier MacDonald is a name I used on New Tahiti before I was frozen. Nobody who ever heard or encountered it would still be alive—but Jason would know the name, because he shares my memory up to five years ago." He looked at Jeff. "And you found absolutely nothing on the girl?"

The young man shook his head. "Whatever passport she's traveling on, it's not Pallas Athene. I bribed a couple of guys to run her Pallas Athene prints and retinagram against every passport application made in the past four years—but that could take weeks."

"All right," said Nighthawk. "We've only got one lead. That makes deciding what to do next very easy."

"I'm coming along," said Cassandra.

"You're staying here," said Nighthawk.

"I have more right than—"

"It's not a matter of rights," said Nighthawk. "He doesn't know we're looking for him, so if he has to send a message, he's not going to send it to *us*. He'll know you're either here or back at your home, and he'll have it routed that way."

She instantly saw the logic behind his statement. "Damn you," she said. "Why do you have to be right?"

"If he *does* contact you, you've got Kinoshita's code. Jeff, give her yours."

"Why do I need another?" she asked.

"What if Kinoshita gets killed?"

"You're the one who seems to be in charge," said Cassandra. "Why not give me yours?"

"I will if you want," said Nighthawk. "But Jeff will give you his as well." He paused. "He's a young man, I'm an old one. If this situation is as dangerous as Jason seems to think, which of us figures to survive the longest?"

"That's what *he'd* say, with that cold, relentless logic," said Cassandra. "I don't like it any better coming from your mouth."

"But you'll stay?"

"I'll stay—but not in the hospital. There's no reason for me to be here. I'll rent a room in town. If anyone tries to contact me here, I'll have it patched through."

"All right," said Nighthawk. He turned to Kinoshita. "Are you sure you want to come?"

"He's my friend—and I've fought beside every Widowmaker. This is my destiny. I'm coming."

"Then let's go."

The aircar took five minutes to get them to the spaceport, and they broke through the stratosphere, reached light speed, and left the Giancola system far behind them in another ten minutes.

"Tell me about Friday," said Nighthawk as the navigation computer took over the ship's controls and pointed it for the Renaissance system.

"He's sleek and slim, a glistening red, almost as if he'd been varnished," said Kinoshita. "And his ears flap. They're no bigger than ours, but when he's excited they look like they're trying to fly off with him."

"Humanoid?"

"Two arms, two legs, walks upright." Kinoshita suddenly made a face. "He eats bugs. Live ones."

"Good protein," said Nighthawk.

"And there aren't a lot of worlds where he'll starve to death," added Jeff approvingly.

"What was he like?"

"Unpleasant," said Kinoshita.

"Then why did Jason tolerate him?"

"We were taking on an entire planet, complete with its security forces and a standing army, with a team that never numbered much more than one hundred, and Friday was an explosives expert." Kinoshita paused. "As for Friday, he didn't even want any pay. All he wanted was the chance to kill as many Men as possible, and he figured working with the Widowmaker afforded him the very best opportunity. He didn't care who won or lost, who lived or died. He just wanted to kill as many humans as he could."

"That's too bad," said Nighthawk.

"What is?" said Kinoshita. "I don't understand."

"Tell him, Jeff."

"If Jason went to Renaissance to try to enlist his help, either Jason's in even worse shape than we think, or Pallas Athene actually underestimated the threat. Why else would he be willing to put up with something like Friday?"

"Who else could he ask?" replied Kinoshita.

"Us."

"Would you have let him come along?"

Jeff smiled and looked at Nighthawk. "He's got a point."

"Maybe."

"Just maybe?"

"What would you have done if he insisted on joining us?" asked Nighthawk. "Shoot him again?"

"Point taken," said Jeff. Then: "But if he knew we wouldn't stop him, why *didn't* he ask for our help?"

"Have you ever asked for help?"

"No."

"He's just another version of you," said Nighthawk. "Why would *he* ask if you wouldn't?"

"Because they cut him open in an operating theater two days ago."

"They did a lot worse to him on Pericles and he never asked for help there either," put in Kinoshita. "I still haven't decided if Nighthawks are bona fide heroes or egomaniacal madmen."

"A little of each, I suppose," said Nighthawk. "Jeff, did you find out what they're executing Friday for?"

"The charge was a little hazy," answered Jeff. "He blew up a building, that much I know."

"Who was in it?"

"It's classified," said Jeff.

"Classified?" repeated Nighthawk. "Probably someone like a planetary governor, and they're keeping it quiet until they can make an orderly transition." A pause. "How much longer until we get there?"

"Six hours," said Kinoshita, checking the computer.

It was hardly worth going into Deepsleep, so they ate, they talked, they napped, and finally the ship touched down on Renaissance V, a colony world with a population of about four hundred thousand, divided almost evenly between Men and aliens. The jail was some forty miles out in a hot, arid desert, and they learned from the shuttle's computer that hard cases from all the nearby systems were brought to the maximum-security prison on Renaissance.

Nighthawk had signaled ahead that they were arriving and wished to speak to the prisoner known as Friday. After they had passed through three different security checkpoints, the warden, an ascetic woman in her sixties, greeted them and led them to the alien section of the prison.

"Friday has suddenly become very popular," she remarked. "He's been here for seven months without a message, a letter, or a visitor. Now he's had four of you in two days. I'd ask you if you were here to find out where he buried the treasure—but there isn't any treasure."

"What *did* he do?" asked Nighthawk. "The computer was a little reluctant to part with that information."

"If it was generally known, we'd have anti-Projasti— and possibly anti-alien—pogroms throughout the cluster." She stared at him. "You're the Widowmaker, aren't you? I recognize your name."

"Yes, I am."

"There are those who think you're just a bloodthirsty man who kills for money," she said. "I don't happen to agree with them. I will tell you, Mr. Nighthawk, but I want your word that you and your companions will keep the information to yourselves. I was not exaggerating about the consequences should it become public knowledge."

"I promise," said Nighthawk. "*We* promise."

"He blew up a school while classes were in session. More than twenty children were killed, and more than one hundred were injured. As far as we can tell, he did it solely because they were human children, and to him that would be twenty children who wouldn't grow to adulthood and become his enemies."

"How did you keep something like that a secret?"

"We couldn't," she replied. "But officially it was blamed on a faulty fusion generator." They stopped at another checkpoint, and suddenly lights blinked and whistles beeped. "You'll have to remove your weapons and leave them at this station," said the warden.

The three men placed their weapons in a series of receptacles and finally passed through the checkpoint. They went down a corridor for perhaps fifty feet, then turned right and suddenly passed a number of cells. There were no doors or bars, but there were glowing force fields across the front of each cell. They walked past a few more cells, then stopped.

"Here we are," said the warden.

A sleek red being sat on a chair that constantly re-shaped itself to fit the contours of its body.

"Friday, you have visitors," announced the warden.

Friday stood up and stared at the three men. "You two look familiar, but I don't know you." He turned to Kinoshita. "I know *you*, though. You are traveling in the wrong company. Your master was here yesterday."

"What did he want?" asked Nighthawk.

"Why ask me when you already know the answer?" said Friday.

"I want to hear it from you."

"Or what?" said Friday with as close to a smirk as his alien face was capable of. "Will you tell the warden to punish me? You are too late. She is already counting the days to my dismemberment."

"You told him what he wanted to know," said Nighthawk.

"Why should you think so?"

"Because if you hadn't, he'd still be here or you'd be dead," replied Nighthawk. "He wouldn't leave without the information if you were still alive and capable of speech." He paused. "And neither will I."

"I am immune to threats."

"Are you immune to pain?" asked Nighthawk.

"You are there. I am here."

"Not for long," said Nighthawk. He nodded to Jeff, who stepped behind the warden, grabbed her, and held her gently but firmly in his arms. "He won't hurt you, but we don't want you to yell or try to hinder us. Ito, hit that circle on the wall— the blue one. My guess is that it kills the cell's force field."

Kinoshita did as he was told, and the force field instantly vanished.

"If he gets out, or if you harm him—" began the warden.

"He's not getting out," said Nighthawk, stepping forward. "And he's not a foolish alien. He knows he's going to tell me what I need to know, and it would be foolish to let me do what I'm planning to do to him first."

"Stop!" said Friday, taking a step back. "You have no right to enter my cell."

"Did you have a right to blow up that school?"

"I will call for help!"

"No you won't," said Nighthawk.

"Why won't I?"

"Because no one will come to help you, and because it would make me very angry. Ask Kinoshita what I'm like when I'm angry." He took another step forward.

"You can't do this!" shouted Friday.

"I'm the Widowmaker," said Nighthawk. "I can do anything."

"There are laws!"

"When did you and I ever care about laws?" said Nighthawk. As he approached, the alien kept backing away. Finally, when he was standing by Friday's cot, he swung his hand down and broke it in half.

"That was metal!" said Friday, his alien eyes wide with fear.

"No," said Nighthawk. "That was practice." He smiled an ominous smile. "You're next."

"All right!" said Friday. "I will tell you what you want to know."

"I know you will."

"Jefferson Nighthawk, who now calls himself Jason Newman, came here yesterday. He had received an appeal for help from Pallas Athene, and because he was in a weakened condition, he sought my help."

"Did he tell you where she was?"

"On Bollander III," said Friday.

"I don't know it," said Nighthawk.

"I do," said Jeff. "Or at least I've heard of it. It's in the Quinellus Cluster."

"And that's where he's going?"

"Yes," said Friday.

"How did he expect you to help him?"

"He offered to free me."

"You've been convicted and sentenced," said Nighthawk, frowning. "There's no bail. Did he offer to break you out? From *this* place? How?"

"I never asked him."

"You didn't think he could pull it off?"

"On the contrary, if the man who now calls himself Jason Newman said he could free me, I have every confidence that he spoke the truth."

"Then why the hell didn't you go with him?"

"Because Bollander III is under attack by the Younger Brothers."

Nighthawk turned to Jeff. "The Younger Brothers? They sound like some mythical gang of cowboys from Earth's Wild West."

"They've started showing up on the bounty lists," answered Jeff. "So far anyone who's gone after them hasn't come back— and that includes some good men."

"You didn't answer me, Friday," said Nighthawk. "He offered to help you break out if you'd help him. Why did you choose to stay here, when you're due for execution?"

"Because I only kill *Men*," said Friday.

"What are the Younger Brothers?"

"Something quite different," said Friday with an enigmatic smile.

26.

"WE'RE DAMNED LUCKY the warden didn't order the guards to arrest us on the way out," said Kinoshita as their ship took off from the Renaissance system.

"When I grabbed her I whispered to her that it was a ruse," said Jeff.

"And she believed it?"

"Obviously."

"She doesn't know Jefferson Nighthawk," said Kinoshita. "Or maybe it was just more convenient for her to believe it. Maybe she didn't want to match her guards up against a pair of Widowmakers."

Jeff shrugged. "It comes to the same thing in the end."

Nighthawk, who had been instructing the navigational computer to head to the Bollander system, finally looked up. "We're running blind," he said.

"There's something wrong with the ship's sensors?" asked Kinoshita.

"I'm not talking about the ship," said Nighthawk. "We're racing hell-for-leather for Bollander III, and we don't have any idea what's waiting for us there."

"The Younger Brothers."

"Yeah, I know—but what *are* the Younger Brothers?"

"Aliens with a price on their head," said Kinoshita.

"We'll go there, we'll kill them, and we'll take Jason back to the hospital," added Jeff.

"I wish someone on this ship besides me would start using his brain," said Nighthawk. "We're not touching down until we know what we're up against."

"Jason's probably there already," said Jeff, "and he might need our help."

"Given the shape he's in, he definitely needs our help," said Nighthawk.

"Well, then?"

"Come on, Jeff," said Nighthawk in annoyed tones. "Start reasoning it out."

Jeff looked confused. "I don't know any more about the Younger Brothers than you do—just that there's a lot of paper on them."

"You know more than that," said Nighthawk.

"Really, I don't."

"Yes, you do," said Nighthawk. "*I* know more than that, and I never heard of them until a couple of hours ago."

"But the only thing Friday told us is that they're aliens," said Jeff.

"Then we didn't learn what we know from Friday, did we?" said Nighthawk.

Jeff lowered his head and concentrated for a few minutes, then looked up helplessly. "Honest to God, Jefferson, I don't know anything else about them."

"Then maybe you should consider what you don't know and extrapolate from that," suggested Nighthawk.

Jeff frowned. "What I *don't* know?" Suddenly he smiled. "Of course!"

"Would someone please tell me what I'm missing?" said Kinoshita.

"By your own testimony, Pallas Athene is almost as good with her weapons as I am," said Jeff. "Yet she felt compelled to ask Jason for help when she—or at least her world—was faced with the prospect of the Younger Brothers. And Jason must have known about them too. Why else would he have left the hospital a day after major surgery if he didn't think he was needed?"

"Jason may or may not have known what they were," said Nighthawk. "Based on what Kinoshita tells us about Pallas

Athene, the mere fact that she asked him for help would have convinced him the situation couldn't wait for him to fully recover from the operation."

"That makes sense," agreed Kinoshita. "I remember Jason telling me before Pericles that if only two people survived, it would probably be him and her. If she put out a call for help, it had to be serious."

"It seems simple in retrospect," said Jeff. "I've got to learn to start thinking like you do."

"You've never had to before," said Nighthawk. "I was a fourteen-year-old kid alone in the galaxy. You were the Widowmaker, in your physical prime, trained by your predecessor." He paused. "Anyway, we've got to find out what the Younger Brothers are, what they can do, why Pallas Athene felt she needed help and why Jason agreed with her. Then we'll be in a better position to do something about them."

"I'll contact the Oligarchy's Bounty Bureau on the subspace radio and see what I can find out," said Kinoshita.

Nighthawk shook his head. "That won't do any good."

"Why not?"

"Tell him, Jeff."

"If anyone in the Oligarchy knew the Younger Brothers were aliens, it would have said so on every Wanted poster," answered Jeff. "And if the Oligarchy doesn't even know they're aliens, how can they know what kind of abilities they have?"

"Right," said Nighthawk. "But *someone* knows."

"Pallas Athene," said Kinoshita.

Nighthawk nodded. "Check with Bollander III and see if you can find out what name she's using these days. Then trace it back through Passport Control and see where she's been in the past year." He looked at Jeff. "You say that they've just recently showed up on the bounty lists?"

"That's right," said Jeff. "I never heard of them six months ago."

"Okay," said Nighthawk to Kinoshita, "then going back a year should do it. See if you can track her movements, then check with the authorities on each planet and find out if the Younger Brothers were there when she was there, what they did, what they're capable of doing."

"I'll get right on it," said Kinoshita, activating the subspace radio.

"Do it in your cabin," said Nighthawk. "No reason why Jeff and I have to listen to you playing detective."

Kinoshita got up, stopped by the galley for a beer, and carted it off to his cabin with him.

"I'm trying to think the way you do, Jefferson," said Jeff. "It's just not coming easy. I work at it and work at it, and then you point out what I'm missing and I feel like such a fool."

"It's just a matter of practice," replied Nighthawk. "In case you don't remember, Kinoshita beat the shit out of you the first couple of weeks he worked with you on your martial arts. Today you could kill him in three seconds."

"I remember."

"How did you feel about it then?"

"Like I'd never be able to hold my own against him."

Nighthawk smiled. "You see?"

"Maybe I should have traveled with Jason for a year or so when I first started, until I learned to think properly," said Jeff.

"It wouldn't have worked," said Nighthawk. "He was busy not being the Widowmaker."

"How can he have these skills and not want to put them to use?"

"I'm sure he puts them to use all the time," said Nighthawk. "He was protecting Jubal Pickett when you came face-to-face with him, remember? He just doesn't want to do it as a Jefferson Nighthawk."

"I don't know why not," said Jeff. "It never bothered me."

"That's because despite your name and your DNA, you're your own man. Jason was literally me—born with my memories, my experiences, my reactions. I don't think it bothered him while I was frozen, but once he knew I was going to be awakened and cured, he didn't want to just be a copy of the Widowmaker—so he kept the skills, but he lost the name and the face." He paused. "He kept me alive at enormous personal cost. I owe him everything I've got, including his privacy and his own identity. And now," he added, "I owe him my best efforts to keep him alive. After all, he did the same for me five years ago."

"He put together an interesting crew back on Sylene IV, didn't he?" said Jeff. "Kinoshita tells me it was mostly aliens."

"So I hear."

"That Friday is a cold son of a bitch."

"He must have been pretty good with those explosives," said Nighthawk.

"I'm surprised Jason put up with him."

"When you're overthrowing a tyrant whose support outnumbers yours thousands to one, you use the weapons you have. Friday was what Jason had."

"I wonder why he didn't try to kill Jason?" said Jeff. "He seems to hate all Men."

"It makes sense when you think about it," answered Nighthawk. "Why kill the one Man who could lead him to multitudes of human targets?" He paused and looked at Jason. "But you're asking the wrong question."

"What's the right one?"

"When we were back on Giancola, you left to find out what you could about Pallas Athene's whereabouts, and you can back empty-handed."

"Yes, I did."

"Well, then?" said Nighthawk. "The question presents itself."

"Of course!" exclaimed Jeff suddenly. "If I couldn't find anything on her, how come Friday knew where she was?"

"You see?" said Nighthawk. "It's not that hard when you get the hang of it."

"Okay, that's the question," said Jeff. "But I don't know the answer to it."

"Sure you do," said Nighthawk. "Sometimes half the trick is knowing the right question. Let's see if we can't dope this out while Kinoshita is talking to the Oligarchy."

"All right," said Jeff. He considered the question. "Either Friday kept in constant contact with her, or he didn't. Since he hates humans, we can assume they weren't friends and rarely if ever saw or communicated with each other. Am I right?"

"Probably. Keep going."

Jeff thought for a moment, then looked up with a troubled expression on his face. "Damn! You knew all along, didn't you, Jefferson?"

"Knew what?"

"That there's a good chance we're not going to find Jason or Pallas Athene on Bollander III."

"That's right," said Nighthawk. "We're going through the motions because so far we're operating on minimal information of questionable value. Jason received her message, so *he* knows where she is—"

"But there's a good chance that Friday was wrong even if he thought he was telling the truth," interjected Jeff.

Nighthawk nodded his agreement. "If Friday wasn't in contact with Pallas Athene—and that's a logical assumption—there are only two ways he could know she was on Bollander III. Either he and she both stayed on Pericles or Sylene long enough for him to learn her new name so that he could trace her through Passport Control, or else he managed to track her down with no more information that we have—and since you couldn't come up with anything at all on her, I think it makes sense that he couldn't either."

"Then why are we going to Bollander III?" asked Jeff.

"She *might* be there," said Nighthawk. "There's always a chance she decided to stay put for a few years. But it's more likely that someone there will know where she went next."

"And in the meantime, Jason Newman gets farther and farther ahead of us," muttered Jeff.

"He won't do anything stupid," said Nighthawk. "I just hope that's enough to keep him alive."

"He's two days out of major abdominal surgery," said Jeff. "He could burst open just from the pressure of his ship's breaking mechanism."

Nighthawk shrugged. "Anything's possible."

"You sound like someone who doesn't give a damn, Jefferson."

"No," Nighthawk corrected him. "I sound like someone who isn't going to waste time worrying about a situation that he can't change or control. When Kinoshita comes out of his cabin, maybe we'll have a situation we *can* do something about."

They fell silent then, each lost in his own thoughts, until Kinoshita emerged almost an hour later, a puzzled look on his face.

"What did you find out?" asked Jeff anxiously.

"I'm not sure," said Kinoshita. "It's very strange."

"Obviously someone knew *something* about the Younger Brothers," said Nighthawk.

"The one thing everyone agrees upon is that they really are brothers, as identical as Jeff and the first clone," said Kinoshita. "They appear human, but no one knows for sure if they are. And they're very efficient killers."

"Then what's so puzzling?" asked Jeff.

"There's something more, isn't there?" said Nighthawk.

Kinoshita nodded. "Beta Campanis III says there are three Younger Brothers, all identical, like I said."

A grim smile crossed Nighthawk's face. "I can see this one coming."

"Greenbriar says there are seven brothers," continued Kinoshita. "Silverbright II claims there are six."

"Get to the kicker," said Nighthawk.

"Benitarus IV says there are more than six hundred of them, and they've got security holos of them to prove it."

27.

THEY KNEW SOMETHING was wrong the moment they touched down and entered the Bollander III spaceport.

Their weapons didn't set off any alarms. The security cameras had been melted, and there were half a dozen armed guards posted around the place.

Nighthawk approached the robot that was in charge of the Customs desk. One of its prismatic eyes was missing, and only a charred hole remained.

"Good day, sir," said the robot with a distinct lisp. "Welcome to Bollander III."

"What the hell happened here?" asked Nighthawk.

"There was a disturbance yesterday," said the robot. "It will not interfere with your stay on beautiful Bollander III, sir."

"What happened to your eye?"

"An unfortunate incident, sir, which need not concern you. I assure you that I am fully capable of servicing you with my one remaining eye."

"Someone burned it out."

"I cannot feel pain, sir."

"I offered an observation, not sympathy," said Nighthawk.

"I apologize, sir."

"You're also the first robot I've ever met who has a speech defect."

"The result of a full-force blast by a sonic pistol, sir."

"From the same man?"

"Yes, sir," replied the robot. "Welcome to Bollander III. May I help you now?"

"What did you do to get him so mad at you?"

"That may be privileged information, sir."

Nighthawk pulled out his bounty hunter's license and showed it to the robot. "I think the man who injured you may be the man I am trying to bring to justice. You will be breaking no law or confidence if you tell me what transpired."

"A man landed his ship and entered the spaceport yesterday, sir," said the robot. "He was carrying a laser pistol, a pulse gun, a sonic pistol, two knives, and a small hand weapon of undetermined properties. Of course the alarm sounded, and I explained that he would not be allowed to pass through the spaceport until he relinquished his weapons. He refused."

"Then what?"

"I explained that the sensors also detected that he was bleeding beneath his tunic, and that even if he disarmed himself he would not be allowed access to Bollander III until he could produce medical documentation that he was not contagious."

"He refused, of course?"

"Yes, sir." A brief pause. "Welcome to Bollander III. How may I help you?"

"You can tell me what happened after the man refused to relinquish his weapons or offer you the medical documentation that you requested."

"I explained that he would have to wait while I contacted my human superior, sir. He replied that he had no time to wait, and began to walk through Customs. Naturally I positioned myself in such a way that he could not pass. He then pulled out a laser pistol and shot me in my left eye. When that had no effect upon me other than to limit my depth perception, he withdrew his sonic pistol and fired it at me from a distance of eleven feet eight inches. This disrupted my circuitry, and I fell backward to the floor. Before I could get up he had disabled all of the sensors and cameras with his weapons. I had of course signaled for help when he disabled my eye, and security personnel arrived shortly thereafter."

"Poor bastards," muttered Kinoshita.

"Welcome to Bollander III," said the robot to Kinoshita. "May I help you, sir?"

"Later," said Nighthawk. "Did the man kill any spaceport personnel?"

"No, sir. He disarmed the first two to arrive with a remarkable display of marksmanship, then warned the others to drop their weapons and leave or he would kill them."

"And?"

"They disarmed themselves and left. He passed through the spaceport two minutes and seven seconds later. The police have not yet apprehended him."

"If they're lucky, they won't," replied Nighthawk. "Aren't you going to welcome me to Bollander III and give me a twenty-four-hour visa?"

"Yes, sir," said the robot. "Welcome to—"

"Here's my passport," interrupted Nighthawk, handing over the small disk.

The robot cleared him in less than a minute, then did the same for Jeff and Kinoshita.

"Robot, I have another question before we leave," said Nighthawk.

"Yes, sir?"

"I'm here to visit an old friend who sometime uses the name of Pallas Athene. Can you tell me how to find her?"

"There is a vidphone directory on the west wall, sir."

"That won't work," said Nighthawk. "My computer couldn't find her, and if she was listed in a directory it would have been able to."

"Then I am unable to help you, sir."

"Don't be so sure of that," said Nighthawk. "How long have you been in operation?"

"Nine years, sir."

"Has your memory been affected by the screecher?"

"'Screecher,' sir?" asked the robot.

"Sonic pistol."

"No, sir. My memory is intact."

"Then search through it and tell me if anyone who has been a resident of Sylene IV at any time in the past has cleared Customs on Bollander III in the past five years," said Nighthawk.

"Searching…yes, sir."

"How many?"

"Just one."

"A woman?" asked Nighthawk.

"Yes, sir."

"What was her name?"

"Helen of Troy, sir."

"How can I contact her?"

"There is a vidphone directory on the west wall of the spaceport lobby, sir."

"Thank you, robot," said Nighthawk. "I hope you feel better soon."

"I cannot feel pain, sir," said the robot as the three men walked off toward the directory.

"Son of a bitch!" muttered Jeff. "Friday was telling us the truth after all!"

"What the hell kind of siege can the planet be under?" asked Kinoshita as they approached the directory screen. "I mean, hell, three days out of surgery and bleeding from his exertion, Jason's done more discernible damage to Bollander than a gang of six hundred aliens."

"Never forget that they're aliens," said Nighthawk. "Until we learn more about them, we can't know what they want, what they're like, what they're capable of."

"Or how to kill them," added Jeff.

"Hopefully Jason will have figured it out by the time we catch up with him," said Nighthawk.

"Unless they figure out how to kill him first," said Jeff.

They reached the directory and scanned it. There was no Helen of Troy and no Pallas Athene.

"Great," said Kinoshita. "The robot was wrong. She's not on Bollander."

"She's here," said Nighthawk.

"What makes you so certain?" demanded Kinoshita.

"Tell him, Jeff."

"Because Jason's still on the planet," said Jeff. "We had to discover where she was, but she called Jason and asked for his help. *He* knew exactly where to go." He paused. "So we know we're on the right world. But I'll be damned if I know what our next step is."

"If they make him mad enough, we could just follow the trail of bodies," said Nighthawk with a wry smile.

"Seriously, Jefferson," said Jeff, "what do we do now?"

"Seriously, Jeff, use your brain," said Nighthawk.

Jeff looked blank. "I don't know—go to the usual places, the bars and drug dens and the like, and see what information we can pick up?"

Nighthawk shook his head. "This world's got a population of a couple of million. There might be two hundred bars, and fifty or sixty drug dens—and we've got a weakened Widowmaker preparing to go up against a gang that is so lethal that the toughest lady Kinoshita ever met felt it was necessary to enlist his help."

"Then what do you suggest?" asked Jeff.

"The answer's inherent in what I just told you," said Nighthawk.

Jeff frowned. "It is?"

"Reason it out," said Nighthawk. "We know she's on Bollander. That's a given. Friday told us so, and Jason came directly here. What's the one other thing we know about her?"

"That she lived on Sylene?"

Nighthawk merely stared at him.

"Oh, I see!" said Jeff suddenly. "Hell, it shouldn't take much time at all."

"Would one of you please tell me what the hell you're talking about?" demanded Kinoshita.

"The one thing we know about Pallas Athene," said Jeff, "the defining fact about her, is that she's almost as lethal as Jason. You've said so often enough."

"So?"

"So I don't know if she drinks or drugs—but I do know the one spot she's *got* to have done business with if she's been here for a few years, the one spot most likely to know where she is."

"And what is that?" asked Kinoshita, still puzzled.

Jeff smiled. "A weapons shop."

28.

THEY TRIED TWO other weapons shops without success before they came to the Sharpshooter. It was run by a pair of elderly women, pudgy, pink, and rosy-cheeked. Each wore a satin ribbon in her hair, they both wore old-fashioned (perhaps, thought Kinoshita, the term should be "ancient-fashioned") spectacles, and they had a pot of tea sitting right on the main counter.

"Good morning, gentlemen," said one of them. "Welcome to the Sharpshooter. May I offer you some tea?"

"That would be very nice," said Nighthawk before his two companions could offend by refusing it.

"I'm Winnifred Dugan, and this is my sister Wilma. I can't tell you how honored we are to have both the original Widowmaker and the newest version in our little shop."

"You know who I am?" said Nighthawk, surprised.

"Bloodletting is our business, in a manner of speaking," said Wilma. "And who is better at it than the Widowmaker? Ah, the sights you've seen!"

"And the men you've killed!" added Winnifred with undisguised enthusiasm.

"And so many have doubtless gone unreported," said Wilma. "You're one of our ideals, Mr. Nighthawk." She turned to Jeff. "And so, of course, are you, young Mr. Nighthawk. Such a record of death and destruction!"

"I prefer to think of it as a record of justice meted out," replied Jeff.

"Of course you do," said Wilma soothingly. "What would you gentlemen like in your tea?"

"Nothing," said Nighthawk.

"Whiskey," muttered Kinoshita too softly for them to hear.

Winnifred poured three cups of tea, placed the delicate cups on a silver serving platter, walked out from behind the counter, and brought a cup to each of them.

"What can we sell you today?" asked Wilma. "We're having a special on pulse guns with both infrared and ultraviolet telescopic sights. Perhaps you'd prefer a pistol with a barrel that will extend at your command; you simply estimate the distance and it will instantly become the proper length to afford you the greatest accuracy. And we have a state-of-the-art burner that will function under thirty-two fathoms of ocean, regardless whether it's composed of water, chlorine, or ammonia."

"What we'd like is some information," said Nighthawk.

"Certainly," said Winnifred, returning to her place behind the counter. "Information is one of our most popular commodities, and always our most expensive."

"We're looking for a woman…"

"There's an excellent upscale brothel on the next block," said Wilma. "If you tell them we sent you, you'll receive a ten percent discount."

"And you'll receive a twenty percent kickback?" asked Nighthawk with a smile.

"Twenty-five," replied Wilma, returning the smile.

"Thanks anyway, but we're looking for a particular woman, and she won't be working in a whorehouse," said Nighthawk. "At various times she's been known as Pallas Athene and Helen of Troy."

The two sisters frowned as one. "It's not a name we're familiar with," said Winnifred at last.

"She's probably changed it again," said Nighthawk. "If I were to ask you who was the deadliest woman on the planet, what would your answer be?"

Wilma smiled. "Our answer would be: five hundred credits."

Nighthawk smiled and pulled out five one-hundred-credit bills.

"We can make a bank transfer from your account if you prefer," said Winnifred.

"Why should you pay taxes on it?" said Nighthawk, placing the money on the counter. "This is a private transaction. It's nobody's business but our own."

"I *knew* I would like you if I ever met you, Mr. Nighthawk!" said Winnifred. "Isn't he thoughtful, Wilma?"

"He's thoughtful and he's courteous," agreed Wilma.

"He's also five hundred credits poorer than he was half a minute ago," put in Nighthawk.

"Oh! Forgive us, Mr. Nighthawk," said Wilma. "We're not used to being in the company of two living legends."

"The name?" said Nighthawk.

"Certainly," said Winnifred. "The deadliest woman—probably the deadliest person on the planet, human or alien—is named Hera."

"No last name?"

"None."

"That's got to be her!" said Kinoshita. "It's yet another name from the Greek myths."

"Well, she's consistent, anyway," said Nighthawk.

"Except that she's not the deadliest person on the planet anymore," said Wilma. "You are—you or the younger you."

"Speaking of younger," said Nighthawk, "have either of you ever heard of the Younger Brothers?"

"Villains from ancient Earth's Wild West," answered Wilma promptly. "Their names were Cole, Bob, and Jim."

"Nothing more recent?"

"I've heard rumors about a gang of that name on the Inner Frontier," said Winnifred, "but no one seems to have any reliable information. Why?"

"Just curious," said Nighthawk. "What can you tell me about Hera?"

"Are you here to kill her?"

"No."

"Then why is the greatest bounty hunter in the galaxy interested in her?"

"I'll be happy to tell you," said Nighthawk. "For five hundred credits."

Winnifred laughed aloud; Wilma merely smiled. "We'd rather think you're here to hunt her down," said Wilma. "It's much more exciting. And it's certainly not worth five hundred credits to us to find out that you're not here on some excessively bloody business."

"As you wish," said Nighthawk. "Are you ready for another five hundred credits?"

"Certainly," said Winnifred. "You want to know where to find her, of course?"

"Of course."

"How come the young Widowmaker hardly speaks?" she asked suddenly.

"He's taking notes."

"And the little man? Wherever a Widowmaker has been seen, he's always there too."

"My name is Ito Kinoshita, ma'am," said Kinoshita, bowing low. "I'm pleased to make your acquaintance."

"What's your relationship to the Widowmakers?" continued Winnifred. "Errand boy or secret master?"

"Friend," answered Nighthawk. "The address?"

"The five hundred credits?"

Nighthawk peeled off five more bills.

"She lives at 43 Macabee Street," said Wilma.

"Where is Macabee Street?"

"Three blocks west of here."

"Thank you," said Nighthawk, turning and taking a step toward the door.

"But you won't find her there," said Winnifred.

Nighthawk stopped and turned back to face the two sisters.

"She went into hiding five days ago," said Winnifred.

"But you know where?"

"Certainly. We shipped a supply of weapons, batteries, and ammunition there before she left Macabee Street, so that no one could intercept them or follow our messenger."

"And how much do you want for that information?" said Nighthawk.

"We don't want any more of your money," said Wilma. "We're merely avaricious, not rapacious."

"Of course not."

"We will freely give you the directions," said Winnifred.

"That's very generous of you," said Nighthawk suspiciously.

"Just as soon as you sign a piece of paper," said Wilma.

"Promising you my life, my fortune, and what else?"

"Merely stating that you always buy your weapons at the Sharpshooter, and that even when you're in the Spiral Arm or out on the Rim or in the Magellanic Clouds, you have them shipped to you from Bollander III."

"You are two of the cuter extortionists it's been my experience to meet," said Nighthawk wryly. "Give me a piece of paper and a stylus."

Winnifred reached behind the counter and promptly withdrew a sheet of paper, while Wilma produced a quill pen. Nighthawk scribbled his endorsement and handed the pen and paper back.

"Map," commanded Wilma, and a printer instantly spat forth a complex map. "No, not of the cluster," she said. "I want a map of Bollander III." Another map instantly appeared. She studied it and frowned. "No, this will never do. It's the whole planet. If I circle the location they need, it could cover ten thousand square miles. Let me try once more. Computer, I want a map of Orbach and Swenson counties on Bollander III, and make sure you include all the major roads." The map appeared two seconds later, and she laid it down on the countertop. "Much better," she said. "I just hate computers, don't you?"

"I never gave it much thought," said Nighthawk.

"Well, *we* loathe them," said Winnifred. "How can you invite a computer to tea, or discuss beauty with it?"

"I got the impression that what you mostly discuss is bloodletting," said Nighthawk.

"But there's a beauty to a well-planned hunt," said Winnifred. "And a certain exquisite mathematical precision to an efficient kill."

"The only beauty is coming out of it alive," said Nighthawk.

"Oh, tosh!" said Winnifred dismissively. "You find the same beauty in it that we do, or else why would you do it?"

"Because I can."

"Now that's an interesting if unexpected answer, Mr. Nighthawk," said Winnifred. "We'll have to think about that very seriously."

"In the meantime," said Wilma, handing Nighthawk the map, "I've circled the place where you'll find Hera, always assuming the man or men—or aliens—she's hiding from haven't found her first. Her location is indicated in red, and our shop is circled in blue. She's quite some distance out of town. In fact, she's in the next county."

Nighthawk handed the map to Kinoshita. "We'll find her."

"May we ask who a woman of her obvious talents is hiding from?" said Winnifred.

"You can ask."

"It's not worth five hundred credits to us," said Wilma apologetically.

"It's worth a lot more than that to me," said Nighthawk. "I wish I knew the answer. I guess there's just one more question, and then we won't bother you ladies any further."

"It's no bother," they said almost in unison.

"What's your question?" added Wilma.

"What weaponry did you ship to Hera's new location?"

"Just the usual."

"Nothing exotic? No molecular imploders, no subatomic vibrators, nothing like that?"

"Even the Inner Frontier is becoming too civilized for weapons like that," said Wilma.

"Which isn't to say that we couldn't get them for the right price," added Winnifred with a wink. "Just in case you ever need one."

"True," said Wilma. "But Hera never asked for them. Just a few extra burners and screechers, a shotgun that fires radioactive pellets, and a supply of batteries."

"Too bad," said Nighthawk. "I'd hoped we could learn a little about what she was facing based on what weapons she needed."

"I have a question," said Jeff. "Are we the first off-worlders to visit your establishment within the past two days?"

"There was one gentleman," said Winnifred. "He looked a little like you two Widowmakers. Not an exact likeness, but maybe like a cousin."

"He was in a bad way," put in Wilma. "He tried to hide it, but there was blood seeping through the front of his tunic."

"What did he buy?"

"That was the interesting thing," continued Wilma. "He bought batteries and bullets for his weapons, but that wasn't all. He bought goggles—"

"Goggles?" repeated Nighthawk sharply. "What kind?"

"Infrared, ultraviolet, night vision...in fact, one of every kind we have in the shop."

"And a radiation meter," added Winnifred. "Don't forget that, sister."

"Yes, a radiation meter," agreed Wilma. "Oh, and sound and vibration detectors, too." .

"Was that all?" asked Jeff.

"I think so. I can have the computer check to make sure."

"Do that, please," said Nighthawk. "And then we'll buy three of everything he bought."

"Let me pour you some more tea while Wilma is gathering the stock," said Winnifred, putting three clean cups on the tray.

"Don't you have a robot to do that for you?" asked Nighthawk.

"We don't trust robots."

He turned to Kinoshita. "Give Wilma a hand."

Kinoshita went off to help her fill the order, while Nighthawk and Jeff sipped their tea and tried to pretend it was simply flat beer. Wilma and Kinoshita returned a few minutes later with a large box, Nighthawk paid for it, and they went off to find the woman who was now known as Hera—and, hopefully, still another Widowmaker.

29.

THEY ELECTED TO rent an aircar. As soon as they were five miles out of town and passing a number of increasingly large farms, Jeff, who was driving, ordered the vehicle to stop and climbed out.

"What now?" asked Kinoshita as Jeff and Nighthawk began examining the aircar inside and out.

"Now we find and disable every safety system that will enable the company that owns the vehicle to track us," said Nighthawk. "We'll have enough trouble with what's in front of us. We don't want to be looking over our shoulders, too."

"Got one," reported Jeff from behind the car.

"And here's one under the seat," added Nighthawk, ripping out the small device.

"Until we know if they left anyone in town, or have any residents beholden to them, it's better than no one knows exactly where we are or what we're doing," Jeff told Kinoshita.

"But the company will know what you've done," said Kinoshita.

"We'll pay for the damage when we get back, and since there's only one spaceport on the planet and our ship is there, they know we can't run out on the bill," answered Jeff. "They won't come looking for us."

"The rest of the interior's clean," announced Nighthawk, climbing back onto his seat. "Let's go."

"Maybe while we're here we ought to discuss what we've learned," suggested Jeff.

"We can do it while we're traveling," said Nighthawk. "It'll take us a couple of hours to reach our destination, and I don't like stopping this close to town. We've gone to the trouble of removing all the sensors and trackers, so why make it easy for someone to follow us?"

"Makes sense," agreed Jeff. He commanded the aircar to shoot forward.

"So what have you learned?" asked Nighthawk.

"Jason knows more about the Younger Brothers than we do, or he wouldn't have stopped at the Sharpshooter."

"True," said Nighthawk. "But he doesn't know enough."

Suddenly Jeff grinned. "I was right. Maybe I *am* learning to use my brain."

"I don't follow you," said Kinoshita.

"He bought a lot of stuff that we wouldn't have bought if we'd landed ahead of him," said Jeff. "That means he knows something we don't know."

"But not enough?" said Kinoshita.

"He knows he's going to need something to enhance his vision, his ability to perceive them—but he doesn't know *what* he'll need. That's why he bought every kind of goggle and vision enhancer they had. He thinks they may show up on a radiation detector. And because he's as careful and methodical as Jefferson, he made sure his pistol won't run out of bullets and his burner and screecher won't run out of power." He paused. "I just wish he'd bought something to patch his incisions before he bleeds to death."

"He probably considers them a minor irritant," said Kinoshita. "He fought the last half hour of the action on Pericles with his hand cut off—not broken, not crushed, but severed."

"What kept him from bleeding to death?" asked Jeff.

"He cauterized it with a burner."

"Damn!" said Jeff. "That hurts even to think about! The man's got guts, I'll give him that. Anyway, it's obvious that he thinks one or more of those items he bought will give him an advantage. Maybe they're nocturnal, and he figures he'll have to face them in the dark. They're aliens; maybe some part of them, some deadly part, is hidden from human sight in the infrared spectrum and he needs the goggles to spot it. Maybe he's learned something about their physical makeup, something that makes him think he can spot them with a radiation detector before they know he's there."

"I hear a lot of 'maybe's," said Nighthawk.

"We can't know until we encounter one," said Jeff.

"True."

Jeff frowned. "But you're not happy with my answer."

"Your answer is fine, as far as it goes," said Nighthawk. "But it's all guesswork and suppositions. Suppose you tell us what we *know*."

"We know Pallas Athene is now Hera, and we've pinpointed her location. We know she's being threatened by the Younger Brothers. We know Jason Newman landed here, caused a commotion at the spaceport, and picked up a bunch of equipment designed to help him spot something that might not be visible to the naked eye. And as far as I can tell, that's *all* we know." Jeff looked at Nighthawk. "What am I missing?"

"The forest."

"The forest?" repeated Jeff, puzzled.

"You've identified all the trees, but you still haven't seen the forest."

"I don't know what you're getting at."

"*Think*, Jeff," urged Nighthawk. "I know you can do it. Put the pieces together."

Jeff frowned. "Whatever it is, you didn't know it before we landed here or you would have mentioned it, or made me reason it out."

"Keep going."

"All right," said Jeff. "What do we know now that we didn't know three hours ago? We know that Jason bought a bunch of stuff, but if some of it is effective, some of it won't be, so we can't learn anything more from that until we actually come up against a Younger Brother. And we know Hera laid in a supply of standard weaponry, but that doesn't tell us a damned thing." He paused, his brow knotted in concentration. "Damn it, Jefferson, that's everything we've learned."

"No it isn't," said Nighthawk. "Keep going. Reason it out."

"She changed her name, but she did that years ago, and then she changed it again sometime before she moved to wherever the hell it is that she's hiding." Suddenly his eyes widened. "That's it, isn't it?"

"The name changes?" asked Kinoshita.

Jeff shook his head. "No, not the name changes. She left the city to go hole up out in the wilderness—and she did it five days ago."

"See?" said Nighthawk with a smile. "I told you you could do it."

"Do what?" said Kinoshita. "What has he figured out?"

"She didn't ask Jason for help until three days ago," said Jeff. "That's when she found out that one of the most wanted gangs of killers on the Inner Frontier, a gang that may number as many as six hundred members, wasn't going to be deterred just because she'd left the city."

"We know that," said Kinoshita.

"Yeah, but we didn't *think* about it," said Jeff. "Or at least, *I* didn't."

"I don't see—"

"Look," said Jeff. "This is a gang that steals millions, that plunders whole cities, that kills on a grand scale. What the hell are they doing hundreds of miles from the nearest city, hunting down a lone woman?"

Kinoshita suddenly looked puzzled. "Retaliation for killing a gang member?" he ventured.

"If she'd killed even one of them, we'd know what we were up against, what race they were. The authorities would spread the word to every bounty hunter on the Inner Frontier." He paused. "I'll bet she didn't have much money when you knew her back on Sylene IV, and I'll bet she doesn't have a hell of a lot more now."

"She had enough to pay her bills, nothing more," admitted Kinoshita. "It never seemed to mean much to her. But how do you know she hasn't hit it rich?"

"You don't really think Jefferson and I are the only people those charming old ladies would offer a molecular imploder to, do you?" replied Jeff. "Hera's worried enough to ask Jason for help. If she had the money, don't you think she'd have bought an imploder?"

"All right, so she doesn't have much money," said Kinoshita. "So what?"

"If she's not living in a city that can be plundered, if she didn't kill a Younger Brother, and if she doesn't have any money, why are they after her?"

"When you put it that way, it doesn't make much sense, does it?" said Kinoshita. "There must be a reason."

"There is," said Jeff. "They don't want *her* at all. Could one woman, even a woman as remarkable as you tell us she is, hold off a well-armed gang with nothing but conventional weapons? Remember: they know she's still here, or she wouldn't have asked Jason to come to Bollander. And they had at least a day's head start on him."

"Then they probably killed her and left before Jason even touched down yesterday."

"They may have killed her," said Jeff. "We won't know that until we reach our destination. But they haven't left."

"Why would they stay?" asked Kinoshita.

"Because they were never after her," said Jeff. "She's just bait. Think back, Ito—what happened five days ago?"

A sudden look of comprehension crossed Kinoshita's face. "Jefferson killed Hairless Jack Bellamy—and then he killed Cleopatra Rome maybe half a day later."

"Right. And while he was doing that, I was taking the Jack of Blades out by the Tarica system. So suddenly there are two Widowmakers, and we're getting more active. Probably we're going to team up to go after some of the bigger gangs, gangs like the Younger Brothers." Jeff smiled. "But they don't know who or where the Widowmakers *are*. All they know is that they think it's time to kill the Widowmakers before we kill them."

"What has Hera got to do with it?"

"Jefferson's been retired for two years. As far as I can tell, he doesn't keep in contact with anyone except his garden supply shops and his antiquarian booksellers. The Younger Brothers don't know about either interest, so they have no idea how to track him down. And me, I'm the new kid on the block. Except for you, I haven't made a friend on the whole Frontier; I've been too busy collecting bounties. So if you were the Younger Brothers and you wanted to find a Widowmaker, you'd learn who actually knew one and lived to tell about it. You'd have heard about the affair on Pericles V. There were only five survivors. Jason and Cassandra changed their names, and you travel with the Widowmaker. Friday was sitting in a maximum-security prison with a death sentence hanging over his head. That left Pallas Athene. If they were ever going to draw the Widowmaker out, the best way was to use her as bait. They want more than one Widowmaker, of course, but at this point they'll settle for what they can get." He turned to Nighthawk. "How am I doing?"

"You've nailed it," said Nighthawk approvingly.

"But I still needed you to point me in the right direction."

"That's what I'm here for."

"I thought it was to kill the Younger Brothers," said Jeff with a smile.

"That, too," said Nighthawk. He did not return the smile.

30.

THE COUNTRYSIDE BECAME more rugged as the farms gradually disappeared. The land was covered by rocky outcroppings, deep gullies and ravines, and dry riverbeds.

"Well, they're probably still alive," said Kinoshita. "There are enough places to hide."

"From men, yes," said Jeff. "From aliens? It depends on their senses and abilities."

He looked to Nighthawk, who nodded his agreement.

"How close are we getting?" asked Kinoshita.

"You are 6.327 miles from your destination," announced the aircar.

"Stop when you're three miles away," said Nighthawk.

"Registered," replied the aircar.

"Three miles over this terrain is a hell of a walk," said Kinoshita. "We'll be lucky if one of us doesn't break an ankle."

"We know it's a trap," said Jeff. "Do you really want us to drive right up to wherever it is she's hiding?"

"I was just remarking," said Kinoshita defensively.

"Besides, we won't find Jason there," continued Jeff.

"Why not?"

"Because he's got sixty years of Jefferson's experiences and memories. If I know it's a trap, so does he."

"That may not stop him," said Nighthawk. "He came here out of loyalty to a friend. Maybe she's just bait, but he'll do what he can to save her anyway. He'll try to protect himself, but he won't stand by and watch them kill her."

Kinoshita donned his infrared and ultraviolet goggles in quick succession, then took them off. "Nothing," he complained. "I can't see a damned thing with them that I couldn't see before."

"It could mean we won't need them," said Nighthawk. "On the other hand, it could simply mean that there aren't any Younger Brothers within your field of vision. You don't really expect a tree or a rock to look any different, do you?"

"No, I guess not."

The vehicle came to a stop and hovered a few inches above the ground. "We are now exactly three miles from your destination."

"Shut down all systems in ten seconds," ordered Jeff, "and reactivate on my command, once you verify my voiceprint."

"Done," said the aircar just before its power went dead.

"What if you're wounded or killed?" asked Kinoshita.

"Jefferson's voiceprint is identical to mine," replied Jeff. "The vehicle will respond to his command."

"And if you're both killed?"

"Then you'll have a long walk back to the spaceport," said Nighthawk.

"Well, shall we begin?" said Jeff, hanging his various goggles around his neck and looping the radiation detector over a shoulder as Nighthawk and Kinoshita did the same.

"Might as well," replied Nighthawk.

With Jeff in the lead the three men began approaching what they assumed would be a cabin or a farmhouse, some dwelling where Hera had planned to make her last stand. They kept to the heavy foliage, walking around the numerous gullies, picking up a number of cuts and scratches from the thick thornbush.

After they'd gone half the distance Nighthawk stopped.

"What is it?" asked Jeff.

"I need to think for a minute."

"What's the problem?"

"I don't think we're looking for a house at all," said Nighthawk. "Consider our surroundings. We haven't seen a road or a landing field in the last eighty miles. This land we're on is as virgin as it gets. And the sisters at the Sharpshooter didn't give us an address; they pinpointed a spot on the map." He paused. "This area is honeycombed with caves. My guess is that Hera's holed up in one. It's more defensible, it's probably connected to half a dozen other caves—escape routes if she needs them. It might even have its own water source. It wouldn't take much to set up a generator for power; she could even run it off a screecher battery so she'd have all the comforts of home."

"There are probably twenty caves that could qualify as the location," said Kinoshita. "How do we tell which one is the right one?"

"We don't bother," said Nighthawk.

"Right," agreed Jeff. "We let *her* find *us.*"

"How?" said Kinoshita.

"We'll go another three-quarters of a mile," said Nighthawk. "Then we'll stop and find a cave that's connected to others."

"And then we'll create enough of a disturbance to let both sides know we're here," added Jeff, "and duck into the cave. She probably knows the cave system inside out, and they don't. She figures to find us before they do."

"Hopefully Jason will be with her," continued Nighthawk, "and if we all put our heads together and trade information, maybe we can figure out just what the Younger Brothers are and what makes them tick—and how to silence that ticking before it silences us."

"Sounds good to me," said Jeff. "Let's get moving."

They proceeded cautiously for another thousand yards, then stopped again. Jeff activated his radiation detector, stared at it, and shook his head.

"Not a damned thing," he said softly.

Kinoshita tried his various goggles again. "I agree—nothing."

"It's quiet, too," said Jeff. "Nothing but the rustling of leaves and some avians whistling to each other." He paused. "I wonder: could the Younger Brothers have killed them both and left the planet already?"

"Oh, I doubt it," said Nighthawk with an amused smile.

"What is it?" asked Jeff, puzzled.

"Look behind you," said Nighthawk.

Jeff spun around and found himself facing Jason Newman. Newman's tunic was streaked with crusted blood, and he'd lost a considerable amount of weight, but it was clearly the same man Jeff had faced on Giancola II.

"Well, well," said Newman. "Who'd ever have guessed it—especially on a nondescript little world like this: a gathering of Widowmakers."

31.

"WHERE'S PALLAS ATHENE?" asked Kinoshita, who was the only one besides Newman who had actually known her.

"She's dead," answered Newman. "I think they killed her once they knew I'd arrived. The body was pretty fresh."

"You left your vehicle a couple of miles away?" said Nighthawk.

"Of course. It was obviously a trap."

"Yet you came anyway," said Jeff.

"It may have been a trap, but her danger was real," replied Newman. "When I asked for help back on Sylene, she was the first to volunteer. How could I turn her down?"

"Before we go any further," continued Jeff, "I want to apologize for what I did back on Giancola."

"There's no need," said Newman. "You're young. You'll outgrow it. *We* both did."

"So what's the setup here?" asked Nighthawk. "Where are they, and just as important, *what* are they?"

"I don't know," answered Newman. "When I got here and walked to the cave she was in, there was only one Younger Brother, or one alien, or one whatever the hell he is. He looked mildly human—two arms, legs, eyes, and ears, but the proportions were wrong. So were the joints; no human arms or legs ever bent like his. But still, there was just the one."

"So are you saying our information was wrong, and that there's no gang, there's only one?" asked Jeff.

Newman shook his head. "No. I'm saying there was just one when I showed up. He ducked out of sight when I approached Pallas Athene's cave. She had it stocked for a long siege: weeks' worth of food and ammunition laid in, and she'd rigged some lights to a couple of screecher batteries. The cave was pretty deep, and there were a number of others connected to it."

"How did the alien get into the cave if it was that well fortified?" asked Nighthawk.

"He didn't," said Newman. "As near as I can reconstruct it, she stuck her head out the front of the cave—maybe to see if they'd gone away, maybe to see if I was coming, maybe for some other reason—and got the top of her head blown off for her trouble."

"Standard weapon?" asked Nighthawk.

"Pulse gun," confirmed Newman.

"What happened then?" asked Kinoshita.

"It was the damnedest thing," said Newman, frowning. "I walked out of the cave, prepared to hunt down and kill the alien—but he was standing out there, maybe fifty yards away, waiting for me."

"So you killed him?" asked Kinoshita.

Newman grimaced. "Yes and no."

"Explain," said Nighthawk.

"When I faced him his whole body seemed to tense—and suddenly I was facing half a dozen identical Younger Brothers. It was like…I don't know…an amoeba, perhaps. All I know is that one second I was facing a single alien, and a second later there were six of them, all armed. I half-thought they were illusions just meant to distract me. I mean, hell, there was no way he *could* make them solid, with real weapons—but I didn't feel like taking any chances, so I killed three of them before the others had even drawn their weapons. They weren't the most accurate gunmen I've ever seen, but the way their bullets kicked up the dirt around me and their burners melted a rock I'd ducked behind, I had to conclude that they were as real as I was. I killed two more, but suddenly new ones, identical in every way, sprang from the corpses, two and three at a time, and I found myself facing over a dozen of them." He turned to Nighthawk. "Did you ever hear of anything like that?"

Nighthawk shook his head. "Never."

"Anyway, I killed a few more. They simply multiplied and came back to life, and I figured that before I either ran out of battery power or created a whole army, I'd better take cover and consider my options. I ducked back into the cave. She'd booby-trapped the entrance, and I set off the charge to explode and seal it off. I spent the next day exploring the various tunnels and caves. It's a goddamned maze, but Pallas Athene had carved coded notations on the walls in Terran, so I always knew where I was."

"Smart woman," remarked Nighthawk. "Thanks to T-packs everyone *speaks* Terran, but precious few aliens can actually *read* it."

"I don't think they even tried," said Newman. "I think they were content to let me wander around under the ground until you two showed up. They couldn't get in through Pallas Athene's cave, of course, but most of the caves are interconnected; they could have entered through another one if they'd wanted to—but I never saw a sign of them."

"I *knew* they wanted us all!" said Jeff.

"Anyway," continued Newman, "the longest tunnel let me out about two hundred yards from here. I had just emerged from it and was trying to get my bearings when I heard you three. I had no idea who you were, but I could tell by the voices you were human. I actually came over to warn you to get the hell away from here."

"So you think the rest of them are still waiting near Pallas Athene's cave?"

"I've been exploring the caves and tunnels for almost a full day, so I don't know where they are," said Newman. "But you can bet they'll have some lookouts posted within a two- or three-mile radius of Pallas Athene's cave."

"We didn't see any," said Jeff.

"You weren't supposed to," said Newman. "They're not there to stop you from approaching; they're there to prevent you from leaving." He smiled grimly. "All the Widowmakers in one fell swoop. I'll bet they can't believe their luck."

"Finding us is a little different from killing us," said Jeff. "Let's see if they still think they're lucky tomorrow morning."

"It's not that easy," said Newman.

"If you killed a few, at least we know they're not invulnerable," said Jeff. "That's a start."

"I must not have made myself clear. You can kill three of them, but if you do, suddenly you're facing six new ones. If you're successful enough, eventually you'll create a whole army of them."

"They've got a weakness," said Jeff.

"Oh?" said Newman. "What is it?"

"I don't know—but if they didn't have one, why would they care whether we live or die? If they want us dead, it's because they can be defeated and they want to eliminate us before we figure out how to do it."

Newman and Nighthawk exchanged looks. "You know," said Newman, "the kid's got a point."

"He's learning," said Nighthawk. "The trick is finding out what that weakness is."

"I don't suppose you know that, too?" Newman asked Jeff.

"Not yet," answered Jeff. "I guess we ought to go have a look at them."

"I suppose so," said Nighthawk. "If they know we're here, they're probably looking for us. Let's at least choose where we meet them." He turned to Newman. "I have a question for you first."

"What is it?"

"The goggles and the radiation detector that you bought at the Sharpshooter—what did you plan to use them for?"

Newman shrugged. "I had no idea. Pallas Athene gave me so many different counts—one day there were ten, one day three, one day seventy-five—I thought some part of them might be beyond the spectrum that the human eye can see, at least under certain conditions. But now that I've seen them myself, I left all that equipment in her cave. They're the strangest aliens I've ever seen, but seeing them isn't the problem."

"Good," said Nighthawk, dumping his gear. "I was getting tired of wearing this stuff anyway." Jeff and Kinoshita followed suit.

"The cave that let me out here is about two hundred yards to the west," said Newman. "There's a tunnel that we can follow back toward Pallas Athene's cave. There's no sense giving them an easy target, so we can spread out, each take a cave, maybe catch them in a crossfire. Except…"

"Except what?"

"Except the last thing we want to do is start killing them until we discover how to make they *stay* dead."

"We'll never discover it by standing here," said Jeff. "Where's the cave?"

"Follow me," said Newman.

"You're in no condition to go back and face them again," said Jeff. "Your shirt is covered with blood, and we know how recently you had your surgery."

"I know you're thinking of me," said Newman, "but they murdered my friend, and the only way you're going to keep me from this is to shoot me again. Are you prepared to do that?"

"Of course I'm not," said Jeff.

"Then stop arguing and follow me."

Newman set off to the west, and in a few minutes they came to the mouth of a cave that was almost hidden by the dense underbrush.

After they had all entered, Kinoshita stopped long enough to pull some branches across the front of the cave. Nighthawk was about to light his atomic torch, but Newman signaled him to put it away.

"She planned well," he said. "There's some element in the walls that exudes a faint glow, quite enough for us to see where we're going, and this way the torch won't announce our presence."

He headed off, and the other three followed him. They saw no sign of life, and after a little more than a mile Newman came to a stop.

"We're within a hundred yards of her cave," he whispered. "It's time to split up." He pointed to a small corridor to his right. "This leads to one of the caves."

"I'll take it," said Jeff, heading off into the tunnel.

Kinoshita took the next cave, about sixty yards farther.

Nighthawk and Newman walked another seventy yards, passing Pallas Athene's sealed cave, then stopped at another small corridor.

"You want this or the next one?" asked Newman.

"This'll be fine," replied Nighthawk. "How are you holding up?"

"I'll live," said Newman. An ironic smile. "Or if I don't, it won't be because of the surgery." The smile vanished. "If I die and you're still around, tell the kid it wasn't his fault."

"I will."

"I'm not Abel, and there's no reason for him to go through life thinking he was Cain."

"You're a good man, Jason."

Newman flashed him a quick smile. "I come from good stock." He turned and began walking farther down the corridor. "I'll see you when it's over."

Nighthawk bent over slightly to avoid bumping his head, then emerged into a small, musty-smelling cave. The walls were damp, and little rodent-like animals scurried into the corners as he walked through it.

As he came to the front of the cave he remembered Newman's description of how Pallas Athene had died, and resisted the urge to stick his head out and look around. He stood back about ten feet and studied what was within his field of vision. There was an open field that approached the huge semicircular outcropping that held most of the caves, but he couldn't see anything moving, just the short brown-green ground cover that passed for grass on Bollander III.

Nighthawk waited for five minutes, then five more. Still no aliens. Finally he decided that there was no sense waiting until nightfall, so he stepped out of the cave, burner in hand, ready for anything. The field was still empty. A moment later Jeff, Kinoshita, and Newman also emerged from their caves, forming a semicircle around the field.

"So where are they?" asked Jeff, who had so much faith in his ability to react that unlike his three companions he hadn't bothered to draw his weapons.

Nighthawk looked around, puzzled. "There's something very wrong here," he said at last.

Newman began approaching him. "What is it?" he asked.

Kinoshita was about to approach him as well when Nighthawk held up his hand. "Stay where you are. No sense making it easy for them."

Kinoshita stood still, and Jeff nodded and also held his ground.

"How many of them did you kill?" Nighthawk asked Newman.

"Eleven."

Nighthawk nodded toward the empty field. "Where are they?"

"I don't know," answered Newman. "There were enough aliens left to carry them off."

"Carry them *where?*"

Newman shrugged. Then suddenly he tensed, staring past Nighthawk to the far end of the field. "Here's someone who can tell us."

A humanoid alien, his skin a reddish brown, his head a little too large, his eyes too wide and too round, his arms with an extra joint in them, his legs bending in the wrong places, approached them.

Nighthawk aimed his burner at the alien, as did Newman and Kinoshita. Jeff merely watched him with arms folded across his chest, still disdaining his burner and his pulse gun.

The alien stopped when he was twenty yards away from Nighthawk. He seemed to be totally unconcerned by the weaponry that was being pointed at him.

"Greetings," said the alien. "I am the Younger Brothers."

"All of them?" asked Nighthawk sardonically.

"Yes," answered the alien. "Do you doubt me?" He seemed to tense and flex his body, and suddenly there were four of him, then eight, then twenty, then more. In less that ten seconds the men found themselves facing an armed band of fifty identical Younger Brothers.

"I'm impressed," said Nighthawk.

"There is no reason why you should be," said the initial alien. "After all, you are capable of the same feat, are you not?"

"Why should you think so?"

"Your DNA is identical to two of these others," said the alien. "All three of you are known as the Widowmaker. All three have collected bounties across the Inner Frontier. You have been doing so for more than one hundred fifty years, which means you are as long-lived as I myself am."

"I assume you have some point to make?"

"Certainly," said the alien. "Why should we be on opposite sides? I kill, you kill. I multiply, you multiply. I am without mercy, you are without mercy. I propose that we band together to plunder that portion of the galaxy known as the Oligarchy."

"You killed my friend," said Newman coldly. "Retribution must be made."

"She was nothing," said the alien. "All that matters is you and me, each of us in our hundreds and thousands."

"I'm flattered that you should think so," said Nighthawk. "But every innocent man you've ever killed matters to me."

"I was afraid that would be your attitude," said the alien. "Then we are enemies, and we shall not permit you to leave Bollander III."

"I don't recall asking for your permission," said Jeff, pulling his burner and killing three aliens before they realized what he was doing. The rest of the Younger Brothers pulled their weapons, and the three dead aliens suddenly split into six living ones. Nighthawk and Newman began firing while retreating to Nighthawk's cave. Kinoshita did the same. Jeff remained in the open an extra few seconds, killing an additional half-dozen Younger Brothers only to see them multiply and join their comrades.

"We can't use your escape route," said Nighthawk. "Now that I've seen what they can do, we can't cut and run, or they'll decimate this world and every world they land on."

"I wonder where the hell they've been," said Newman between shots with his burner. "They couldn't have escaped notice until just these last few months."

"He's got to be some kind of mutant with powers no other member of his race has. If it was a normal ability, we'd have been overrun by them eons ago." Nighthawk stepped back as a pulse of energy crashed into the side of the cave, spewing dust and rocks on them. "It doesn't matter. One of these bastards is more than enough."

"If I can get through the tunnels to Pallas Athene's cave, at least I can get us a supply of energy and bullets," said Newman. "Can you hold them off for about ten minutes?"

"Don't bother," said Nighthawk. "That's just extending the battle. We need to find a way to win it."

"I know," said Newman. "But how the hell do you win a battle where every time you kill your enemy you create more of him?"

"There has to be a way, or they wouldn't have gone to so much trouble to get us all here," replied Nighthawk. "Jeff had to be right about that."

"Maybe they really thought we'd join them," suggested Newman. He grimaced and shook his head. "No, of course not. That was just a shot in the dark on their part. They know we're bounty hunters."

A laser beam began cutting through the outer wall of the cave.

"If we give them enough time, they can cut through anything we use for cover," observed Nighthawk.

"I'm searching my memory—and yours," said Newman, picking off another Younger Brother. "I can't remember any situation that was remotely like this."

"I'd be willing to bet there's never been one," said Nighthawk grimly. He finally spotted the alien that was carving through the cave wall and put a bullet between his eyes.

And then, suddenly, all the shooting stopped. Nighthawk and Newman exchanged puzzled looks.

"What now?" murmured Nighthawk.

"It's the kid," said Newman, pointing.

Jeff walked into their line of sight, his hands raised above his head. Every alien weapon was trained upon him.

"I've got a proposition for you," said Jeff when he had halved the distance between himself and the Younger Brothers.

"A partnership?" asked one of the aliens.

"A contest," said Jeff.

"Explain," said another.

"Why continue the killing?" said Jeff. "It serves no purpose. Instead, I propose a battle of champions—yours against ours." He tapped his chest with his thumb. "I'm ours." He looked across the row of aliens facing him. "Here's the deal: if you win, my companions will agree to join you and follow your orders."

"And if you win?"

"You lay down your arms, leave the Inner Frontier, and promise never to return."

"He's crazy!" muttered Newman. "As quick as he kills whoever he's facing, it'll just split in two and start shooting again."

"No!" whispered Nighthawk excitedly. "He *knows* something! He's spotted something we've missed!"

"What?"

"I don't know—but *he* knows!"

Out in the field, Jeff took a few more steps forward. "Do you mind if I lower my hands now?" he asked. "It's a hot day, and it's awkward to keep them over my head."

"If you touch your weapons we'll kill you," said four of the Younger Brothers in unison.

"I won't touch them until you've chosen your champion and we face each other."

All fifty aliens chuckled at that. "We are identical, as are you."

"Me?" said Jeff. "I'm just a beginner. Those two guys"—he gestured toward Nighthawk's cave—"are the real Widowmakers. Killing your champion is just my training exercise."

One of the aliens stepped forward. "I will be our champion," he announced.

"Whatever makes you happy," said Jeff.

"This will be a battle to the death," continued the alien, "not to first blood. Do you understand and agree?"

"I do," said Jeff.

"That means if he kills one and it becomes two new ones, the fight's not over," said Newman.

"I trained him," replied Nighthawk. "I've got to trust him."

Jeff and the alien stood about fifteen feet apart, facing one another. The alien's hand was poised above its weapon. It showed no fear or nervousness, nor could Nighthawk see any reason why it should. Death seemed to be something entirely different to the Younger Brothers than to anything else he'd ever encountered.

"Are you ready?" said Jeff.

"I am ready."

Jeff drew his burner and had it in his hand before the alien had even touched his own weapon—but instead of shooting the alien he was facing, he pivoted and fired at one of the aliens who was standing near the middle of the band of Younger Brothers. The alien screamed once and fell to the ground, dead, a smoking black hole between his eyes.

And suddenly the other aliens simply popped out of existence. One moment they were there, solid and three-dimensional, armed with functioning weapons, and the next they were gone.

Nighthawk and Newman raced out of their cave and ran up to Jeff. Kinoshita joined them a moment later.

"What the hell did you do?" asked Nighthawk.

"They all sprang from the original, the one who first approached us," explained Jeff. "I don't know how he gave them form and substance, but I knew it had to come from him."

"Why?" asked Nighthawk.

"Like I said before, if they didn't have a weak spot, they wouldn't have bothered trying to kill us. *He* had to be the weak spot."

"They all looked alike," said Kinoshita. "How did you know which one to kill?"

"He was the only one who wasn't shooting at us," answered Jeff. "I figured he had to be too busy controlling all the others. The problem was that I couldn't get a clear shot at him from my cave, so I had to come up with that cock-and-bull challenge. It was the only way get close enough to be sure I wouldn't miss. I knew I'd only get one chance, because if the first shot didn't kill him, he'd realize he'd given himself away and I'd never be able to spot him again."

"I never saw that," admitted Nighthawk.

"Neither did I," added Newman.

"I can't think of a better time for you to have started using that brain of yours," said Nighthawk.

"Thanks," said Jeff. "That means a lot." He turned to Newman. "I hope this helps make up for what happened on Giancola II."

"It's forgotten," said Newman.

"Well, I guess we can get back to the spaceport," said Kinoshita.

"You three go ahead," said Newman. "I've got work to do."

"Here?" asked Jeff.

"I've got to bury Pallas Athene." He jerked his head toward the alien. "I think I'll leave him to the insects and the worms, or whatever passes for them on Bollander."

"Do you need any help?" asked Nighthawk.

"She was my friend. I'd rather do it alone."

"Good-bye, Widowmaker," said Jeff.

"I'm out of the Widowmaker business. My name's Jason Newman." He turned to Nighthawk. "I always wondered what you'd be like. Now I know. If you're ever on Murchison III, maybe we'll have a drink together."

Then he was in a cave, heading for the tunnel that would lead him to Pallas Athene.

"Not the warmest person in the galaxy, is he?" remarked Jeff as they headed back toward the aircar.

"Hardly surprising," said Nighthawk with a self-deprecating smile. "He's just another version of me."

"I don't know if I agree," said Jeff. "After all, I'm just another version of you too."

"No," said Nighthawk, throwing an arm around the young man's shoulders. "I have a feeling that you may be an improvement."

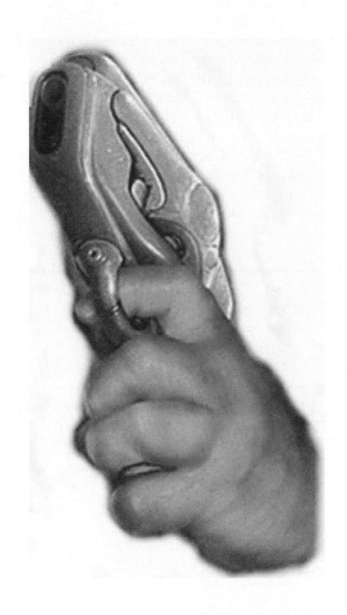

Epilogue

THE TWO BOYS peeked cautiously around the corner of the building.

"It's *him*!" said the first boy excitedly.

"It couldn't be," said the second. "Why would he be here? We're just an unimportant little world."

"Not anymore," said the first boy with conviction. "Not if *he's* here."

"Who's the little guy with him?"

"I don't remember his name, but I know that they always travel together."

"Well, I don't think it's him," said the second boy.

"I'm telling you it is!"

"He's too young."

"It's the same face I've seen in the holos," said the first boy.

"I don't care. He's too young to have done all the things they say, and besides, he'd never come to our world."

"I'll ask him."

"I dare you!" said the second boy.

The first boy swallowed hard. He pursed his lips, took a deep breath, and stepped out into the street just in front of the two men who were riding the slidewalk from the spaceport.

"Hi," said the young man, amused at the boy's discomfiture.

"Are you him?" asked the boy. "Are you the Widowmaker?"

"I'm working at it," answered the young man.

AUTHOR BIOGRAPHY

Locus, the trade journal of science fiction, keeps a list of the winners of major science fiction awards on its web page. Mike Resnick is currently 4th in the all-time standings, ahead of Isaac Asimov, Sir Arthur C. Clarke, Ray Bradbury, and Robert A. Heinlein.

Mike was born on March 5, 1942. He sold his first article in 1957, his first short story in 1959, and his first book in 1962.

Mike and Carol discovered science fiction fandom in 1962, attended their first Worldcon in 1963, and 81 SF books into his career, Mike still considers himself a fan and frequently contributes articles to fanzines. He and Carol appeared in five Worldcon masquerades in the 1970s in costumes that she created, and won four of them.

Carol has always been Mike's uncredited collaborator on his science fiction, but in the past few years they have sold two movie scripts—SANTIAGO and THE WIDOWMAKER, both based on Mike's books—and Carol *is* listed as his collaborator on those.

Since 1989, Mike has won four Hugo Awards (for "Kirinyaga", "The Manamouki", "Seven Views of Olduvai Gorge", and "The 43 Antarean Dynasties"), a Nebula Award (for "Seven Views of Olduvai Gorge"), and has been nominated for 25 Hugos, 11 Nebulas, a Clarke (British), and six Seiun-shos (Japanese). He has also won a Seiun-sho, a Prix Tour Eiffel (French), 2 Prix Ozones (French), 10 Homer Awards, an Alexander Award, a Golden Pagoda Award, a Hayakawa SF Award (Japanese), a Locus Award, 2 Ignotus

Awards (Spanish), a Futura Award (Croatian), an El Melocoton Mechanico (Spanish), 2 Sfinks Awards (Polish), a Fantastyka Award (Polish), and has topped the Science Fiction Chronicle Poll six times, the Scifi Weekly Hugo Straw Poll three times, and the Asimov's Readers Poll four times. In 1993 he was awarded the Skylark Award for Lifetime Achievement in Science Fiction, and in 2001 and 2004 he was named Fictionwise.com's Author of the Year in open competition with Dan Brown, Stephen King, Robert Ludlum, Louis L'Amour, Robert A. Heinlein, Ray Bradbury and Isaac Asimov.

ARTIST BIOGRAPHY

Jim Burns was born in Cardiff, South Wales in 1948. He developed a passion for drawing—in particular for creating strange, imaginary scenes, weird lifeforms and futuristic machinery whilst still at primary school—a passion which has never left him.

In terms of a career however, his first inclinations were towards flying, airplanes probably being an even greater passion than drawing during those teenage years and with this in mind he successfully applied to the Royal Air Force to train as a pilot in 1966. Despite eventually soloing on jet trainers he proved to be a less than inspired pilot, the RAF demanding nothing short of the absolute best of its trainees, and with some heaviness of heart elected to leave the service (rather than stay on in some other non-flying capacity) and apply to Newport School of Art for a year's foundation course.

He was accepted and then went on to complete a 3 year Diploma in Art and Design course at St. Martin's School of Art in London. He left St Martins with a pretty poor grade (there wasn't much enthusiasm for this 'science fiction nonsense') but had already been signed up by the recently established illustration agency, Young Artists (1972). He has been with this agency, later re-named 'Arena', ever since.

In the 28 years since then, Jim Burns has never been without work, mostly in the science fiction field (his personal passion), and has produced jackets for many hundreds of books both in the U.K. and the U.S.A. He has also had some involvement with conceptual design for films, notably in 1980 when he spent 10 weeks in Hollywood working on the film *Blade Runner*.

He has won the Art Hugo award twice—the only non-American ever to have won it—and has also picked up 12 BSFA awards (The British Science Fiction Award presented annually at the largest British S.F. convention, Eastercon). This is more than anyone else—including writers.

Jim Burns tends to paint mostly in acrylics these days, though he has gone through career phases using gouache and oils. He would like to return to oils eventually, particularly if he can ever find the time to do more personal work!

Jim Burns lives in rural Wiltshire in a 300 year old cottage with his wife of 27 years, Sue (They met at art college!). He has four children—Elinor, Megan, Gwendolen and Joseph.